Toronto Noir

TORONTO NOIR

EDITED BY
JANINE ARMIN & NATHANIEL G. MOORE

AKASHIC BOOKS
NEW YORK

This collection is comprised of works of fiction. All names, characters, places, and incidents are the product of the authors' imaginations. Any resemblance to real events or persons, living or dead, is entirely coincidental.

Published by Akashic Books

Series concept by Tim McLoughlin and Johnny Temple
Toronto map by Sohrab Habibion

ISBN-13: 978-1-933354-50-7
Library of Congress Control Number: 2007939597

First printing

Printed in Canada

Akashic Books
PO Box 1456
New York, NY 10009
info@akashicbooks.com
www.akashicbooks.com

ALSO IN THE AKASHIC NOIR SERIES:

Baltimore Noir, edited by Laura Lippman
Bronx Noir, edited by S.J. Rozan
Brooklyn Noir, edited by Tim McLoughlin
Brooklyn Noir 2: The Classics, edited by Tim McLoughlin
Chicago Noir, edited by Neal Pollack
D.C. Noir, edited by George Pelecanos
Detroit Noir, edited by E.J. Olsen & John C. Hocking
Dublin Noir (Ireland), edited by Ken Bruen
Havana Noir (Cuba), edited by Achy Obejas
Las Vegas Noir, edited by Jarret Keene & Todd James Pierce
London Noir (England), edited by Cathi Unsworth
Los Angeles Noir, edited by Denise Hamilton
Manhattan Noir, edited by Lawrence Block
Miami Noir, edited by Les Standiford
New Orleans Noir, edited by Julie Smith
Queens Noir, edited by Robert Knightly
San Francisco Noir, edited by Peter Maravelis
Twin Cities Noir, edited by Julie Schaper & Steven Horwitz
Wall Street Noir, edited by Peter Spiegelman

FORTHCOMING:

Brooklyn Noir 3, edited by Tim McLoughlin & Thomas Adcock
D.C. Noir 2: The Classics, edited by George Pelecanos
Delhi Noir (India), edited by Hirsh Sawhney
Istanbul Noir (Turkey), edited by Mustafa Ziyalan & Amy Spangler
Lagos Noir (Nigeria), edited by Chris Abani
Manhattan Noir 2: The Classics, edited by Lawrence Block
Mexico City Noir (Mexico), edited by Paco I. Taibo II
Moscow Noir (Russia), edited by Natalia Smirnova & Julia Goumen
Paris Noir (France), edited by Aurélien Masson
Phoenix Noir, edited by Patrick Millikin
Portland Noir, edited by Kevin Sampsell
Richmond Noir, edited by Andrew Blossom,
Brian Castleberry & Tom De Haven
Rome Noir (Italy), edited by Chiara Stangalino & Maxim Jakubowski
San Francisco Noir 2: The Classics, edited by Peter Maravelis
Seattle Noir, edited by Curt Colbert
Trinidad Noir, edited by Lisa Allen-Agostini & Jeanne Mason

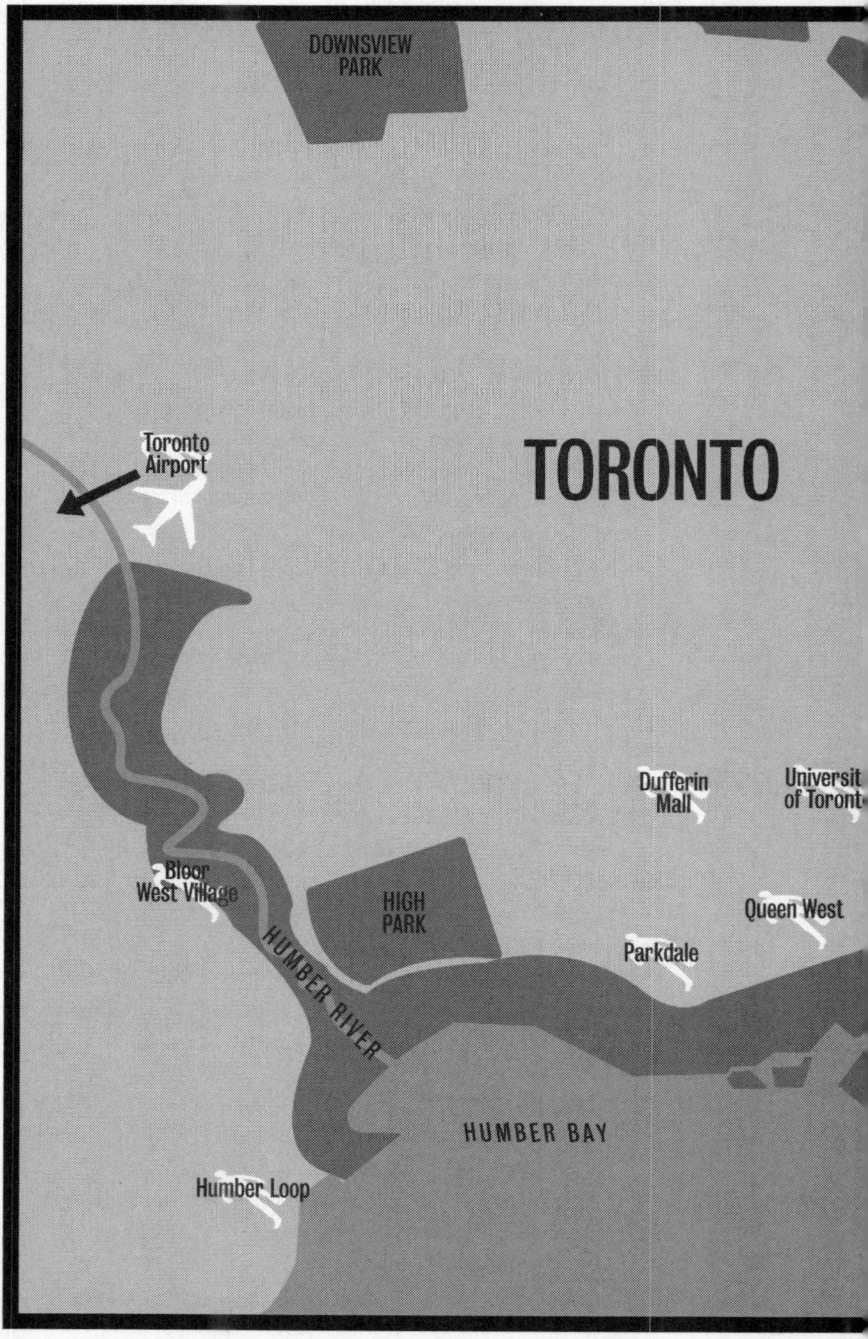

DOWNSVIEW
PARK

TORONTO

Toronto
Airport

Dufferin
Mall

Universit
of Toront

Bloor
West Village

HIGH
PARK

Queen West

Parkdale

HUMBER RIVER

HUMBER BAY

Humber Loop

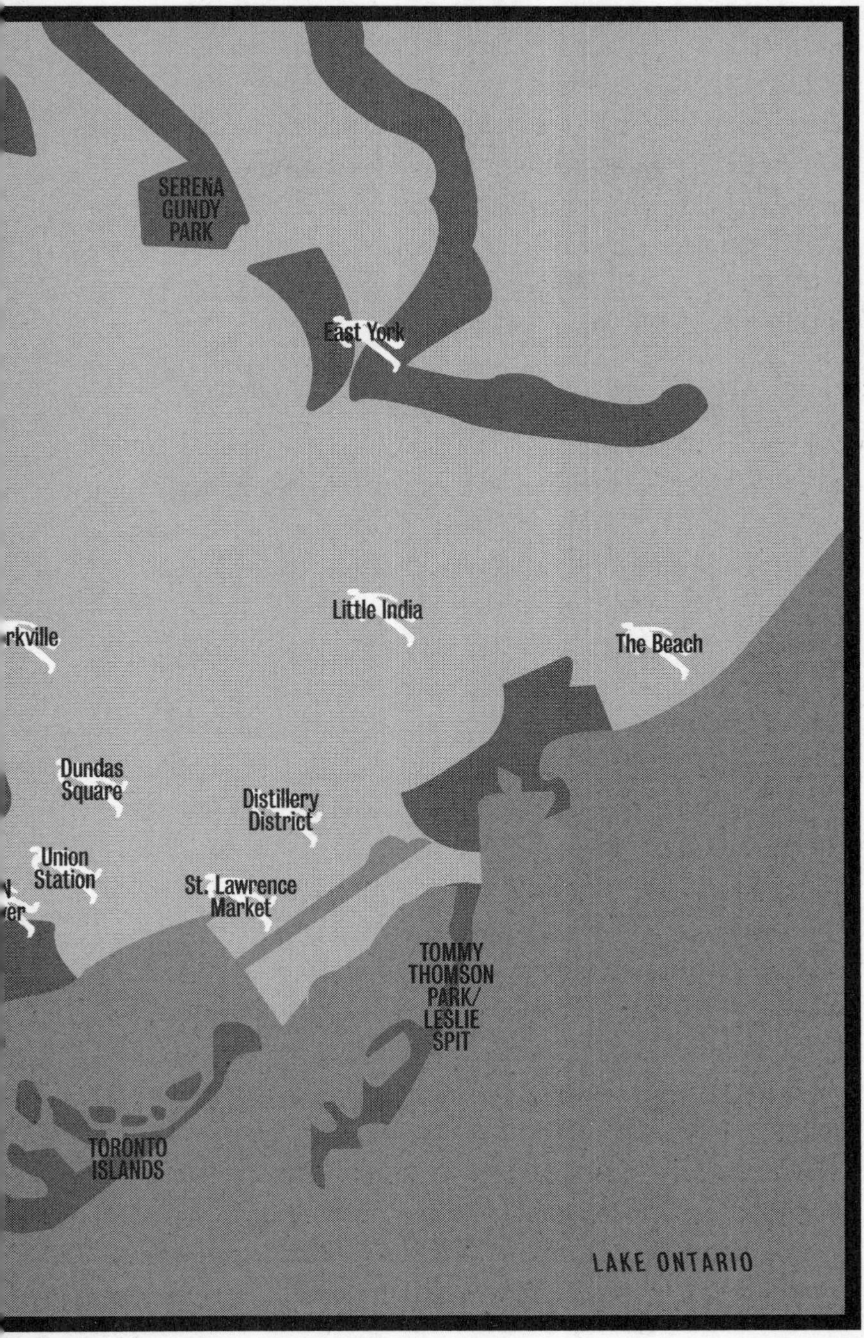

SERENA
GUNDY
PARK

East York

Little India

rkville

The Beach

Dundas
Square

Distillery
District

Union
Station

er

St. Lawrence
Market

TOMMY
THOMSON
PARK/
LESLIE
SPIT

TORONTO
ISLANDS

LAKE ONTARIO

Table of Contents

PART III: ROAD TO NOWHERE

PART IV: FLATLAND FLATLINE

INTRODUCTION

To Noir a Good Night

In 1834, York, city of mud and canons, became Toronto, city of trauma and free refills. Depending on what side of the CN Tower you stand under, Toronto is histrionic or claustrophobic, gelling or uncool. It's the 1967 Stanley Cup champion Maple Leafs; it's a fading World Series Blue Jays souvenir cup. It's gaggles of language-starved landfill stalkers who text and Facebook and spit wads of bubble gum onto the world's cleanest tarmac.

With its simple gestures, a stolen blue bike, a red balloon caught by a fraying string on Oakland Avenue, Toronto bids for more than the Olympics. Frustrated and frustrating, it teems with forensic experts and film-set extras trying to interpret our troubled conscience.

Even though it's North America's most multicultural metropolis outside of Miami, it's more commonly known for its cold winters, strong beer, and variety of transportation options. Perhaps that's why it's so disorienting. As Gail Bowen notes in "The King of Charles Street West," *Come in and get lost* is strategically emblazoned on Toronto's landmark five-and-dime Honest Ed's. The Toronto Transit Commission has moved over twenty-five billion people since 1921, almost four times the world's population. And while the transit monopoly searches for its next light rail train, others search for their next breath, meal, or kiss.

Toronto Noir lets a bit of moonlight contour the ever-mobile city, allowing a glimpse, a brief catch and release. Sentimentality and deception bring these stories together. Dog-ear this book, use it as foreplay for further encounters on your coffee table. Sift through the stiff pages written by people who inform and present their city in a way no double-decker gimmick bus whizzing past the Rogers Centre and Casa Loma could ever hope to do. It is in our emergency rooms and carrying our groceries home that we are Torontonians.

Some of our youth emulate high-octane luxury-car drag racing video games and kill taxi cab drivers one day shy of becoming a Canadian citizen. Others try and steal Michael Stipe's microphone when he passes it down to the audience during a free concert at Dundas Square. Some nights we listen and judge, while others, the air has a pulse and bodies clog the carb-heaving arteries of concrete. Some nights, living isn't enough and words are all we have; they blow them out without leaving a note or forwarding address.

Some leave us, while others like Margaret Atwood, Michael Ondaatje, and Ken Dryden carry the torch. The city is haunted by ghosts that sometimes get parks named after them: Gwendolyn MacEwan, Oscar Peterson, Jeff Buckley, Timothy Findley. Musically, Toronto spars with New York. The Barenaked Ladies, Broken Social Scene, Ron Sexsmith, Gordon Lightfoot, Glass Tiger, Platinum Blonde, and Triumph all got their starts here.

Not that anybody knows. Toronto grounds itself in its unknowing.

Working and living under the Great North, *Toronto Noir*'s authors share the weight of the unseen and the dying. Music binds Mark Sinnett to self-erasure and Peter Robinson inflects domestic problems with the twist of a foreign knife. Heather

Birrell takes us to Ecuador and shows us how maternal longing can be an evil thing.

"A writer uses a pen instead of a scalpel or blowtorch," says Ondaatje. Here, Peter Street's clubland spawns nightly crime-scene sound bites. In the West End, bucolic mansions are usurped by halfway houses. Bollywood screenings warm up Little India on murderously cold winter nights, while cadavers conceal their wares in cemetery-riddled East York.

In the end, physical acts and written acts share a parasitic need to enjoy and to tolerate. So clash away, city by the lake, it all comes down to communal passions: crimping your hair, making deviled eggs, varnishing the deck, not calling someone back, ever.

These stories capture encounters that happen every day. They resurrect the brutish moments displaced by high school graduations and taxi strikes, preserve them in metaphor, wrap them in gauze. Except here we let the carnivorous parchment swell heavy: a panting mascot, tied outside a bank, awaiting the return of its owner.

Come in, and get lost.

Janine Armin & Nathaniel G. Moore
Toronto, Ontario
February 2008

PART I

East York Enders

THE KING OF CHARLES STREET WEST

BY GAIL BOWEN

Dundas Square

Toronto was in the tenth day of a garbage strike when Billy Merchant came back into my life. The city was sweltering, and the stench that rose from overflowing cans, fetid dumpsters, and cardboard boxes swollen with rotting produce hung above the hot pavement like a poisoned cloud. We were a city ripe for a plague, so it was no surprise when I picked up the *Toronto Star* that morning and saw Billy's photo staring up at me. I hadn't seen him in forty years. If he'd let Mother Nature take her course, I wouldn't have recognized him, and he could have kept his empire for himself. But Billy never met a mirror he didn't like, and he was rich enough to believe he could defeat time. Judging by the picture in the *Toronto Star*, he had either discovered the fountain of youth or invested in a perpetual makeover: His hair was still thick and black as the proverbial raven's wing; his body was toned; his jawline smooth and his smile dazzling.

He didn't look young—he looked carved, like one of those figures at the Movieland Wax Museum in Niagara Falls. Except, unlike the wax Jack Nicholson or the wax Harry Potter, Billy Merchant hadn't been captured in his most memorable scene ever—at least, not the one I remembered. Billy with his cool, slender fingers around my throat whispering, "If you ever tell anybody what you saw, I'll kill you."

I hadn't doubted him for a moment. Billy had his weaknesses, but he wasn't given to idle threats. Besides, twenty feet away from me, at the bottom of the basement stairs of the rooming house where we lived, there was a dead man and I had watched as Billy killed him.

"It's hard to make predictions—especially about the future."
—Allan A. Lamport, Mayor of Toronto

For four decades, I'd kept our secret. I had my reasons, but when I saw the cutline under Billy's photo calling him *The King of Charles Street West,* something stirred inside me. A preacher or a poet might have called that stirring a thirst for justice, but I wasn't a preacher or a poet. I was an ordinary woman who lived in a nice house off the Danforth with too many pictures of my son and too many memories, so I did what an ordinary woman does when she contemplates blackmailing a murderer: I made myself a cappuccino, peeled an orange, and sat down to read the paper.

The article about Billy was nice—inspiring even. Much of it was in Billy's own words—about how forty years ago, as a twenty-year-old with a high school education and two years working construction under his belt, he moved to Toronto, found a place to live in a rooming house on Charles Street West, got a job waiting tables, worked hard, and saved every penny. According to Billy, his landlord, a Russian immigrant without living kin, admired his work ethic, and the men developed what Billy characterized as a father-son relationship. Then came the happy ending. When the older man died, it turned out that he'd left Billy his house. Starting with the property he'd inherited on Charles Street West, Billy began to sell, mortgage, lease, invest, and purchase until he owned an impressive chunk, not just of Charles Street West, but of Metropolitan Toronto.

City Success Story was the heading above the continuation of the story on page three. There was a photo there too: It was of Billy standing in front of the Charles Street West property in 1967 with "an unidentified woman." The unidentified woman was me.

Except for a strip of joke pictures of Billy and me mugging in the instant photo booth at Union Station, this was the only photo of the two of us together. I realized with a pang that it had been taken by our landlord, Vladimir Maksimovich Chapayev, known to us as Vova, and murdered by Billy on a soft September evening in 1967. It wasn't hard to figure out how the picture had made its way into the paper. When it came to his triumphs, Billy was as sentimental as a schoolgirl. He would have cherished this photo of himself on the cusp of his brilliant career. The fact that he had killed the man who took the photo and threatened to kill the woman who stood beaming beside him would have been of no more consequence to Billy than the clippings his manicurist snipped from his fingernails.

"*Nuts to you.*"
—Motto of Toronto's Uptown Nuthouse
(now defunct)

If you're going to travel fast, you have to travel light. That's what Billy always said. But it was possible Billy had underestimated the power of things he left behind. I had resources. The $64,000 question was whether I still had the nerve to use them. For forty years, I had wrapped myself in respectability, believing that each act of quiet duty separated me from the girl who believed the sun rose and set on Billy Merchant and who stood at the top of the cellar steps, heart pounding with fear and love as Billy knelt over Vladimir Maksimovich Chapayev and pinched the nostrils of his thick, maddeningly persistent snorting peasant nose until the old Russian stopped breathing forever.

As I propped Billy's photo against my cappuccino cup, my hands were shaking. Maybe, after all, the last laugh would be Billy's. Maybe in that instant when he silenced Vova, he had silenced me. It was possible that all the years of cautious living in my pleasant house off the Danforth had smothered the raw nerve I would need to bring Billy to his knees. I looked at Billy's picture again. And against logic and good sense, I drew strength from it.

In my quiet, sunny kitchen, I could almost hear Billy's voice, silky as one of the ties he was fond of fingering at Holt Renfrew: "Bring it on, babe. You're tough, but I'm tougher. I can take you."

"You take a chance the day you're born. Why stop now?"
—Billy Merchant's motto,
appropriated from the movie *Golden Boy*

I moved into the Charles Street West house on June 21, 1967: the first day of what the world would remember as the summer of love. There were no flowers in my hair, but there should have been. I was a virgin ripe for experience, ready for plucking. When I saw Billy, shirtless, his thin chest glistening with sweat as he mowed the postage-stamp lawn in front of the house, my loins twitched. He gave me one of his bullet-stopping grins, asked if he could carry in my luggage, and I was a goner.

That night Billy took me to see *Golden Boy* at a cheap theater that showed old movies. When Barbara Stanwyck told William Holden to follow his dream, Billy's hand squeezed mine as if someone had shot 300 kilovolts of electricity through his body. Afterwards, Billy stood under a streetlight, arms extended like an actor. "Sooner or later, everybody works for the man," he said. "And babe, you are looking at the man that, sooner or later, everybody is going to work for." That was my 300 kilovolt moment.

From the day we met, Billy and I seized every possible second together. Vova lived on the first floor of the rooming house. A gentle accountant who spent his evenings and weekends making scrapbooks of the Royal Family lived on the third floor. Billy and I shared the kitchen and bathroom on the second floor. His bedroom was at the front and mine was at the back, but even the long summer evenings weren't long enough for us, and by Canada Day, Billy and I knew the squeaks and hollows of one another's mattresses as intimately as we knew the contours of one another's bodies.

We might have been short on money, but we were long on dreams. I earned nine dollars a day selling costume jewelry at the Robert Simpson Company on the corner of Queen and Yonge. My dream was to go to Shaw's Business College and become a private secretary. Billy earned nine dollars a day (and tips) at Winston's on Adelaide Street West. Winston's was the restaurant where the Bay Street elite ate prime rib and talked money. Billy, who dreamed of becoming a millionaire before he was twenty-five, said that every day at Winston's was worth a year of college education.

That summer, he and I explored the city, not just our

neighborhood—all the neighborhoods. On payday, we bought ten dollars' worth of subway tokens, and after work, we'd hop on the subway and take turns choosing which stop we'd get off at and which bus or streetcar we'd board. Every night was an adventure. As we traveled through the muggy evenings, Billy would sit with his forehead pressed against the window looking out at the unfamiliar streets with the hunger he had in his eyes when he looked at my body.

"Toronto is the engine that drives Canada."
—Mel Lastman, Mayor of Toronto

When he talked about Toronto, Billy was like a lover: His voice grew soft; his hands trembled; his eyes glittered with lust. He needed, physically, to touch every part of the city, so he could penetrate her secrets. He had a shoebox filled with the spiral notebooks in which he recorded what the men who lunched at Winston's were saying about his city, and the information he had was pure gold. The men who drank icy martinis at Winston's had insider information about which crumbling town houses and firetrap warehouses were going to be torn down and where new freeways might be built; they knew where the subway might be expanded, and which cheap rural land would be developed as suburbs for the people flocking to live the dream. The men with icy martinis knew what nobody else knew: They knew where Toronto was going.

"Nobody knows where the hell downtown Toronto is. But everybody's going to know where downtown North York is."
—Mel Lastman, Mayor of Toronto

Even though Billy didn't understand what they were talking about, he wrote it down. Later, when we rode the public transit out to the edges of the city, Billy put the pieces together, and he floated his extravagant dreams. He was a man obsessed. Many years after that, I was reminded of Billy when I read my child the story of Icarus who dreamed of touching the sun and stuck feathers to his shoulders with wax so he could fly. When Icarus flew too close to the sun, the wax melted and he fell into the sea, but Billy was smart enough to calculate the odds. Nothing could bring him down.

"I'm lost, but I'm making record time."
—Allan A. Lamport, Mayor of Toronto

During the summer of love, Toronto was filled with kids who'd hitchhiked to Toronto to get stoned in Yorkville and enjoy a little loving wherever they found it. One steamy Sunday, Billy and I were walking through Queen's Park. As always, someone in the crowd was playing a guitar badly and the sweet smell of pot was heavy in the air. The lawns were littered with sleeping bags where girls with sunbursts painted on their cheeks and dreamy unfocused eyes were pressing their bodies against jean-clad barefoot boys with straggly beards. Billy stepped over them as if they were excrement.

We'd just passed the statue of Edward VII on his horse, when I tripped over a boy in a sleeping bag and lost my footing. Billy caught me before I fell, but the boy rolled over lazily, gave me the look boys give girls, and patted the place beside him on the sleeping bag. In a flash, Billy dropped to his knees and began to pummel the boy. When I heard the sound of fist against bone, my stomach heaved, but I managed to pull Billy back, and he pushed himself to his feet. For a beat, Billy and I stood side by side, looking down at the boy as he felt his jaw. I was sure there'd be trouble, but the boy just smiled and flashed us the peace sign.

For some reason, the gesture enraged Billy. The blood drained from his face and he aimed a kick at the boy's leg. "That's right, asshole," he said. "Peace and love."

Some of the other kids were emerging from their sleeping bags, rubbing their eyes and trying to get their heads around what was going on. Billy's wiry body was a coiled spring.

"Keep it up, you sorry little pieces of shit!" he yelled. "The more you smoke and screw, the more useless you become. And that works for me. You don't know who I am, but I know who you are. Every day I serve your fathers their lunch. While you're lying in parks getting crabs and blowing your minds, your fathers are transforming this city from Toronto the Good into Toronto the Great. Go ahead and laugh, but you're the reason I'm going to be part of Toronto the Great. You want to know why? Because you're breaking your fathers' hearts. You're the reason they order double martinis every day and get loose-lipped about the projects that are going to change this city forever."

The jaw of the boy Billy hit was starting to swell, but he kept the faith. It was an effort for him to form the words, but he managed. "Chill, brother," he said.

Billy shot the boy a look of pure hate. "Fuck you," he said, then he grabbed my hand and dragged me after him out of the park.

"If I had $1,000,000 I'd be rich."
—Toronto musicians The Barenaked Ladies

Billy was silent till we got to Bloor Street. "Are you okay?" I said finally.

When he turned toward me, there was a new darkness in his eyes. "Yeah, I'm okay. I'm more than okay. I'm terrific. I deserve to make it. When Toronto's a world-class city, I should be one of the kings. I'm smart. I've got drive and I've got nerve. The only thing I don't have is money." His voice broke, and for a terrible moment I thought he was going to cry. "I know where this city is headed. And I've got plans—great plans—I just don't have the money to get started. And that means I'm fucked."

"You can save," I said.

"From what I earn at Winston's? Fuck!" He laughed. "Only one thing to do. Wait for Vova to die."

"What would that change?"

His laugh was short and bitter. "I'm in Vova's will. It's supposed to be a big secret, but I'm the heir. Vova lost touch with his people in Russia years ago. He says they're probably dead by now. Anyway, one night when he got drunk, he started obsessing about how the government was going to take his house after he died. I told him that if he had a will, the government couldn't touch his property. So he poured himself another shot and wrote out a will leaving everything to me."

"How come you never told me?"

"Because I made a promise to Vova." Billy's voice was suddenly weary. "Also because it doesn't fucking matter. Vova has the heart of an ox. He'll live to be a hundred."

"He drinks a lot."

Billy shook his head. "Yeah, maybe I'll get lucky, and some Saturday night he'll get loaded and walk under the wrong ladder."

"Things work out for the best," I said, but for once my mind wasn't on Billy's future. It was on my own. My period was three weeks late, and as a rule, I was regular as clockwork.

"Come in and get lost."
—Slogan of Honest Ed's Discount House,
Bloor and Bathurst

Years later, when my son came home from school and told me that the flapping of a butterfly's wings can cause a chain of events that ultimately causes or prevents a tornado, I thought of the summer of 1967, when the flapping of the wing of a single butterfly in Russia changed four lives in Toronto.

By the time the Canadian National Exhibition opened at the end of August, I still hadn't told Billy we were going to have a baby. For days, his mood had been as sullen as the weather. He had a line on some land north of Toronto that was going cheap, but the regular customers at Winston's were on holidays, and tips were down. For the first time since he came to the city, Billy had been forced to dip into his savings to make ends meet, and his anger was building. I could see it in the set of his jaw and in the new fierceness of his temper. When I suggested we forget our troubles by spending an evening on the midway, he tensed and balled his fists. I flinched, and Billy saw my fear and gave me a melting smile.

"Okay, babe. Tomorrow's Saturday. I'll have my Saturday night drink with Vova—got to keep on his good side. Then after I pour him into bed, we'll go to the Ex. We'll eat some cotton candy. I'll win you one of those fancy satin dolls on the midway; then we'll take in the fireworks. Good times!"

Good times. But for Billy and me, good times always carried a price. The next day, when I came home from work, Billy was waiting for me on the front steps. He was ashen. As soon as he spotted me, he grabbed my hand and dragged me away from the house.

"My fucking luck," he said, his voice cracking. "I answered the phone today when Vova was out doing errands. It was long distance, and I couldn't make out what the person on the other end was saying. We yelled at each other for a couple of minutes trying to make one another understand, then somebody who said he was Vova's nephew came on the line. *His* English was excellent. He told me that he was crying with happiness to finally locate his uncle, because he had found a way to get to Canada and be reunited with Vladimir Maksimovich. So that's that. The nephew comes to Toronto. He gets the house, and I get the shaft. My fucking luck."

Billy was as low as I'd ever seen him, so I did what girls in the movies did when their men were down. I put my arms around him and murmured encouragement. "You always tell me people make their own luck," I said.

I was a naïve nineteen-year-old trying to make the man I loved feel better, but my words transformed Billy. It was as if I'd ignited a fuse in his brain and the possibilities were shooting forth. He pounded his fist into his hand. "You're right. We make our own luck." His eyes were burning, absorbed in a vision that only he could see. He grabbed me by the shoulders. "Babe, you're going to have to make yourself scarce for a while."

"What about the fireworks?"

"We'll make it in time for the fireworks. I promise you." His grip on my shoulders tightened.

"Billy, you're hurting me."

"If we don't do this right, you're going to be hurting a lot more. Now don't ask questions. Just follow instructions. Go up to your room, stay there, and listen for the phone downstairs in the hall. If it rings, grab it—quickly. Tell whoever it is that Vova's not here."

"But if you and Vova are in the kitchen, he'll hear the phone."

"I'll put the radio on the crazy station that plays Russian music and crank it up."

"Billy, what are you going to do?"

He shrugged and gave me a sly smile. "Same thing I do every Saturday night—have a drink with my pal, Vova."

"Toronto will never be the same again."
—Phil Givens, Mayor of Toronto

I did what Billy told me to do. I went to my room, opened the window, and sat staring into the sultry twilight, listening. The weekly drinks were a ritual. Vova never opened a bottle until Saturday night, and then he drank till the bottle was empty. Billy's job was to pour the vodka, listen, and get Vova safely into bed. It never took long. Vova put in long hours, and he drank fast. That night, I could hardly breathe as I listened to the mournful tunes of Russian radio and the voices of the two men: Billy's baritone, playful, deferring; Vova's bass, booming louder as the level of the bottle dropped. Our landlord's conversational topics were limited: his hatred of all government; his contempt for rules and regulations; his pride in his self-reliance and accomplishments. As I heard the familiar litany, I relaxed. It was just another Saturday night, after all. Then the phone downstairs in the hall rang, shrill and insistent, and my heart began to pound. I raced to answer it. It was long distance. I broke the connection, and left the phone off the hook. In that instant, I knew that nothing would ever be the same again.

The kitchen door was closed. I crept down the hall and opened it a crack. Vova and Billy were sitting at the kitchen table. Vova was slumped over the table, his broad back toward me. Billy looked up when the door opened. I nodded, and Billy stood, went to Vova, dragged him from his chair, and began moving toward the basement stairs. The old man came to and started grumbling. "What the hell?"

"Time for bed," Billy said, coolly.

Vova laughed. "Hey, you make mistake. That's the basement way. What the hell? I'm the drunk one." He laughed again; then Billy pushed him. For a beat there was silence, then a dull thud as Vova's body hit the concrete at the bottom of the stairs. Billy disappeared after him. Mesmerized, I moved across the kitchen floor to the door that led to the cellar. I saw it all: Vova's body splayed on the floor, twitching like a grotesque abandoned puppet; Billy sitting back on his heels, breathing hard and watching. When the twitching didn't stop, Billy leaned forward and pinched Vova's nostrils shut until finally he was still. As Billy came back up the stairs toward me, I felt a wash of relief; then his fingers were around my throat. The stench of death and rage that poured off his skin was overpowering.

"If you tell anybody what you saw, I'll kill you," he said. And I knew he would.

Billy was a man who kept his promises—all of them. That night, as Vova lay dead in the basement, Billy took me to the fireworks at the CNE. As the rockets ignited and threw Billy's profile into sharp relief, he was so beautiful I couldn't imagine my life without him. But the moment passed. The last exploding star arced across the sky, and the dark, cheerless night closed in on us. Coming home on the subway, we leaned against each other, exhausted by the events of the day. The house on Charles Street West was silent, and like children in a fairy tale who suddenly find themselves in peril, Billy and I held hands as we climbed the stairs. That night Billy made love to me with a violence that thrilled and terrified me. When he was through, he fell away like a sated animal and slept the sleep of the innocent.

I didn't sleep. I couldn't. My mind was assaulted by images that I knew not even time could erase, and I was terrified that I might have, somehow, harmed my baby. When Billy's breathing became deep and rhythmic, I slipped out of bed and started for the door. Obeying an impulse I didn't understand, I took the shoebox that contained the spiral notebooks Billy had filled with his plans and ideas. Then I went to my room, packed my suitcase, and walked out the front door of the house on Charles Street West for the last time.

It's always been easy for a woman to disappear in Toronto, especially if no one really wants to find her. The day after I left Billy, a childless widower in his late fifties hired me as his companion/housekeeper. Six weeks later I married him. When my son was born, I named him after my new husband: Mark Edward Lawton.

My husband was a generous and loving father, but naming a child after a man does not make the baby that man's son. From the day he was born, Mark was Billy's boy. As I knelt on the floor of my bedroom closet and pulled out the shoebox that held the spiral notebooks in which Billy had recorded his dreams and secrets, I knew that Billy's boy needed his dad.

"It's my city. I don't have to consult anyone."
—Mel Lastman, Mayor of Toronto

I didn't go downtown often. I could buy everything I needed on the Danforth; besides, when I got off the subway at Bloor, I felt lost. Nothing stayed the same. It was as if a sorcerer who was never satisfied had taken over the old neighborhood, replacing the solid brick houses and tiny lawns with buildings that soared and shone brightly until the sorcerer waved them away and conjured up buildings that soared even higher and shone even more brightly.

It must be hard to keep focused in a world that's constantly shifting. Perhaps that's why Billy, in a gesture that the *Toronto Star* praised, located his offices on the site of the house that Vova left him. I thought I would feel a pang when I returned to the place I had run from in the early hours of that hot night of love and death. But I felt nothing. The sleek shops and gleaming high-rises that lined Charles Street West made it so uniformly perfect that there was nothing left to recognize.

Billy's office was on the fifty-first floor. I was counting on the elevator ride to give me time to compose myself, but the smooth soundless glide was over in seconds, and when the doors opened, I found myself in Billy's world. The reception area of Merchant Enterprises was designed to impress and intimidate: Everything was hard-surfaced, sharp-edged, and high gloss. The woman behind the reception desk fit right in. Whippet-thin, porcelain-skinned with red-red lips and red-red nails, her close-fitted sharkskin suit had been cut to showcase her perfection. She gave me a quick, assessing look, decided I wasn't worth her time, and glared. When I asked to see Billy, she was brusque, almost rude. "Mr. Merchant isn't available."

"May I leave something for him?"

She nodded.

I pulled the spiral notebook from my purse, ripped out a page upon which Billy had written the words *KILL VOVA* a dozen times in the margins, and handed it to her. "Give this to Billy," I said. "Tell him it's from the woman who was standing beside him in the picture in the paper this morning."

She held the grimy ripped page between her thumb and forefinger and looked at it with distaste.

"Better get a move on," I said.

She narrowed her eyes at me, decided I meant business, and then pressed a button with one of her perfectly shaped nails. "Mr. Merchant, there's a person here to see you. Her picture was in the paper with you this morning."

"Nicely done," I said. Then I sat down to wait. Time-wise, Billy's sprint from his office to the reception area must have been a personal best, but he wasn't even breathing hard. He looked me up and down, gave me his bullet-stopping grin, and held out his arms. "It's been a long time."

When I didn't walk into his embrace, Billy turned to his receptionist. "Nova, cancel the rest of my appointments for this morning and hold my calls." He placed his fingertips on my elbow. "Why don't we go down to my office? I have a feeling you and I've got a few things to discuss."

We were silent as Billy guided me down the hall, opened the door, and led me inside. For the first time since he'd spotted me in the reception area, Billy seemed uncertain. "I didn't think I'd ever see you again, but you've always had a way of surprising me."

"I'm not through yet," I said. Two walls of Billy's office were floor-to-ceiling glass, and the view of the city was spectacular. For a few moments, I looked down on Toronto, getting my bearings.

"So what's the verdict?" Billy asked.

"It's a great city," I said. "But you always knew that, didn't you?"

"Yeah, and from up here you can't smell the garbage."

There was something different about Billy that I couldn't put my finger on. Up close, there was no doubt that his hair was dyed, and the skin around his eyes had the strange tightness that comes from too much plastic surgery. But the change in Billy was more than cosmetic. Underneath the thousand-dollar suit, there was a weariness that no amount of tailoring could disguise. And his voice was different—lower and flatter. It didn't take long for the truth to hit me. For the first time in his life, Billy Merchant had stopped looking forward to the future. There were no more mountains for him to climb. Billy met my gaze. "Time marches on, eh?"

"Yes," I said. "Time marches on."

"You don't look half bad for an old broad."

I laughed. "Still a charmer."

"So shall we cut to the chase?" Billy examined the paper I'd ripped from his notebook. "*Kill Vova,*" he said. His laugh was short and bitter. "Do you know I truly don't remember writing those words?"

"You think I faked this?"

He shook his head. "No, that's my handwriting. And I'm assuming there's more where this came from."

"You're right. The morning I left, I took your notebooks with me. Anyone who wants to know the real story of the King of Charles Street West would find those notebooks very valuable."

Billy's gaze didn't waver, but as he pulled out his checkbook and pen, his hands were shaking. "You're not capable of pulling this off," he said quietly. "There are two kinds of people in the world: the ones who betray and the ones who get betrayed. If you were going to betray me, you would have done it long before now." He tried a smile. "That doesn't mean you're not going to get a payoff. You deserve something for keeping quiet all these years. So who do I make the check out to?"

"Mark Edward Lawton," I said.

Billy's eyes narrowed. "Jesus, that little putz! What's your connection with Mark Lawton?"

"He's my son."

Billy sighed. "No offense, but he's a shit. Aggressive. Arrogant. Ruthless. He and I are in a bidding war over some warehouses. I was in a meeting with him all morning. I've got him beat, but he won't back down."

"He takes after his father," I said.

Billy took the lid off his pen. "Who's his father?"

I shrugged. "He's a real killer. Aggressive. Arrogant. Ruthless. You know what they say, Billy. *The apple doesn't fall far from the tree*."

"Meaning?"

"Meaning, no matter what I did, I couldn't keep Mark from turning out like his father."

"Am I supposed to know this guy?"

"Every morning when you shave, you see him in your mirror." Billy froze. "You're not saying I'm your kid's father. That's impossible. I've been married three times. Never knocked up any of my wives. I've been tested. I don't shoot blanks, but I'm not exactly a potentate."

Despite everything, I laughed. "Oh god, Billy, do you even know what a potentate is?"

"Sure," Billy said. "A guy who's potent. Which apparently I am not." He leaned across the desk. His face softened. "Or am I? Do you have proof?"

"No," I said. "My husband was listed as Mark's father on

the birth certificate. But Mark was born six months after the night Vova died, and Mark wasn't premature."

"Those premature babies are little, right?"

"Right," I said. "Mark weighed almost ten pounds. He was a full-term baby. I was three months pregnant the night I left the house on Charles Street West."

I could see the hope in Billy's eyes. "Jesus, I can't believe this. I always thought that when I cashed in my chips, it would be the end of Merchant Enterprises, but if I have a son . . . that would change everything."

"It could," I agreed.

"I'll get one of those paternity tests," Billy said.

"Be my guest. Or you could just look into Mark's eyes or listen closely to his voice. He's your boy, Billy."

Billy shook his head in wonder. "I have a son."

"Are you going to hand out cigars?" I said.

He grinned. "Why not? Better late than never, eh? At last, the King of Charles Street West has an heir." He came around the desk and took my hand. For a moment, I glimpsed the Billy I loved. "So when are we going to tell my boy the truth? I'm trying not to be a prick here, but Mark should know who his real father is."

I felt a stab of panic. "I'll be taking a chance," I said. "I've heard Mark talk about you, and what he says isn't flattering. If he discovers you're his father, I could lose him."

"That's not going to happen. Mark may be a putz, but he's smart. You and I are a great package deal. I've got money, and you've got class. He won't walk away from that."

"Guaranteed?"

Billy reached out and stroked my cheek. "Babe, there are no guarantees in life. It's like I always say, *You take a chance the day you're born. Why stop now?*"

I removed his hand from my cheek. "Actually, the first person to say that line was Barbara Stanwyck in *Golden Boy*. Maybe you should start acknowledging her."

Billy raised an eyebrow. "Why would I do that? It's my signature line." He held out his arm. "Time to move, our son is waiting." He took a camera from a shelf near the door.

"Planning to take a family portrait?" I said.

Billy slung the camera around his neck. "This morning when I had that meeting with Mark, I noticed this abandoned shoe factory near his office. It's a rat-trap, but a great location. If we're going to be in the neighborhood, I might as well snap some pictures. People would pay big money to be that close to the lake." His eyes were sparkling with the old lust for the future. "Do you know what a pied-à-terre is?"

"It's a small second home rich people have in cities they love."

Billy nodded admiringly. "You always were sharp. Anyway, everybody loves Toronto. Mark and I could turn that shoe factory into a bunch of little condos—except instead of calling them condos, we'll call them pieds-à-terre. If we give our little shoeboxes a French name, people will be creaming their jeans to get in on the ground floor." Billy smoothed my hair. "We're going to make a killing. Now come on, babe. Time for you to introduce me to my son."

Then Billy and I, the betrayer and the betrayed, linked arms and together we rode the elevator that took us to the shining doors that opened to the city. When we stepped outside, Billy handed the doorman his camera and a twenty-dollar bill. "Take our picture, would you?" he said. "And be sure to get a nice shot of the building."

As we stepped into position, I put my lips next to Billy's

ear and whispered, "The last person to take a picture of the two of us together was Vova."

Billy turned and craned his neck so he could see the top of his office tower. "Wouldn't that old man be amazed if he could see what I've done?"

As he had so often, Billy took my breath away. For a moment, I felt light-headed. I took his arm and inhaled deeply, and the moment passed. Even on the tenth day of a garbage strike, there's something restorative about the smell of Toronto in summer. It's as seductive as the scent of a lover you can never really bring yourself to leave.

WALKING THE DOG

BY PETER ROBINSON

The Beach

The dog days came to the Beaches in August and the boardwalk was crowded. Even the dog owners began to complain about the heat. Laura Francis felt as if she had been locked in the bathroom after a hot shower as she walked Big Ears down to the fenced-off compound on Kew Beach, where he could run free. She said hello to the few people she had seen there before while Big Ears sniffed the shrubbery and moved on to play with a Labrador retriever.

"They seem to like each other," said a voice beside her.

Laura turned and saw a man she thought she recognized, but not from the Beaches. She couldn't say where. He was handsome in a chiseled, matinee-idol sort of way, and the tight jeans and white T-shirt did justice to his well-toned muscles and tapered waist. Where did she know him from?

"You must excuse Big Ears," she said. "He's such a womanizer."

"It's nothing Rain can't handle."

"Rain? That's an unusual name for a dog."

He shrugged. "Is it? It was raining the day I picked her up from the Humane Society. Raining cats and dogs. Anyway, you're one to talk, naming dogs after English children's book characters."

Laura felt herself flush. "My mother used to read them to me when I was little. I grew up in England."

"I can tell by the accent. I'm Ray, by the way. Ray Lanagan."

"Laura Francis. Pleased to meet you."

"Laura? After the movie?"

"After my grandmother."

"Pity. You do look a bit like Gene Tierney, you know."

Laura tried to remember whether Gene Tierney was the one with an overbite or the large breasts and tight sweaters. As she had both, herself, she supposed it didn't really matter. She blushed again. "Thank you."

They stood in an awkward, edgy silence while the dogs played on around them. Then, all of a sudden, Laura remembered where she had seen Ray before. Jesus, of course, it was *him*, the one from the TV commercial, the one for some sort of male aftershave or deodorant where he was stripped to the waist, wearing tight jeans like today. She'd seen him in a magazine too. She had even fantasized about him, imagined it was him there in bed with her instead of Lloyd grunting away on top of her as if he were running a marathon.

"What is it?" Ray asked.

She brushed a strand of hair from her hot cheek. "Nothing. I just remembered where I've seen you before. You're an actor, aren't you?"

"For my sins."

"Are you here to make a movie?" It wasn't as stupid a question as it might have sounded. The studios were just down the road and Toronto had almost as big a reputation for being Hollywood North as Vancouver. Laura ought to know; Lloyd was always telling her about it since he ran a post-production company.

"No," Ray said. "I'm resting, as we say in the business."

"Oh."

"I've got a couple of things lined up," he went on. "Commercials, a small part in a new CBC legal drama. That sort of thing. And whatever comes my way by chance."

"It sounds exciting."

"Not really. It's a living. To be honest, it's mostly a matter of hanging around while the techies get the sound and light right. But what about you? What do you do?"

"Me?" she pointed her thumb at her chest. "Nothing. I mean, I'm just a housewife." It was true, she supposed: "Housewife" was about the only way she could describe herself. But she wasn't even that. Alexa did all the housework, and Paul handled the garden. Laura had even hired a company to come in and clear the snow. So what did she do with her time, apart from shop and walk Big Ears? Sometimes she made dinner, but more often than not she made reservations. There were so many good restaurants on her stretch of Queen Street East—anything you wanted, Japanese, Greek, Indian, Chinese, Italian—that it seemed a shame to waste them.

The hazy bright sun beat down mercilessly and the water looked like a ruffled blue bedsheet beyond the wire fence. Laura was feeling embarrassed now that she had openly declared her uselessness.

"Would you like to go for a drink?" Ray asked. "I'm not coming on to you or anything, but it *is* a real scorcher."

Laura felt her heart give a little flutter and, if she were honest with herself, a pleasurable warmth spread through her lower belly.

"Okay. Yes, I mean, sure," she said. "Look, it's a bit of a hassle going to a café or a pub with the dogs, right? Why don't you come up to the house? It's not far. Silver Birch. There's cold beer in the fridge and I left the air-conditioning on."

Ray looked at her. He certainly had beautiful eyes, she thought, and they seemed especially steely blue in this kind of light. Blue eyes and black hair, a devastating combination. "Sure," he said. "If it's okay. Lead on."

They put Big Ears and Rain on leashes and walked up to Queen Street, which was crowded with tourists and locals pulling kids in bright-colored carts, all OshKosh B'Gosh and Birkenstocks. People browsed in shop windows, sat outdoors at Starbucks in shorts drinking their Frappucinos and reading the *Globe and Mail*, and there was a line outside the ice-cream shop. The traffic was moving at a crawl, but you could smell the coconut sunblock over the gas fumes.

Laura's large detached house stood at the top of a long flight of steps sheltered by overhanging shrubbery, and once they were off the street, nobody could see them. Not that it mattered, Laura told herself. It was all innocent enough.

It was a relief to get inside, and even the dogs seemed to collapse in a panting heap and enjoy the cool air.

"Nice place," said Ray, looking around the modern kitchen, with its central island and pots and pans hanging from hooks overhead.

Laura opened the fridge. "Beer? Coke? Juice?"

"I'll have a beer, if that's okay," said Ray.

"Beck's all right?"

"Perfect."

She opened Ray a Beck's and poured herself a glass of orange juice, the kind with extra pulp. Her heart was beating fast. Perhaps it was the heat, the walk home? She watched Ray drink his beer from the bottle, his Adam's apple bobbing. When she took a sip of juice, a little dribbled out of her mouth and down her chin. Before she could make a move to get a napkin and wipe it off, Ray had moved forward just as far as it took, bent toward her, put his tongue on the curve under her lower lip, and licked it off.

She felt his heat and shivered. "Ray, I'm not sure . . . I mean, I don't think we should . . . I . . ."

The first kiss nearly drew blood. The second one did. Laura fell back against the fridge and felt the Mickey Mouse magnet that held the weekly to-do list digging into her shoulder. She experienced a moment of panic as Ray ripped open her Holt Renfrew blouse. What did she think she was doing, inviting a strange man into her home like this? He could be a serial killer or something. But fear quickly turned to pleasure when his mouth found her nipple. She moaned and pulled him against her and spread her legs apart. His hand moved up under her long, loose skirt, caressing the bare flesh of her thighs and rubbing between her legs.

Laura had never been so wet in her life, had never wanted it so much, and she didn't want to wait. Somehow, she maneuvered them toward the dining room table and tugged at his belt and zipper as they stumbled backwards. She felt the edge of the table bump against the backs of her thighs and eased herself up on it, sweeping a couple of Waterford crystal glasses to the floor as she did so. The dogs barked. Ray was good and hard and he pulled her panties aside as she guided him smoothly inside her.

"Fuck me, Ray," she breathed. "Fuck me."

And he fucked her. He fucked her until she hammered with her fists on the table and a Royal Doulton cup and saucer joined the broken crystal on the floor. The dogs howled. Laura howled. When she sensed that Ray was about to come, she pulled him closer and said, "Bite me."

And he bit her.

"I really think we should have that dog put down," said Lloyd after dinner that evening. "For God's sake, biting you like that. It could have given you rabies or something."

"Don't be silly. Big Ears isn't in the least bit rabid. It was an accident, that's all. I was just a bit too rough with him."

"It's the thin end of the wedge. Next time it'll be the postman, or some kid in the street. Think what'll happen then."

"We are not having Big Ears put down, and that's final. I'll be more careful in future."

"You just make sure you are." Lloyd paused, then asked, "Have you thought any more about that other matter I mentioned?"

Oh God, Laura thought, not again. Lloyd hated their house, hated the Beaches, hated Toronto. He wanted to sell up and move to Vancouver, live in Kitsilano or out on Point Grey. No matter that it rained there 364 days out of every year and all you could get to eat was sushi and alfalfa sprouts. Laura didn't want to live in Lotus Land. She was happy where she was. Even happier since that afternoon.

As Lloyd droned on and on, she drifted into pleasant reminiscences of Ray's body on hers, the hard, sharp edges of his white teeth as they closed on the soft part of her neck. They had done it again, up in the bed this time, her and Lloyd's bed. It was slower, less urgent, more gentle, but if anything, it was even better. She could still remember the warm ripples and floods of pleasure, like breaking waves running up through her loins and her belly, and she could feel a pleasant soreness between her legs even now, as she sat listening to Lloyd outline the advantages of moving the post-production company to Vancouver. Plenty of work there, he said. Hollywood connections. But if they moved, she would never see Ray again. It seemed more imperative than ever now to put a stop to it. She had to do *something*.

"I really don't want to talk about it, darling," she said.

"You never do."

"You know what I think of Vancouver."

"It doesn't rain that much."

"It's not just that. It's . . . Oh, can't we leave it be?"

Lloyd put his hand up. "All right," he said. "All right. Subject closed for tonight." He got up and walked over to the drinks cabinet. "I feel like a cognac."

Laura had that sinking feeling. She knew what was coming.

"Where is it?" Lloyd asked.

"Where is what, darling?"

"My snifter, my favorite brandy snifter. The one my father bought me."

"Oh, that," said Laura, remembering the shattered glass she had swept up from the hardwood floor. "I meant to tell you. I'm sorry, but there was an accident. The dishwasher."

Lloyd turned to look at her in disbelief. "You put my favorite crystal snifter in the *dishwasher*?"

"I know. I'm sorry. I was in a hurry."

Lloyd frowned. "A hurry? You? What do you ever have to be in a hurry about? Walking the bloody dog?"

Laura tried to laugh it off. "If only you knew half the things I had to do around the place, darling."

Lloyd continued to look at her. His eyes narrowed. "You've had quite a day, haven't you?" he said.

Laura sighed. "I suppose so. It's just been one of those days."

"This'll have to do then," he said, pouring a generous helping of Remy into a different crystal snifter.

It was just as good as the one she had broken, Laura thought. In fact, it was probably more expensive. But it wasn't *his*. It wasn't the one his miserable old bastard of a father, God rot his soul, had bought him.

Lloyd sat down and sipped his cognac thoughtfully. The next time he spoke, Laura could see the way he was looking at her over the top of his glass. *That* look. "How about an early night?" he said.

Laura's stomach lurched. She put her hand to her forehead. "Oh, not tonight, darling. I'm sorry, but I have a terrible headache."

She didn't see Ray for nearly a week and she was going crazy with fear that he'd left town, maybe gone to Hollywood to be a star, that he'd just used her and discarded her the way men did. After all, they had only been together the once, and he hadn't told her he loved her or anything. All they had done was fuck. They didn't really *know* one another at all. They hadn't even exchanged phone numbers. She just had this absurd feeling that they were meant for each other, that it was *destiny*. A foolish fantasy, no doubt, but one that hurt like a knife jabbing into her heart every day she didn't see him.

Then one day, there he was at the beach again, as if he'd never been away. The dogs greeted each other like long lost friends while Laura tried to play it cool as lust burned through her like a forest fire.

"Hello, stranger," she said.

"I'm sorry," Ray said. "A job came up. Shampoo commercial. On-the-spot decision. Yes or no. I had to work on location in Niagara Falls. You're not mad at me, are you? It's not as if I could phone you and let you know or anything."

"Niagara Falls? How romantic."

"The bride's second great disappointment."

"What?"

"Oscar Wilde. What he said."

Laura giggled and put her hand to her mouth. "Oh, I see."

"I'd love to have taken you with me. I know it wouldn't have been a disappointment for us. I missed you."

Laura blushed. "I missed you too. Want a cold beer?"

"Look," said Ray, "why don't we go to my place. It's only a top floor flat, but it's air-conditioned, and . . ."

"And what?"

"Well, you know, the neighbors . . ."

Laura couldn't tell him this, but she had gotten such an incredible rush out of doing it with Ray in *her own bed* that she couldn't stand the thought of going to his flat, no matter how nice and cool it was. Though she had changed and washed the sheets, she imagined she could still smell him when she lay her head down for the night, and now she wanted her bed to absorb even more of him.

"Don't worry about the neighbors," she said. "They're all out during the day anyway, and the nannies have to know how to be discreet if they want to stay in this country."

"Are you sure?"

"Perfectly."

And so it went on. Once, twice, sometimes three times a week, they went back to Laura's big house on Silver Birch. Sometimes they couldn't wait to get upstairs, so they did it on the dining room table like the first time, but mostly they did it in the king-size bed, becoming more and more adventurous and experimental as they got to know one another's bodies and pleasure zones. Laura found a little pain quite stimulating sometimes, and Ray didn't mind obliging. They sampled all the positions and all the orifices, and when they had exhausted them, they started over again. They talked too, a lot, between bouts. Laura told Ray how unhappy she was with her marriage, and Ray told her how his ex-wife had ditched him for his accountant because his career wasn't exactly going in the same direction as Russell Crowe's, as his bank account made abundantly clear.

Then one day, when they had caught their breath after a particularly challenging position that wasn't even in the *Kama Sutra*, Laura said, "Lloyd wants to move to Vancouver. He won't stop going on about it. And he never gives up until he gets his way."

Ray turned over and leaned on his elbow. "You can't leave," he said.

It was as simple as that. *You can't leave*. She looked at him and beamed. "I know," she said. "You're right. I can't."

"Divorce him. Live with me. I want us to have a normal life, go places together like everyone else, go out for dinner, go to the movies, take vacations."

It was everything she wanted too. "Do you mean it, Ray?"

"Of course I mean it." He paused. "I love you, Laura."

Tears came to her eyes. "Oh my God." She kissed him and told him she loved him too, and a few minutes later they resumed the conversation. "I can't divorce him," Laura said.

"Why on earth not?"

"For one thing, he's a Catholic. He's not practicing or anything, but he doesn't believe in divorce." Or more importantly, Laura thought, his poor dead father, who *was* devout in a bugger-the-choirboy sort of way, didn't believe in it.

"And . . . ?"

"Well, there's the money."

"What about the money?"

"It's mine. I mean, I inherited it from my father. He was an inventor and he came up with one of those simple little additives that keep things fresh for years. Anyway, he made a lot of money, and I was his only child, so I got it all. I've been financing Lloyd's post-production career from the beginning, before it started doing as well as it is now. If we divorced, with these no-fault laws we've got now, he'd get half of everything. That's not fair. It should be all mine by rights."

"I don't care about the money. It's you I want."

She touched his cheek. "That's sweet, Ray, and I wouldn't care if we didn't have two cents between us as long as we were together, honest I wouldn't. But it doesn't have to be that way. The money's there. And everything I have is yours."

"So what's the alternative?"

She put her hand on his chest and ran it over the soft hair down to his flat stomach and beyond, kissed the eagle tattoo on his arm. She remembered it from the TV commercial and the magazine, had thought it was sexy even then. The dogs stirred for a moment at the side of the bed, then went back to sleep. They'd had a lot of exercise that morning. "There's the house too," Laura went on, "and Lloyd's life insurance. Double indemnity, or something like that. I don't really understand these things, but it's really quite a lot of money. Enough to live on for a long time, maybe somewhere in the Caribbean? Or Europe. I've always wanted to live in Paris."

"What are you saying?"

Laura paused. "What if Lloyd had an accident? . . . No, hear me out. Just suppose he had an accident. We'd have everything then. The house, the insurance, the business, my inheritance. It would all be ours. And we could be together for always."

"An accident? You're talking about—"

She put her finger to his lips. "No, darling, don't say it. Don't say the word."

But whether he said it or not, she knew, as she knew he did, what the word was, and it sent a delightful shiver up her spine. After a while, Ray said, "I might know someone. I did an unusual job once, impersonated a police officer in Montreal, a favor for someone who knew someone whose son was in trouble. You don't need to know who he is, but he's connected. He was very pleased with the way things worked out and he said if ever I needed anything . . ."

"Well, there you are then," said Laura, sitting up. "Do you know how to find this man? Do you think he could arrange something?"

Ray took her left nipple between his thumb and forefinger and squeezed. "I think so," he said. "But it won't be easy. I'd have to go to Montreal. Make contact. Right at the moment, though, something a bit more urgent has come up."

Laura saw what he meant. She slid down and took him in her mouth.

Time moved on, as it does. The days cooled, but Ray and Laura's passion didn't. Just after Thanksgiving, the weather forecasters predicted a big drop in temperature and encouraged Torontonians to wrap up warm.

Laura and Ray didn't need any warm wrapping. The rose-patterned duvet lay on the floor at the bottom of the bed, and they were bathed in sweat, panting, as Laura straddled Ray and worked them both to a shuddering climax. Instead of rolling off him when they had finished, this time Laura stayed on top and leaned forward, her hard nipples brushing his chest. They hadn't seen each other for a week because Ray had finally met his contact in Montreal.

"Did you talk to that man you know?" she asked after she had caught her breath.

Ray linked his hands behind his head. "Yes," he said.

"Does he know what . . . I mean, what we want him to do?"

"He knows."

"To take his time and wait for absolutely the right opportunity?"

"He won't do it himself. The man he'll put on it is a professional, honey. He knows."

"And will he do it when the right time comes? It *must* seem like an accident."

"He'll do it. Don't worry."

"You know," Laura said, "you can stay all night if you want. Lloyd's away in Vancouver. Probably looking for property."

"Are you sure?"

"He won't be back till Thursday. We could just stay in bed the whole week." Laura shivered.

"Cold, honey?"

"A little. Winter's coming. Can't you feel the chill?"

"Now that you mention it . . ."

Laura jumped out of bed and skipped over to the far wall. "No wonder," she said. "The thermostat's set really low. Lloyd must have turned it down before he went away." She turned it up and dashed back, jumped on the bed, and straddled Ray. She gasped as he thrust himself inside her again. So much energy. This time he didn't let her stay in control. He grabbed her shoulders and pushed her over on her back, in the good old missionary position, and pounded away so hard Laura thought the bed was going to break. This time, as Laura reached the edges of her orgasm, she thought that if she died at that moment, in that state of bliss, she would be happy forever. Then the thermostat clicked in, the house exploded, and Laura got her wish.

TWO DOGS PERISH IN BEACHES GAS EXPLOSION, Lloyd Francis read in the *Toronto Star* the following morning. *HOUSE-OWNERS ALSO DIE IN TRAGIC ACCIDENT.*

Well, they got that wrong on two counts, thought Lloyd. He was sitting over a cappuccino in his shirtsleeves at an outdoor café on Robson Street in Vancouver. While the cold snap had descended on the east with a vengeance, the West Coast was enjoying record temperatures for the time of year. And no rain.

Lloyd happened to know that only one of the house's owners had died in the explosion, and that it hadn't been an accident. Far from it. Lloyd had planned the whole thing very carefully from the moment he had found out that his wife was enjoying a *grand passion* with an out-of-work actor. That hadn't been difficult. For a start, she had begun washing the bedsheets and pillowcases almost every day, though she usually left the laundry to Alexa. Despite her caution, he had once seen blood on the sheets. Laura had also been unusually reluctant to have sex with him, and on the few occasions he had persuaded her to comply, it had been obvious to him that her thoughts were elsewhere and that, in the crude vernacular, he had been getting sloppy seconds.

Not that Laura hadn't been careful. Lord only knew, she had probably stood under the shower for hours. But he could still tell. There was another man's smell about her. And then, of course, he had simply lain in wait one day and seen them returning together from the beach. After that, it hadn't been hard to find out where the man, Ray Lanagan, lived, and what he did, or didn't do. Lloyd was quite pleased with his detective abilities. Maybe he was in the wrong profession. He had shown himself to be pretty good at murder too, and he was certain that no one would be able to prove that the explosion in which his wife and her lover had died had been anything but a tragic accident. Things like that happened every year in Toronto when the heat came on. A slow leak, building over time, a stray spark or naked flame, and *BANG*!

Lloyd sipped his cappuccino and took a bite of his croissant.

"You seem preoccupied, darling," said Anne-Marie, looking lovely in a low-cut white top and a short denim skirt opposite him, her dark hair framing the delicate oval face, those tantalizing ruby lips. "What is it?"

"Nothing," said Lloyd. "Nothing at all. But I think I might have to fly back to Toronto today. Just for a short while."

Anne-Marie's face dropped. She was so expressive, showing joy or disappointment, pleasure or pain, without guile. This time it was clearly disappointment. "Oh, must you?"

"I'm afraid I must," he said, taking her hand and caressing it. "I have some important business to take care of. But I promise you I'll be back as soon as I can."

"And we'll look into getting that house we saw near Spanish Beach?"

"I'll put in an offer before I leave," Lloyd said. "It'll have to be in your name, though."

She wrinkled her nose. "I know. Tax reasons."

"Exactly. Good girl." It was only a little white lie, Lloyd told himself. But it wouldn't look good if he bought a new house in a faraway city the day after his wife died in a tragic explosion. This called for careful planning and pacing. Anne-Marie would understand. Marital separations were complicated and difficult, as complex as the tax laws, and all that really mattered was that she knew he loved her. After the funeral, he might feel the need to "get away for a while," and then perhaps Toronto would remind him too much of Laura, so it would be understandable if he moved somewhere else, say Vancouver. After a decent period of mourning, it would also be quite acceptable to "meet someone," Anne-Marie, for example, and start anew, which was exactly what Lloyd Francis had in mind.

* * *

Detective Bobby Aiken didn't like the look of the report that had landed on his desk, didn't like the look of it at all. He worked out of police headquarters at 40 College Street, downtown, and under normal circumstances, he would never have heard of Laura Francis and Ray Lanagan. The Beaches was 55 Division's territory. But these weren't normal circumstances, and one of Aiken's jobs was to have a close look at borderline cases, where everything *looked* kosher but someone thought it wasn't. This time it was a young, ambitious beat cop who desperately wanted to work Homicide. There was just something about it, he'd said, something that didn't ring true, and the more Bobby Aiken looked at the files, the more he knew what the kid was talking about.

The forensics were clean, of course. The fire department and the Centre for Forensic Sciences had done sterling work there, as usual. These gas explosions were unfortunately commonplace in some of the older houses, where the owners might not have had their furnaces serviced or replaced for a long time, as had happened at the house on Silver Birch. An accident waiting to happen.

But police work, thank God, wasn't only a matter of forensics. There were other considerations here. Three of them.

Again, Aiken went through the files and jotted down his thoughts. Outside on College Street it was raining, and when he looked out of his window all he could see were the tops of umbrellas. A streetcar rumbled by, sparks flashing from the overhead wire. Cars splashed up water from the gutters.

First of all, Aiken noted, the victims hadn't been husband and wife, as the investigators and media had first thought. The husband, Lloyd Francis, had flown back from a business trip in Vancouver—giving himself a nice alibi, by the way—as soon as he had heard the news the following day, and he was doubly distraught to find out that not only was his wife dead, but that she had died in bed with another man.

No, Lloyd had said, he had no idea who the man was, but it hadn't taken a Sherlock Holmes to discover that his name was Ray Lanagan, and that he was a sometime actor and sometime petty crook, with a record of minor fraud and con jobs. Lanagan had been clean for the past three years, relying mostly on TV commercials and bit parts in series like *Da Vinci's Inquest*, before the CBC canned it, and *The Murdoch Mysteries*. But Aiken knew that didn't necessarily mean he hadn't been up to something. He just hadn't been caught. Well, he had definitely been up to one thing—screwing Lloyd Francis's wife—and the penalty for that had been far more severe than for any other offense he had ever committed. He might have been after the broad's money too, Aiken speculated, but he sure as hell wasn't going to get that now.

The second thing that bothered Aiken was the insurance and the money angle in general. Not only were the house and Laura Francis's life insured for hefty sums, but there was the post-production company, which was just starting to turn a good profit, and Laura's inheritance, which was still a considerable sum, tied up in stocks and bonds and other investments. Whoever got his hands on all of that would be very rich indeed.

And then there was Lloyd Francis himself. The young beat cop who rang the alarm bell had thought there was something odd about him when he had accompanied Lloyd to the ruins of the house. Nothing obvious, nothing he could put his finger on, but just that indefinable policeman's itch, the feeling you get when it doesn't all add up. Aiken hadn't talked to Lloyd Francis yet, but he was beginning to think it was about time.

Because finally there was the one clear and indisputable fact that linked everything else, like the magnet that makes a pattern out of iron filings: He found out that Lloyd Francis had spent five years working as a heating and air-conditioning serviceman from just after he left school until his early twenties. And if you knew that much about gas furnaces, Aiken surmised, then you didn't have to bloody well be there when one blew up.

Lloyd felt a little shaken after the policeman's visit, but he still believed he'd held his own. One thing was clear, and that was that they had done a lot of checking, not only into his background, but also into the dead man's. What on earth had Laura seen in such a loser? The man had *petty criminal* stamped all over him.

But what had worried Lloyd most of all was the knowledge that the detective, Aiken, seemed to have about his own past, especially his heating and air-conditioning work. Not only did the police know he had done that for five years, but they seemed to know every job he had been on, every problem he had solved, the brand name of every furnace he had ever serviced. It was all rather overwhelming. Lloyd hadn't lied about it, hadn't tried to deny any of it—that would have been a sure way of sharpening their suspicions even more—but the truth painted the picture of a man easily capable of rigging the thermostat so that it blew up the house when someone turned it on.

Luckily, Lloyd knew they had absolutely no forensic evidence. If there had been any, which he doubted, it would have been obliterated by the fire. All he had to do was stick to his story, and they would never be able to prove a thing. Suspicion was all very well, but it wasn't sufficient grounds for a murder charge.

After the funeral, he had lain low in a sublet condominium at Victoria Park and Danforth, opposite Shopper's World. At night the streets were noisy and a little edgy, Lloyd felt, the kind of area where you might easily get mugged if you weren't careful. More than once he'd had the disconcerting feeling that he was being followed, but he told himself not to be paranoid. He wouldn't be here for long. After a suitable period of mourning he would go to Vancouver and decide he couldn't face returning to the city where his poor wife met such a terrible death. He still had a few colleagues who would regret his decision to leave, perhaps, but there wasn't really anybody left in Toronto to care that much about Lloyd Francis and what happened to him. At the moment, they all thought he was a bit depressed, "getting over his loss." Soon he would be free to "meet" Anne-Marie and start a new life. The money should be all his by then too, once the lawyers and accountants had finished with it. Never again would he have to listen to his wife reminding him where his wealth and success came from.

The Silver Birch explosion had not only destroyed Lloyd's house and wife, it had also destroyed his car, a silver SUV, and he wasn't going to bother replacing it until he moved to Vancouver, where he'd probably buy a nice little red sports car. He still popped into the studios occasionally, mostly to see how things were going, and luckily his temporary accommodation was close to the Victoria Park subway. He soon found he didn't mind taking the TTC to work and back. In fact, he rather enjoyed it. They played classical music at the station to keep the hooligans away. If he got a seat on the train, he would read a book, and if he didn't, he would drift off into thoughts of his sweet Anne-Marie.

And so life went on, waiting, waiting for the time when he could decently, and without arousing suspicion, make his move. The policeman didn't return, obviously realizing that he had no chance of making a case against Lloyd without a confession, which he knew he wouldn't get. It was late November now, arguably one of the grimmest months in Toronto, but at least the snow hadn't come yet, just one dreary gray day after another.

One such day Lloyd stood on the crowded eastbound platform at the St. George subway station wondering if he dare make his move as early as next week. At least, he thought, he could "go away for a while," maybe even until after Christmas. Surely that would be acceptable by now? People would understand that he couldn't bear to spend his first Christmas without Laura in Toronto.

He had just decided that he would do it when he saw the train come tearing into the station. In his excitement at the thought of seeing Anne-Marie again so soon, a sort of unconscious sense of urgency had carried him a little closer to the edge of the platform than he should have been, and the crowds jostled behind him. He felt something hard jab into the small of his back, and the next thing he knew, his legs buckled and he pitched forward. He couldn't stop himself. He toppled in front of the oncoming train before the driver could do a thing. His last thought was of Anne-Marie waving goodbye to him at Vancouver International Airport, then the subway train smashed into him and its wheels shredded him to pieces.

Someone in the crowd screamed and people started running back toward the exits. The frail-looking old man with the walking stick who had been standing directly behind Lloyd turned to stroll away through the chaos, but before he could get very far, two scruffy-looking young men emerged from the throng and took him by each arm. "No you don't," one of them said. "This way." And they led him up to the street.

* * *

Detective Bobby Aiken played with the worry beads one of his colleagues had brought him back from a trip to Istanbul. Not that he was worried about anything. It was just a habit, and he found it very calming. It had, in fact, been a very good day.

Not because of Lloyd Francis. Aiken didn't really care one way or another about Francis's death. In his eyes, though he hadn't been able to prove it, Francis had been a cold-blooded murderer and he had received no less than he deserved. No, the thing that pleased Aiken was that the undercover detectives he had detailed to keep an eye on Francis had picked up Mickey the Croaker disguised as an old man at the St. George subway station, having seen him push Francis with the sharp end of his walking stick.

Organized Crime had been after Mickey for many years now but had never managed to get anything on him. They knew that he usually worked for one of the big crime families in Montreal, and the way things were looking, he was just about ready to cut a deal: amnesty and the witness relocation plan for everything he knew about the Montreal operation, from the hits he had made to where the bodies were buried. Organized Crime were creaming their jeans over their good luck. It could mean a promotion for Bobby Aiken.

The only thing that puzzled Aiken was why? What had Lloyd Francis done to upset the mob? There was something missing, and it irked him that he might never uncover it now that the main players were dead. Mickey the Croaker knew nothing, of course. He had simply been obeying orders, and killing Lloyd Francis meant nothing more to him than swatting a fly. Francis's murder was more than likely connected with the post-production company, Aiken decided. It was well-known that the mob had its fingers in the movie business. A bit more digging might uncover something more specific, but Aiken didn't have the time. Besides, what did it matter now? Even if he didn't understand how all the pieces fit together, things had worked out the right way. Lanagan and Francis were dead and Mickey the Croaker was about to sing. It was a shame about the wife, Laura. She was a young, good-looking woman, from what Aiken had been able to tell, and she shouldn't have died so young. But those were the breaks. If she hadn't being playing the beast with two backs with Lanagan in her own bed, for Christ's sake, then she might still be alive today.

It was definitely a good day, Aiken decided, pushing the papers aside. Even the weather had improved. He looked out of the window. Indian summer had come to Toronto in November. The sun glinted on the apartment windows at College and Yonge, and the office workers were out on the streets, men without jackets and women in sleeveless summer dresses. A streetcar rumbled by, heading for Main station. Main. Out near the Beaches. The boardwalk and the Queen Street cafés would be crowded, and the dog-walkers would be out in force. Aiken thought maybe he'd take Jasper out there for a run later. You never knew who you might meet when you were walking your dog on the beach.

NUMBSKULLS

BY GEORGE ELLIOTT CLARKE

East York

I.

Bad men? No, not really. But they were no good. Or they were good-for-nothing ne'er-do-wells. Three goofs.

As one might expect, their childhoods were good for adult-only nightmares. Their parents were ratty in style and snaky by nature. Their dads' mouths were only half-toothed: The rest had been punched or kicked loose and lost. Their moms had craved abortions, but, addled, had said, "Ablutions," and had been served a lot of alcohol instead. Not as bad as thalidomide, but not helpful either.

The East Coast trio's pernicious sociology provides only dismal insight into the disgusting episode of savagery perpetrated in East End Toronto last May. Not even the excuse of primitivism mitigates the horror and stench of the crime, the abomination the three Nova Scotians wrought.

The names of the ex-Haligonians—once sailors turned truckers, who had migrated to East York following their dismissals from Her Majesty's Royal Canadian Navy—will not be forgotten by anyone alert to the reality of monsters. Bruno Bellefontaine, 25, Peter Purdy, 34, and Scott "Scalpel" McAlpine, 27, were turfed from the naval service because they were constantly sinking in rum. Disordered by drink, they disobeyed orders. The three tough guys, muscular bullies, made better boxers and wrestlers than they did seamen. They swore an oath to The Queen, yes, but they swore constantly at their officers too.

(Their officers had hoped to ship the trio to Afghanistan, to be shot down or blown up by the irregulars of the opium warlords. Unfortunately, as shipbound sailors, they would have faced little danger from either narco-terrorists or Islamist drug smugglers. Indeed, plenty of other Canucks were being dynamited and decimated, all without even an apologetic letter from The Queen, but it was quite impossible to ensure the same fate for the water-borne warriors.)

Following their jettisoning from Her Majesty's service, just last September, the three men drifted into the hard-driving, high-pay trade of trucking. Wanting to "get the hell out of the lousy Maritimes," where they were infamous for brawls and extra-toxic intoxication and for getting punched out in every grotty pub or murky tavern in which they exposed their mugs, they eagerly enlisted with Great Lakes–Atlantic Ocean. They began transporting goods among the spaced-out (distant) cities of Halifax, Montreal, Toronto, Windsor, and Thunder Bay.

The three boys loved the job, but could not steer clear of the sauce. They had the awful habit of spiking their coffee thermoses with Pusser's Navy Rum. To drive, just a little drunk, was okay, for it kept them pepped up, making their rigs smoke nonstop from payload to payload.

Off the road, the guys bunked in Toronto. It was terrific: not very French, not very English either. It was a fine place to unwind.

They found a three-bedroom apartment in the only affordable, near-downtown place left in Toronto: East York. The location nudged them, by a mile or so, a bit closer to the real East Coast, and they were only a few blocks away from a semblance of Atlantic Canada: the Beaches. (Yes, the burg was hoity-toity, but the sand was sand and the water was sky-blue.) Their corner was Coxwell and Danforth: a critical mass of taverns, cafés, diners, and medical facilities, everything from hospitals to funeral homes.

(In fact, to pass the north-south artery of Donlands Avenue and bear east along the Danforth is to encounter a horde of cripples wielding canes, gripping walkers, or speeding motorized wheelchairs along sidewalks or across streets. Between Donlands Avenue and Coxwell Avenue, the Danforth is a parade of invalids, interspersed with exotic immigrants, including strays from Atlantic coastal Canada.)

One truly funky hangout for the boys was the Terminal Diner, so-called because it was, three decades ago, a veritable bus terminal. Its decor was walls of black-and-white photos of undying Hollywood idols: Marilyn, Jack & Jackie, Lola Falana. The ceiling boasted vintage record album covers. Marilyn could wink at the boys as they slurped an extra-creamy milk shake; if they looked up, they could see Doris Day, Sammy Davis, Jr., Frank Sinatra, and Harry Belafonte beaming down at their french fries and chicken burgers, as if they were actual deities who could (and did) provide blessings for such greasy, sugary fare. No matter, the Terminal Diner was a cozy site for ostentation, semi-private smoking, and low-toned, public fuming.

Bruno, Peter, and Scalpel also loved checking out the Racetrack Tavern. But the best entertainment in the whole world was to sit on a park bench across from the Toronto East General Hospital and watch obscenely beautiful nurses pass in and out in white stockings, coats, skirts, dresses, and shoes, to eye the most interestingly limping, wobbling, or staggering patients, ideally women, also make their way outside to smoke, inside to die; their spastic motions; their disturbed, yet ballet-like movements; their flounces and jerks rendered them haunting to the point of arousing obsession.

Then again, none of the East Coast truckers were consummately paired with ladies. No, their unions were weekend flings or weeklong traumas. Their primary commitment was to the road, the rig, the rigmarole of work and drink and chat and card games, *not* to dames, who were great to eyeball but could only bring bad luck and babies.

The guys liked their low-rise apartment building on Monarch Park. Its rent was manageable on their three paychecks, and it was, for Toronto, unusually clean of cockroaches. The super—a Sicilian workaholic—was almost a stereotypical housewife, the way he fussed over every nook and cranny of the building, purging it of bugs, getting rid of "low-life scum" of all sorts, clearing out the garbage, and mopping and sweeping as if this were the exterminating duty of a soldier.

The boys didn't even have to trouble themselves about who used the "can" first, last, always: Their road schedule ensured they were seldom "home" together. However, when they were all about, they'd recall their Navy days, and go out and get shit-faced smashed.

They could don dark sunglasses anytime and cruise the Beaches scoping out the pointed erections of breasts—or even, if very lucky, actual topless nudity (legal in Ontario for a decade or more). Or they could jaunt up to the Plaza, at Victoria Park and Danforth, and try the fries at Burger King, pick up porn from the Adult Store, or, when weepingly sentimental, buy Newfie ballads from World of Song. Or they could hit the swanky section of the Danforth—Greek Town—and oil their throats with ouzo while salting them with lemony calamari.

Although the three lads could still drink to the acme of absurdity, they did not scuffle much now. In Toronto, unfriendly waitresses and waiters would simply summon the police, who were neither as forgiving nor as helpfully fanatical about fisticuffs as were the Halifax bobbies. Hogtown's finest would simply wade into an orchestra section of fists, swing their batons like mad conductors, or taser discordant miscreants, and then hogtie offenders' wrists as if they were closing up a garbage bag. Prison was a likely outcome of a Toronto to-do. After all, the Tories had thrown up a lot of jails during the '90s and the first years of the '00s. So it was better to sucker punch a foe in an alley and scram. Bruno, Pete, and Scalpel were awfully quick with the slick, dirty knuckle throw.

But the biggest difference between Good Toronto and all the smaller cities, including *Allô Police* Montreal, was the presence of many more "people of color" (as the newspapers said) and the extra-delicate women, a plush rainbow of dreams. The boys had gone to school with a black woman here, a yellow one there, but they had concentrated their adolescent, juvenile lusts on the Britannic brunettes, the Germanic blondes, the undecided Acadians. Yet Toronto expanded "poontang" possibilities exponentially, from the trim copper goddess in a sari to the golden divinity in a T-shirt and shorts. The truest benefit of the city's multiculturalism was its cosmopolitan smorgasbord of potential sex partners. Even the local cable TV monopoly sang the praises of this cornucopia of copulation possibilities, serving up such titles as *Chocolate Sticks and Vanilla Licks, Bollywood Busts and Hollywood Lusts, Asian Gals and Caucasian Pals* . . . When the guys weren't drunkenly veering their rigs between Gog and Magog, they were only stopping to view their hotel room TV screens, always tuned to a Cubist dazzle of body parts, an orgy of conjunctions and subtractions, plusses and minuses, as clear as the frank numerals of a tax return.

During his days and nights at home on Monarch Park, Scalpel would supplement his TV movie purchases by peering discreetly from behind the living room Venetian blind at the across-the-street neighbors, a piquant blend of Greek *pater* and Sri Lankan *mater*, issuing in a daughter, a teen delicacy of cocoa-butter tastefulness, a seeming satin smoothness of skin, black hair as jet and as long as licorice, two eyes as soft as sable, almond-shaped, and dark brown, and lips of a raspberry pink and strawberry plushness. She usually wore a Catholic uniform of uncomfortable (for Scalpel) brevity of skirt. Her *couture* was peculiar, if visually exciting, for her papa was Greek Orthodox, at least in terms of how *his* mother dressed (in comprehensive black, save for a strand of white pearls about her neck). In contrast, the neighbor girl's mother was not a devotee of modesty, for she, like her daughter, kept her hemlines and heels high. She was also transfiguringly beautiful, vaunting skin that was pure, sensuous sable in color and *imagined* feel, contrasting nicely with the honey-gold appeal of her daughter.

From his vantage point behind the Venetian blind, Scalpel could survey the thirty- to forty-second passage of the daughter from the house, her quick step to either the corner store or the parental car. On one memorable morning, a blast of wind had uplifted the skirts of both mother and daughter, revealing identical underthings of white lace. *French?*

Scalpel's surveillance was a private recreation, but he was also studious. He paid careful attention to the caramel girl and the chocolate woman (decidedly *not* a matron), to the extent that he heard the mother call the daughter's name, Diva, and the husband call the wife's name, Godiva. Then he spied a story in the *Scarborough Reflection*, wherein Diva Galatis was front and center—color photo and surname—because she had won her school's trophy for most valuable athlete, in field hockey, for the second triumphant year in a row. The photographer didn't seem to care that Diva's white bra gleamed through the pink threads of her tight top, along with the pointed suggestion of her curving femininity, but Scalpel cared. He kept the newspaper page folded in his wallet.

Come one special April dawn, Scalpel, the dark-haired, bespectacled, and solidly huge (but not fat) man, was padding along the sidewalk of Monarch Park, heading home from the Coxwell subway station, when he saw Diva, winsome in sneakers and womanish short skirt, stepping nonchalantly in his direction. His heart howled such thunder he was sure she would hear it and denounce him as a deviant. But no, she glanced at him, pursed her lips as she blew and cracked a bubblegum dirigible, smiled wanly, and said, "Hi." She was the epitome of curves. Scalpel could only mumble, or nearly moan, his reply. Immediately after she passed, he turned around and was greeted with the sweet vision of her plaid skirt swishing across her scrumptious derriere.

Thus, his surreptitious flirtation continued. Even Scalpel's two eighteen-wheeler mates, Bruno and Pete, were ignorant of his lurid, selfish panting after Diva, this angel goddess who commandeered his fantasies. And life went on.

II.

Then struck calamity: Diva, the immortally beautiful (and probably virginal) woman was felled in the middle of a game by an uplifted field hockey stick that hit in pure, malicious chance against her skull. The blow had enough force to kill her instantly, but somehow not enough to scar or bruise her soft tender skin; Diva had dropped where she stood, in the exact instant of an additional triumph, in her sneakers, red-and-green plaid skirt, and white knee socks.

The death of the athlete, only eighteen (her whole life and its eventual decline now void), became principal news on TV, radio, the Internet, and even on the front page of the *Toronto Star*. East York Holy Angels High School announced a full day of mourning presided over by grief counselors, who would painstakingly explain that death could befall even a popular, good-hearted, and good-looking athlete—even a teenage one. *Yes, no one was safe.*

But Scalpel was personally broken. Not decimated, devastated. He felt he'd given his granite heart to Diva, and now she was gone, and he'd never touched her, never felt her. He'd merely breathed in her direction, and, at that moment, he'd been breathless.

Pete and Bruno found Scalpel in the dark apartment, a bottle of Tito's Hand-Made Vodka handily half-empty and their buddy slobbering, slurring his words, reducing them to spit. He was moaning, moaning, "Diva was really, really, really unique."

They wondered who this mystery lady was, this inspiration for their pal's epic drunk. Scalpel drooled out his explanation, and his mates became intrigued. They too had noticed, now and then, the high school gal's succinct skirts that didn't so much cover anything as hover tantalizingly about. And they had also noticed Diva's extraordinary features and had, quite involuntarily, grunted inside their own minds. Being white-bread boys, they mused normally about the pale, anorexic waitresses and big-mouthed, big-assed, whey-faced whores and the wholesome, buxom, pie-faced cashiers at Tim's. Usually, they only vaguely appreciated the hot, ice cream–like colors of the "foreign hers."

But Scalpel's grief brought them, not to tears, but to lust for the dead neighbor, the Cinnamon Virgin of the Spice Isles. *What could she have been like?*

Pete studied the cute face in the obituary section. Diva did not belong among all the black-and-white oldsters slain by one casual cancer after another, whose mourning relatives (publishers in this case) all forbade flowers, desiring that sorrow be totaled in the form of a tax-deductible donation to a medical research charity. Diva glowed in full color, brilliant enough that her face seemed to lift from the drab newsprint and illuminate the room. Pete felt moisture in his long dried-up tear ducts. It was hard for him to believe that this fresh-faced chippie was lying waxen and cold in a mahogany chest in the Toronto East Funeral Chapel. Yet there were younger faces on the page too, and there was even a write-up about an unfortunate infant.

As Scalpel rocked and sobbed and wept into Bruno's chest, Pete opened the cold beer and began to gulp it down. *What was to be done?*

He was not moved by altruism. When charities knocked on the apartment door, seeking money to stop the polar ice caps from melting, or to buy polar bears better food, Pete enjoyed lecturing the do-gooders with this tale:

"A woman's German shepherd expired, and she wanted to take the corpse to the SPCA for disposal, but she didn't have a car. She called every cab company in the city to find a driver to take her and her dead dog to the pound. But every cab company—all of them superstitious—refused, often rudely, to help. The poor lady had to sacrifice her best suitcase, cram her dead dog Daisy inside, and take the subway over to Yonge and Queen. Climbing up the stairs to the street level, she was huffing and puffing and sweating like she was raining. A man approached her and offered to help her upstairs with the case. She smiled and accepted. After hefting the suitcase up one flight of stairs, the man stopped and exclaimed, 'Hey, lady! This suitcase is real heavy. What you got in here?' She didn't dare admit that it was a dog, so she lied: 'Oh, just my old computer.' The man grinned, and with instant vigor, bolted up the last several steps and ran off with his imagined booty."

After concluding this saga, Pete would swing the door shut in the faces of the Latter-day Saints, the Witnesses, the Greenpeaceniks, and even the collectors of money for Little League baseball uniforms. What he'd never say was that he was the man who'd stolen the useless corpse of a dog. He was no charitable son of a bitch. But Scalpel was his friend. And the dead girl was, well, a tartlet, who would now be devoured by worms, a most criminal and dismal rape. Simple, crude animals would munch all her loveliness, snacking on eyes, ass, everything soft and vulnerable. This truth seemed to Pete suddenly intolerable and royally vile. He had seen her once, up close, her long black hair cascading over a white blouse, and he had felt lust polysyllabically sully his heart. *How could this beauty be permitted to break down into loathsome slime?* The strange impudence of maggots should not prevail where a man can frustrate their insults. *Innocence topples to the tomb as easily as vice*—this was a truth as unpleasant as a dirty rag. *Something had to be done.*

Pete felt repulsed by Scalpel's panting, his tearful ejaculations, his blunt weeping, his vodka-addled fanaticisms, his clumsy hysterics. His friend's liquored-up agony required a succession of vodka shots—but also a deed so nude in meaning as to be unprintable. Pete planned a Gothic and gay catharsis to mollify Scalpel's drunken grimness. He felt a twinge of revulsion at his own idea, thinking, *I am a bad man. I am the wrong man. I am a natural man—the worst type.* Pete then communicated his scary amusement to Bruno, his shoulder wet with Scalpel's tears and snot: Time for relief from (and for) their sad-sack pal. The trio could have a riot . . .

III.

The entry was not fastidious. The three men were burly, and Pete's practiced crowbar jimmied open a basement window as easily as giving a teat to a baby. And just like they suspected, the sign in the window advertising *The Police Alarm Company* was fake—i.e., a lie. Not even a Toronto funeral home feared robbery.

Worried about a potential guard dog, Bruno took the crowbar and he swung it a few times, just for the feel of how it might waste a violent canine. But no saber-toothed poodle showed up.

Pete's flashlight transformed the trio into three ghouls, but soon they had ascended from the musty basement—the warehouse of caskets, including some needing repair—and broken out onto the main floor. They made their way carefully to the viewing rooms and began cracking open the coffins, one by one, to see where Diva lay. The blubbering Scalpel got sick, throwing up vodka-scented spit over the plushly carpeted floor and onto the cuffs of Bruno's pants. The big man wanted to slug Scalpel, but he simply snarled, "You're such a fuckin' slug."

Scalpel shrugged. He couldn't help feeling sick. One of the coffins they had just pried open was that of a blonde-gray woman, fiftyish. The problem was, in the flashlight's concentrated beam, the cadaver resembled his mother. Logically, he knew that this corpse was not her, for she was still kicking up her heels, so to speak, with her second hubby, in Come-by-Chance. But, emotionally stricken, he had to vomit.

Two false starts on, the boys found the gleaming mahogany, one-room place that was Diva Galatis's last redoubt on the planet. When Bruno pried up the casket lid like an unholy deity reviving—but not repairing—the dead, a gasp seized in all three throats, mouths, and lungs: The girl *was* awesomely beautiful, and the magic of makeup and preservatives had merely enhanced her natural perfection. She seemed to have simply walked off the street, stepped into this miniature bed, and gone to sleep. Blissful. Her funeral dress was simple, a white silk sheath, with discreet pads cupping the perfectly circular, if yet immature breasts. Her gold flesh shone through the filmy white of her grave bridal dress. Diva's hands were set to hold flowers at her chest, and the brown fingers flashed brilliant magenta nail polish. Her almond-shaped eyes were closed under dark-almond-colored lids, and the eyelashes were lustrously sable. Her slender legs tapered down to white schoolgirl socks and flat-soled black shoes. Death was an obvious crime in this case.

"Feast your eyes there, bud!" Pete croaked at Scalpel, whose porcine hands were now stroking, with the most delicate delicacy, the fine, though cool, cocoa-tinted skin of his beloved, his desire, his child-bride, only fifteen years his junior. No-nonsense Bruno, a man of practicality, tore free the satin lining the girl lay upon and, encasing her in this material, lifted her, with little strain, from the box, with Pete holding her legs straight, while Scalpel, disbelieving his joy, tore off his jacket and set it on the floor, as an act of homage for the gently descending corpse. Now, holding the flashlight, Scalpel watched as his two friends arranged the woman, still in a state of fine repose, upon the floor, using the coffin lining as a makeshift bridal suite sheet, while Scalpel's jacket was bunched into a pillow.

Bruno and Pete pried at Diva's legs, which parted stiffly, wafting the insidious smell of formaldehyde. The two men rolled up her dress, revealing a flawless anatomy, including a nicely wispy black brush of hair at her sex.

Excited, Pete snatched the flashlight and yelled at Scalpel, "DO it! DO it! We ain't got forever!"

Scalpel felt queasy, but Diva looked delectable. His desire overthrew all scruples. Besides, with a big-hearted laugh, Bruno was tugging down Scalpel's pants, and then encouraging him to kneel before the prone treat. Scalpel surged—he felt his blood and flesh surge—forward. Next, he realized Diva's smooth, cool thighs against his hot, hairy ones. Now he felt for the sex of the dead girl, believing that she would be kindly tight, if dry, and exquisitely gripping.

Bruno hollered, "Get her wet, boy!"

At this moment, Scalpel withdrew while Pete anointed the cadaver's unblemished sex with drippings from a flask. It gleamed; the whiskey glinted.

Ready, Scalpel thrust himself into the corpse; it shook and jiggled coldly upon the floor. But a pathetic delirium gave him pause: He understood that he was raping his beautiful neighbor, this luxurious pinnacle of womanhood, even as he adored the whiteness of his manhood as it drove into the inert brown once-woman, in a parody of copulation.

Pete reveled in this cocky farce, this murky but arousing debauch. The girl was sweetly akimbo, and utterly pretty, but Scalpel was jiggling and wriggling and snorting like a swinish monkey. No, Scalpel was like a busy eel, spasmodic, darting in and out of the unexpected luxury of the virgin spoil, until his nasty, brutal sallies should attain their vain objective. Suddenly he was groaning. Pete spat icily, "Don't cuss the chill! Pal the gal, man, and laugh." Pete stared, as if drooling at the seesawing transports of his buddy.

After five crazy minutes, a climax shook Scalpel and he

fell away from the icy doll. He was satisfied, but sobbing, then vomiting under the empty ripped-up casket, still held up at chest level upon its trolley.

Pete growled, "Sloppy seconds for me!" After some perfunctory cleaning with tissue taken from the nearby washroom, he was also soon moaning, "Diva, Diva, Diva," as he writhed and shivered. How memorably thrilling it was to have this highly polished cadaver, this ready-made, unblushing, yet virtuous excellence!

Looking, still weeping, at Pete's infernal coupling with the dead girl, Scalpel knew it was not devotion, but desecration. Pete's insistent, unstinting strokes, executed not an ordinary vulgarity, but a fantastically monstrous treason—like someone befouling the face of The Queen with a bodily emission. Scalpel regretted his own too-immediate yielding to Pete, for the dude was grinding into Diva as if she were a pencil sharpener. Scalpel sulked like an emperor forced to accept democracy. *Okay, so none of us are Christ! Does that mean Pete has to play a cockroach?* Scalpel imagined only one remedy for his escalating distaste for Pete's violence: hatred for the man himself. Diva's ravishing would have to prove costly. Scalpel could not let the snake dump his venom into the defenseless girl.

Immersed in Diva's swank vise, Pete felt like an opulent Vandal sacking Rome. This defilement was delirious. He thought, *I am dreaming. I am desiring. I am bad.* He was a phallic angel—no, a reckless devil—now building up to an inevitable nicety. Athletic, untiring, he steadily pumped away at the cold woman's core, that moist gleam in the cylindrical light showing up his dark driving. It was a signal plunder, though the victim was as sticky as mud. A billy goat stench, Pete's, hovered over the scene.

Still shadowy, beyond the flashlight beam in Bruno's hand, Scalpel stealthily retrieved the crowbar and struck wildly but heavily at Pete. The iron bar swung. One blow would pulverize Pete's petal-soft skull.

Bruno saw a long, black object sweep down into the white flashlight illumination and sink, cracking, splashing, into the crown of Pete's head. Bruno did not even have enough time to let the flashlight shake or flicker as some black liquid shot from Pete and dirtied his own face and clothes. Bruno felt rueful, but Scalpel had been ruthless.

In an instant, Pete went from fornication to celibacy. A sizzling convulsion. Black gore pissed up from the pointedly indented skull. Ominous. *Here is real bullshit, some real horse manure*, Bruno thought.

Bruno switched off the flashlight just in case Scalpel wanted to take a swipe at him with the bloody bat. He wasn't sticking around. He dropped the light and hauled ass back to the basement stairwell.

Freaked out by the murder of his buddy, by another buddy, because both had copped with a corpse, and shaking anyway, Bruno lost his footing on the dark stairs. He pitched into the void and came up twisted, his neck broken.

Not the type to quail before a dog's breakfast of a crime, Scalpel retrieved the flashlight, and, in the dimming beam, pulled Pete off their victim and pushed his pal's body into the drying vomit under the dolly hoisting Diva's gutted casket.

Now Scalpel held Diva's head on his lap. The girl remained for him perfectly pure, despite her bloody, ruined dress and the outrages lately visited upon her otherwise preserved perfection. His pitiful tears rendered hers beautiful.

FILMSONG

BY PASHA MALLA

Little India

The door of the Taj opened and two men came in. They moved past Aziz and stood at the sweets counter in the back. The only other customer was some old guy waiting for a take-out order. He was sitting at a table near the door, watching Gerrard Street through the window. It was close to 6 o'clock and getting dark. The streetlamps had come on and cars flashed by hissing through the slush with their lights on.

A young girl was working. Thursday nights were quiet. It was just her up front and her mum cooking in the back. She glided over and leaned her elbows on the counter.

"Ras malai," said one of the men.

"With saffron," said the other.

"We don't do them with saffron," said the girl. "Sorry."

"What the hell, *don't do them with saffron*," said the first man. His voice was loud now. "First it's minus bloody twenty-thirty degrees in your country. Benchod, you freeze your bloody nuts off! Now we ask ras malai with saffron, but you say no saffron."

The girl whisked a stray bit of hair back from her forehead. "Yeah, no saffron. We've only got plain. You should try the gulab jamun. They're good. Really fresh."

The second man whispered something to the first man. Aziz scooped rogan josh into his mouth with his fingers, but didn't take his eyes off the two men. They were dressed similarly: collared shirts—tucked into their jeans and unbuttoned to reveal great thrusts of chest hair—and leather jackets. The louder one had a mustache. The other didn't. They both wore red threads tied around their wrists.

The second man, the clean-shaven, quiet one, said, "Gulab jamun, too sweet."

"Try the jalebi," said the girl.

The first one made a noise. "Benchod, even sweeter! You have ras malai, you add saffron, not too sweet. We want not too sweet." He turned to Aziz. His eyes went from Aziz's face to a poster above the table where Aziz was eating. On it was the actor Shahrukh Khan, mugging for the camera in sunglasses. "Is it right, Shahrukh?"

"Sorry?" said Aziz.

"Come on, Shahrukh." He was getting into it now. "You want sweets, Shahrukh? You're a film hero, which sweets will you order? You eat jalebi?"

Aziz looked at the girl on the other side of the counter. She looked back.

"Um," said Aziz.

The two men advanced toward him. "What, Shahrukh?" said the one with the mustache. "Come on, yaar."

The other one said something in what Aziz guessed was Marathi. Both men laughed. They were at his table now. The loud one poked his tin plate with a fingertip. "You eat meat, Shahrukh? You are Mussulman, just like the real Shahrukh?"

Aziz glanced down at his plate, at the half-eaten lamb. He looked up at the one man, then the other. They leaned toward him. There was beer on their breath. When the one with the mustache breathed his nose made a whistling noise.

Then a bell rang from the back. "Chicken tikka, naan, mattar paneer," called the girl.

The old guy at the front of the restaurant got up. Aziz and the two men watched him move past their table and collect a paper bag from the girl. "Thanks," he said.

The old guy left. Outside the snow was blowing in golden squalls in the light of the streetlamps. The two men turned back to Aziz. "Shahrukh," said the loud, mustachioed one, "we are looking for a journalist. Do you know this journalist? His name is Meerza."

"Shahrukhji," said the other, "we work for a Mussulman. In Mumbai. We are not communalists. Our friends are Mussulman, Parsi, Hindu, Jain, Christian, whomever."

The two men sat down across from Aziz. "I am Prem, this is Lal," said the one with the mustache.

"Do you know this man, this Meerza?" asked Lal. He pulled out a photograph and slid it across the table. Aziz looked at the image. It was his neighbor, smiling before a typewriter. Aziz knew this man as Durani, the name written on his box in the building's mailroom, and not Meerza. "We are journalists also," said Lal. "We have come from India to meet this man."

Aziz stared at the photograph. Once he had locked himself out and Durani had taken him into his own apartment until the superintendent arrived. The place had been empty except for a mattress on the floor and a few piles of books. While they were waiting Durani had prepared chai in the Kashmiri style, with almonds, cinnamon, and cardamom. Aziz had said nothing about this, nor had he mentioned the many books of Urdu poetry stacked around the room. The building, just west of Greenwood, was the sort of place where everyone had left a story behind somewhere else. The residents shared this, along with the understanding that no one needed to stir them up here.

In the photograph Durani looked different. There were no bags under his eyes. The skin on his face seemed less sallow. He appeared gregarious and happy, full of energy. His shirt was clean and freshly pressed. This was not how he looked now. But it was him.

"Do you know this Meerza?" asked Prem. He laid a clammy hand on Aziz's arm. The knuckles bristled with hair. There was a time when Aziz would have taken that wrist between his fingers and snapped it like a twig. Instead, all he did now was resist the urge to yank his own arm away.

Aziz looked at the photograph again, then up at Prem. "No," he said. "I don't know anyone named Meerza."

Prem and Lal sat there for a moment before Lal took back the photograph. "Okay."

"What is playing at the cinema, Shahrukh?" said Prem, letting go of Aziz.

"At the Beach or at the Gerrard?"

"The one just there." Prem motioned with his hand down the street. The gesture traced Aziz's walk home, past the tikka houses and stores of religious paraphernalia, past the Ulster Arms with its coterie of drunks smoking in the parking lot, streetcars clattering by in both directions.

"The one that shows Hindi films," said Lal.

"The Gerrard?" The cinema had reopened recently after years of dereliction. Durani worked there as an usher. Aziz often saw him leaving for work in the starchy uniform, bow tie and all. "I think that place is closed."

"No," said Prem. "Definitely not closed, Shahrukh. Is it, Lal?"

"No," said Lal.

"No, we are quite certain that it is open. In fact, we have come all the way from India especially to make a visit there."

"We have heard the films are very good," said Lal. "First-class Hindi films."

"Perhaps you are starring, Shahrukh?" Prem grinned. A single gray tooth appeared like a tombstone amidst a row of white. Aziz stared at it. It was a dead thing.

Lal slapped the table with both hands. The smack made Aziz jump. It was a sudden, swift act of violence from the quiet man. "We will go to the cinema then," said Lal. "What is playing, it does not matter. We will go for the songs."

The two men stood. "Finish your meal, Shahrukh," said Prem. "Enjoy your meat."

They headed out into the night. The snow whirled into the restaurant on a blast of cold air as they left, and then the door closed. Through the window Aziz watched the two men zip their coats and turn their collars up against the snow, then move off down the street.

Aziz turned back to his meal. He stirred the rogan josh with his fingertips. The lamb had gone cold.

The man in 8B whom he knew as Durani answered Aziz's knock in his shirtsleeves. He looked at Aziz without speaking, hiding most of his body behind the door. Aziz dripped melting snow onto the landing, his eyelashes trapping beads of frost.

"There are two men looking for you," said Aziz. "From Bombay."

Durani stared at Aziz. He said nothing.

"They've gone to the cinema where you work. I thought you'd want to know."

Durani nodded. "Thank you," he said. He went as

though to close the door, then paused. "Will you come in for a moment?"

The inside of the apartment hadn't changed since Aziz had been there last. The bed sat in the center of the room, neatly made. Perhaps there were more books, spilling in piles around the place: Hindi books, English books, Urdu books, books in Arabic, even a few in French. Outside, the wind howled and rattled the windows in their frames.

Durani had been making tea. He brought Aziz a cup, once again in the Kashmiri style. It was warm and sweet and made Aziz think of home, a place he likely had in common with this Durani. They sat cross-legged across from one another on the floor, teacups in their laps. Durani peered at Aziz, then set his teacup down and began digging through a stack of books. He produced a sheaf of typewritten papers stapled together, and passed it to Aziz.

The papers were galleys of an article written for a prominent Canadian newsmagazine, authored by a certain S.B. Meerza and annotated with a few edits in blue ink. Accompanying the text was a picture of the man sitting across from Aziz.

"Read," said this man.

What Aziz read was a profile of a certain highly reputable Bollywood actress—an actress he knew well and whose films he had enjoyed before moving to Toronto. Now he didn't go to the cinema. He woke up, went to his job at the bread factory, had a meal, and then headed to his job at the ice rink. He came home late and slept. Little by little, he was saving money to bring his brother to Canada.

This actress, the article explained, had recently achieved international prominence. She was a fixture now on TV entertainment programs otherwise specializing in Hollywood news, although she had yet to appear in an American movie. But she was on billboards and in magazine ads for perfumes and cosmetics in New York, London, Toronto, all heavy-lidded eyes and glistening lips. There was regular talk of her, even outside India, as "the most beautiful woman in the world."

The first few paragraphs detailed this increasing global fascination with the girl from Malabar Hill. Aziz was familiar with her story. Everyone was. But he could feel the article moving toward something else. There was a subtle irony to how her career was being explained. And the urgency on the face of the man opposite, the author—his tea untouched and going cold—only added to these suspicions.

Sure enough, the article began to pose questions. How had it all happened so quickly? Why were international markets suddenly taking interest? India had been producing screen beauties for generations. There were countless other Bollywood starlets just as stunning, as talented, as charismatic. Why this one?

And then things turned. The actress, claimed the article, had enlisted Mob help: Producers had been threatened, politicians bribed, corporations extorted. A murder led to another, which led to another, which resulted in all-out gang warfare on the streets of Bombay. The article linked the previous year's communal riots to the actress's growing success. A bomb had derailed a commuter train while she presented an award at a film festival in Italy, killing dozens.

None of what the article discussed, Aziz knew, was anomalous in the Indian film industry. But glancing up occasionally at the man across from him—Durani, Meerza, whoever he was, huddled there on the floor in his empty apartment with his tea—he could see the consequences of trying to publish it in a North American publication, of smearing Bollywood's great international hope. That it had never seen the newsstand spoke to the power of the Mob. All its author had left were a bed on the floor, a pile of books, and a galley copy of a piece that never was.

The article ended with a description of the actress making an appearance at the Toronto Film Festival on the arm of a celebrity music producer. The reader was left in a blinding array of flashbulbs and glamour. Aziz flipped the pages back into order and handed the article to Meerza.

"No," the neighbor said, waving his hand. "You keep it."

Aziz paused. He didn't want this thing, and the responsibility it represented. He was doing fine. "Are there other copies?"

"No," said Meerza. "They destroyed my computer and the magazine's files were deleted. This is all that is left."

"I can't take it," said Aziz.

"Please. They've found me."

"You can't run? Or tell the police?"

"These are goondas only. If I say anything about these, and even if police action is taken, more will come. Now that they have found me outside India I will be easy to track. Every move I make will be known."

"So what will you do?"

"I will wait."

"Here?"

"Where else? Perhaps they just want to talk to me, see how I am doing." Meerza swept a hand around the apartment, sketching its emptiness with his fingers.

Outside on the street the snow had stopped. The sky was still and purple. Aziz walked west along Gerrard, snow crunching and squeaking under his boots. In one pocket was Meerza's article, folded into thirds. In the other was the knife. As a streetcar rattled past, Aziz wrapped his gloved fingers tightly around the handle, careful not to pop the blade.

At the Gerrard Cinema he stopped. The marquee twinkled. It cast a dome of yellow light onto the street. Aziz bought a ticket to the early show, which had started nearly an hour ago. The woman working told him this but he waved his hand: no matter. He wanted to see this picture. There was an actress in it who was important to Aziz.

The cinema was dark save the band of light twirling out from the projector, silent save a sad violin and the rattle of the film threading from reel to reel. On screen, the famous Indian actress was praying silently before some sort of altar. It was night. The moonlight in the film was blue. Aziz stared at the screen for a moment, at the woman up there. Then he sat down at the end of an empty row near the door, looking around.

Less than half the seats were occupied. People were scattered around the theater, mostly in groups of two. Aziz glanced from one pair of heads to the next: a woman and her son, two elderly Sikhs, a young couple with their arms around one another. But then, there they were. Prem and Lal were only four rows up, against the wall on the left side of the theater. There was a seat separating the two men, but it was definitely them—the shorn heads gave them away. Aziz fingered the article in his pocket with one hand and the knife with the other.

The action in the film had moved to a battlefield. A handsome soldier was loading his gun while bombs exploded all around. Aziz watched as either Prem or Lal stood in the dark and shuffled his way up the aisle. He lowered his face as the hired thug walked by. The man had a mustache; it was Prem.

Aziz waited until Prem had exited the theater, then slipped out of his seat.

In the bathroom there was one stall, a sink, and a single urinal. The door to the stall was closed. Between it and the floor were jeans hiked to reveal mismatched socks: one blue, one black. Aziz leaned against the sink and unfolded the article from his pocket.

"*Last year's communal violence that erupted on the streets of Bombay,*" he read aloud, "*can be directly attributed to the involvement of gangs in the film industry. The startling rise to the top of one actress, in particular, is irrevocably linked to an ongoing war between certain rival production studios and their respective Mob affiliations.*"

From the stall there was no sound. The feet didn't move.

Aziz continued: "*North American audiences might be interested to know that the Indian actress whose 'exotic' look sells them cosmetics, soft drinks, and high fashion—the international face of Bollywood—has achieved prominence in her home country not by talent, or even looks, but by a methodically implemented strategy of extortion, blackmail, and even murder.*"

More silence from behind the stall door. Aziz flipped the pages until he found the passage he was looking for.

"*The efforts of Bombay's police to curtail the rising violence have been compromised not only by organized crime syndicates, but also by the financial backers of the film industry, who pay off the city's lawmakers to turn a blind eye to their activities. One officer who refused to be bribed was executed, as an example to his colleagues, in broad daylight on Jehu Beach, where he was walking with his wife and daughter.*"

Aziz lowered the article.

"This was my brother," he told the feet beneath the stall. "Our father was an officer in Kashmir, and when the troubles became too much, we moved south to Jammu, and my brother and I both enrolled in the academy. When we graduated, I stayed in Jammu. He went to Bombay."

The toilet flushed. Aziz tensed.

But then nothing happened. The stall door didn't open. The feet remained where they were. Aziz thought back to Prem's hand on his arm, the hair on his knuckles and the touch of his skin, cold and wet. That dead gray tooth.

A minute passed. Another. Still the feet remained motionless. Laying the article on the counter by the sink, Aziz pulled the knife from his pocket. He flicked the blade. The noise it made was crisp and clean. He breathed, he blinked, he stared at those mismatched socks underneath the stall door, and he waited.

PART II

THE MILD WEST

WANTED CHILDREN

BY HEATHER BIRRELL

Bloor West Village

Beth knew Paul would not leave her. It would be up to her.

"Did you see this?" He cocked his head to the side, then skewed it aggressively toward his laptop, which he had perched on a pile of old newspapers on the kitchen table.

"See what?" Beth refused to turn from her careful work at the counter. The naturopath had said six drops of the kava root tincture and three of the impatiens, star of Bethlehem, cherry plum, rock rose, and clematis. In spring water. She squeezed the top of the dropper delicately. Two drops fell, followed by a narrow quicksilver dribble. The precision of it all, the crucial measurements and ratios, the equilibrium and relative concentration and dilution—it was doing her in a bit. But the naturopath had said it would help her regain a sense of her place in the world, settle her nervous system, her overactive mind, and her frequently aroused nether regions. She would feel better, centered, the healer had promised.

Beth smiled. The water clouded then cleared. She lifted the glass to her mouth, and let the mixture slide home. It tasted like moss, mold, cheap perfume sunk deep into cheaper upholstery. She gagged and grabbed the edge of the sink, then closed her eyes without thinking—as if shutting off one sense might dull another—and listened to Paul like he was bearing a message from a fleeting and inconsequential dream.

"Beth, I'm serious."

She opened her eyes and looked out the window. It was summertime in Bloor West Village, and the purple finches, with their wine-speckled plumage, were regular visitors to the feeder. *As if they've been dipped in raspberry juice*, she remembered reading in a guidebook. The birds flitted and pecked, then retreated from a domineering grackle.

Paul whistled through his teeth and Beth watched him sit back hard in his chair. "Check this out," he said. Something had scared him a little, and it was this that finally drew Beth to the screen.

It was an abstract, staged photo, something someone with too much studio time and grant money had cooked up. A black river with creatures rising sluggishly from its depths. Swamp monsters—perhaps it was a movie trailer? Beth shook her head. "So?"

"It's Cuyabeno," Paul replied. "It's your river, Beth."

The trip had been Paul's idea. They'd been trying for two years to conceive, then stopped, then succeeded, then miscarried. Then there were too many options dangled before them, too many well-meaning, putty-faced friends at the door. Paul began to clear out corners in the basement; Beth took long walks in Etienne Brûlé Park. The park was a long strip of winding land on either side of the Humber River, one-time superhighway for the coureur de bois of the park's name. Brûlé was only twenty-three when he became the first European to see Lake Ontario from the mouth of the Humber. What must he have been thinking as he stared out into that inland ocean, surrounded by his Huron Indian brothers? The fall of 1615: Toronto was nothing more than a carrying place, a spot to heave burdens onto strong backs and into hardy canoes.

Yonge Street, longest street in the world, that broad boulevard of strip clubs, fast food, head shops, and hairdressing salons had nothing on the Humber in its heyday—explorers, missionaries, and traders vying for bewildered souls, the softest of fur pelts, the prospect of getting there *first*. Oh, it was romantic and incorrect, she knew, but when Beth visited the park she often thought of Brûlé, and would forego the two landscaped paths for the less manicured trail that ran right smack up against the river's edge.

The alternative was the commercial strip on Bloor where for weeks they attempted to distract themselves, buying crumbly, extravagantly priced cheeses from the new high-end deli, top of the line BC and Australian wines from the LCBO, and organic beef from the butcher. Their neighborhood was a town unto itself, the welcome signs and the real estate pages proclaimed, and it did seem its own little satellite village, not quite suburb, but not entirely of the city either. Quaint, functional, and quietly fantastical, it had an air of the hobbit—hobbit with Eastern European roots, with lingering Ukrainian bakeries and specialty shops. Even the homeless folk tipped their hats with one hand while they held out the other for change. The buskers strummed mournful Ukrainian folk tunes on battered guitars, and on Sundays the loudspeaker at Saint Pius X played stately choral music, designed, it seemed, to chide and cajole the wayward. God was already smiling on Bloor West Village; there was no pressing need for prayer.

And on every street corner and tidy parkette, Beth spotted the strollers. For her they were little buggies of anguish—their sturdy wheels and bright utilitarian fabric, their multitude of clipped-on accessories and soft, cushioned interiors. She wanted to puncture their tires, spray paint their protective sides, slash their UV-blocking visors. Paul knew this, he saw this, and he said, "Let's go away. Somewhere where people don't think this way, the way we think."

Beth had nodded, semi-entranced by Paul's ability to imagine quick fixes and to act on them with a kind of jittery intensity. When he suggested Ecuador, the emerald light and mercurial moisture of the rain forest, she had shrugged then wondered sheepishly, "Isn't it a bit, I dunno, cliché?"

"It won't be cliché for long," he said grimly. "It will be gone."

"That's what I mean," she said. "It's like we're peering in at a dying, caged animal, isn't it?"

"Maybe," said Paul in a way that suggested he hated himself, "there is a way of helping."

He looked like he wanted to stick forks in his eyes, so Beth agreed to go. Paul had a friend who had been through the region with an NGO. The friend gave them tips and details: what to bring, whether to tip or haggle, which immunizations to endure and delicacies to sample. They were to spend two weeks in the Amazon basin, in Cuyabeno National Park.

The trip had been literally breathtaking, fourteen days and nights where Beth spent whole minutes trying to teach herself to breathe again. Was it the humidity or simply the intensity? They called it the world's pharmacy, an Eden: sweet balm and scourge, the innocence and viscera of new beginnings. But it was also something more sinister, something cloying and stealthy. To say it was unlike anything Beth had ever experienced might have been inaccurate—there were woods in northern Ontario whose fog of blackflies and sneering impenetrability came close, maybe. But where the native people of her northern province had been decimated by white man's guilt, these jungle lands were still inhabited by their original denizens—men and women with wide implacable faces and smooth, rubbery skin who clambered up the banks of the river with ease, clutching plastic jugs of gasoline, babies strapped to their backs with long strips of cloth.

Miguel, their tour guide, was such a man. Short and compact in body, barrel-chested, with a few uneven black sprigs of hair for a beard, he had a thin, rosy scar along his jawline and the haircut of a more urban, moneyed man. When he smiled, Beth noted his strong, small, pointy teeth.

This was in a café in Lago Agrio, way-station for travelers, frontier town for the desperate and entrepreneurial. She and Paul had been waiting a long time on a patio, clinking their cups of Nescafé against their saucers.

"Do you think that's him?" Paul pointed toward the street, where a mocha-skinned man was pulling a trolley. They were to expect a guide who spoke five languages, a war veteran, friendly and "uninhibited," the keen teenager who booked their trip had reassured them. When Miguel appeared it was from within the rendezvous restaurant; his arms made his T-shirt bulge with their baseball-sized biceps and he was sporting cheap orange flip-flops, which he continued to wear for the duration of the journey, exposing his long, yellowy-tough toenails, and making the rest of the tour group, in their beige, super-tread hiking shoes, feel subtly, wonderfully mocked.

On the bus to the oversized, motorized canoe, which was to take them to their campsite, the dust from the window made Beth cough, and the rutted roads caused the bus to jump. The inside of her head was all jangly with priorities and survival, and she felt sunburned although she had not been in the sun. She nodded to the two Germans who had joined the group, and then pushed past Paul, who was sleeping, a thin line of spittle reaching from his bottom lip to the strap of his day pack, which he had, wary of pickpockets, left attached to his back.

"Do you mind?" She motioned to the vacant aisle seat next to Miguel.

"Not at all," he said. "You are welcome."

She sat next to him, not speaking, trying to catch her breath.

"You are having some difficulty, some respiratory difficulty?" He turned toward her, face creased with concern and something else—amusement or maybe lust?

"I'm fine," she said, and took in a big lungful of air, right down into her diaphragm, as she'd learned in a few yoga classes and tricky situations.

"Good," he said and went back to his book.

Beth closed her eyes, but that made her dizzy, so she opened them. It was difficult, sitting on the aisle, to find a place to look. Straight ahead meant a row of seatbacks, brown vinyl and grimy. It meant absorbing the reality of the interior of the bus, a rollicking, wretched press of passengers, bulky bags, boxes, and bound chickens. It meant considering which qualifications, exactly, were required to drive a bus in this *strange* country. And looking outside, well, that would involve craning over Miguel to the window so that her head was positioned directly above his crotch.

Also, Beth was experiencing traveler's terror—the pervasive notion that each moment represented a small treasure trove of noteworthy difference, of sights, sounds, smells completely and utterly foreign to what she had ever encountered, and that she would *never pass this way again*. She pivoted her body and her breast grazed Miguel's arm. She muttered an apology, and squinted out at the side of the road. Outside was both hazy with dust and excessively green. The foliage looked prehistoric—gigantic ferns bowing chaotically to the palms reaching high up into the cloudless sky. This was it—the jungle. Miguel shifted to turn the page of his book and she felt obliged to speak. "What are you reading?"

He closed the book to show her the cover, a sepia-toned watercolor of a barn with a fair-haired woman standing in the foreground looking to the horizon. In the top right-hand corner of the book was a gold seal. Beth peered at it. It was one of Oprah's book club picks. Miguel was watching her.

She had no idea what to say. The man in the tour agency had told them Miguel still had a bullet in his thigh from fighting in the border dispute with Peru. Finally she settled on, "Any good?"

Miguel nodded eagerly. "Very good, and it helps me to practice, to stay fluent, use new words." He opened the book to the page he was on. "What does this mean?" He pointed to a word.

Beth did not know what the word meant. She took the book from Miguel and read the blurb on the back. A multigenerational saga set in the American Midwest with a complicated, malevolent patriarch at its core. "Must be dialect," she said, shaking her head. "Sorry."

"It's okay."

But she knew she had fallen in his estimation. She glanced out the window again. There were black pipes running alongside the road that seemed to be made out of the same plastic used to make heavy-duty sports drink bottles. The pipes didn't look very serious, especially next to the profusion of vine and leaf that surrounded them. They passed a length of pipe covered in white spray paint. Beth caught the word OXY repeated in messy, angry capital letters. "What is that?"

Miguel closed his novel, placing a purple bookmark in

its pages. "Oil pipelines," he said. "My people, the people of the river, the Siona, they want the oil companies out. They're sabotaging our home. We have stopped them before. We are well-organized, and although it is not entirely in our nature, we protest peacefully."

"Is it true you have a bullet in your thigh?" Beth blurted, somewhat fanatically.

Miguel nodded. "My partner was not so lucky," he said.

From across the aisle, Beth heard what sounded like a deliberate sniff from Paul. Perhaps it was warranted. But she was mesmerized by Miguel's offhand manner, his apparent obliviousness to his own glaring, gaudy contradictions.

She wondered where Miguel was now, envisioned him paddling valiantly, hopelessly through the unthinkable sludge his river had become. Or maybe not. Instead: in a hotel room in town, his head between the legs of one of the other "uninhibited" citizens of El Oriente. The women of Lago Agrio had been as colorful and intent as the jungle birds; their tight green leggings, pink stilettos, and bands of quivering exposed flesh spoke mostly of joy and heat.

Paul was speaking to her, saying something about the political situation in South America. "It was Occidental, Beth. You know, the one they've been protesting for years. Here, then, is irony. Finally, they get them to admit their free trade has been anything but. They manage to oust them from the land, to reclaim what is theirs. And then, this. I wouldn't be surprised if it's the Man simply asserting his dominance. Oops, spilled some oil in your fresh, piranha-infested, life-giving waters. Sorry about that, but you shouldn't have asked us to leave so rudely. We were, after all, your guests. And were we not gracious? Did we not give your people training and jobs?

Oh, we know. The rule of law. But what about the rule of the jungle?" Paul was clicking around the website as he spoke, searching madly for clues.

She still could not quite grasp what he had shown her. There were ramifications, she knew, delicate ecosystems, butterflies on one side of the world flapping their diaphanous blue wings, while on the other side lucky humans sampled sushi; everything explained by a near-invisible knotted string you could follow back to a few greedy men with polished scalps and eyes like hunks of coal dreaming of the ninth hole and profit charts that explained their own lives to them in triplicate.

And then panic pushed like a spring shoot through the loam of her thoughts. She remembered Miguel, as she had been remembering him suddenly and without apparent justification, since she returned to her house on Willard Avenue with her husband of thirteen years, in the west end of Toronto, here amidst some tall buildings, next to a river and a lake, where she lived and would maybe die. Since childhood she had pinned herself to this map. It reassured her to know the order of her own locale. She knew the earth did not belong to her but to her grandchildren, and perhaps not even to them. But what if there were no children, no grandchildren, and the generational link was lost? One day she would be old, bereft, still angry . . . The image of that other equatorial river she had also begun to call her own, lying like a dark, drugged serpent, flashed into her mind. She turned to Paul. "I'm going to the river."

"I'll follow," he said, with a knowing, almost servile condescension.

She shrugged, thought for a moment about what she might need, then shrugged again. She took Colbeck Street over to

Jane, held out her hand at the crosswalk, then marched across like a trusting fool. From there it was a short hike down to the entrance of the park, and down the short steep hill at Humberview Road, and the longer sloping hill of Old Mill Drive. She reached the parking lot running, had to stop and crouch to catch her breath. The day was overcast and humid; she could feel the threat of rain in her sinuses. The scattered copses of trees and fertile patches beneath the bridges had the look of hiding places for humans. It was the sort of day bad men chose to bury body parts.

Paul caught up with her. She turned for a moment to look into his familiar, fretful face. He was stuttering out facts like a telegraph machine: "You know, it's Petro-Ecuador now. The Ecuadoreans managed to wrest back control, but only after a long and underhanded battle. It was the Americans first. Occidental. They were the ones who invaded what was essentially forbidden territory. And then they did sneaky things like sell part of their shares to EnCana, a Canadian company, Beth, who then sold to the Chinese. If you think we are blameless in all of this you are wrong. We Canadians drift in on the Americans' wake. Oil or diamonds—it doesn't matter, we'll take their sloppy seconds with our shadowy lesser dollar."

She scrambled her way down the concrete wall that had been built to counter flooding, found a log designed for sitting, and looked toward the stone bridge, the site of the Old Mill, its ruins pressed up against a new spa and condos. A fisherman was standing under the bridge, his hip waders making him large and mournful. He baited his hook, cast into the deeper waters downstream, and hooked a salmon while Beth watched. In the fall, the salmon would be running thick through these waters, leaping with every ounce of their life force to clear the man-made steps that had been installed to control the flow of the river. Their connection to their home, to their little patch of earth and rock and water, was that compelling, that terrifying and true.

The water was higher than it had been for weeks; there had been fierce, unseasonal rains while they were away, then in late July the sun had come out and the river had receded, but the most recent downpour had lifted it once again. Above them, a subway train went rumbling by. Out of the corner of her eye, Beth saw a small black airborne shape, a scrap of red. And there it was: familiar, dogged by its Ecuadorean shadow, its strange tropical double. Here—a red-winged blackbird darting out. And there—a toucan decimating a small hard fruit with its unlikely beak. Here—a pair of squirrels trapezing through the low branches of a maple. There—a monkey grooming his mate, bold and fastidious, perched on his very own Amazonian awning.

Paul tapped her shoulder. "Let's not stay here, Beth."

He didn't appreciate the river the way Beth did. Six months ago, four boys had mugged him and two of his friends on a Saturday night as they strolled and took turns toking like teenagers. The boys held a long serrated knife to Paul's throat; they fancied themselves gangsters. Later, close to dawn, the police found three of the four hiding in a gully. They were peppered with red ant bites, their pockets clanking with change.

"Beth, I'm taking you home. You're in no condition to be traipsing around down here like some goddamned explorer of yore." He grabbed her arm.

Beth shook free, but could not remain sitting. She got up and swatted at the seat of her pants, but nothing was clinging there. She had to cut back up to the main path before she could make it down to the beaten sandy trail next to the water again. Paul zigzagged behind her, panting and driven by loyalty.

On the far shore, a night heron was picking through pebbles and bits of trash. The bird stepped carefully over a soda can. Beth stopped to trail her hand in the water. At the edges, the river was lukewarm, but in the center, in the depths, it would be cold. A man had drowned here, having jumped in after his dog. The dog survived.

That first night in the jungle, she and Paul had huddled close on their mattress, flicking the flashlight on and off like schoolchildren, peering out through the mosquito netting at the matte surface of the night and the six other gauzy, tented sleeping areas.

"They're like bridal beds, aren't they?" Beth said.

"Or ghost ships," Paul replied, and Beth turned to him, surprised. They kissed then, softly shocked kisses that helped them both to sleep, despite the rustlings, the constant exchange of information and emotion under the canopy, despite the scurrying geckos and dazed spiders Miguel had warned them might come tumbling from the rafters. Despite their recent history and despite themselves, they kissed and slept like gentle dragons, until the clear commands of the camp cook woke them.

And then there was the issue of moving from sleep to waking, selecting the appropriate attire without parading around as God and all of nature had intended. Paul managed to pull on a pair of shorts and wriggle a T-shirt over his head before emerging to introduce himself to the German couple who had farted unself-consciously as the morning light crept in, and the group of cheery Spaniards sitting on the steps smoking cigarettes. Beth put on her quick-dry pants in a supine position but had to stand to do up the zipper. She ran her hands over her abdomen as had become habit. As if rubbing

Aladdin's lamp, she caressed the pouch of flesh above her belly button. She looked up because she thought she could feel Miguel watching her across the expanse of swamp that separated the sleeping shelter and the dining area, peering out toward her, silhouetted against the mosquito netting like a shadow puppet. Perhaps they all appeared this way, funny outlines backlit by their particular cultures trampling their way through the jungle, laughing and drinking around the slab of a wooden table, starting comically at all the same sights—the tarantulas waving their chubby arms, the sloths hanging like overstuffed handbags from the branches of ancient trees. Watching Miguel watch her, she was overcome by modesty; she had not yet thought to put on a shirt, and she could feel sweat beginning to accrue underneath her breasts. She reached for her bra.

It had been concluded that there was nothing technically wrong with either of them. At first Paul had scoffed, said something about natural selection, overpopulation, all for the best, and she had felt an odd pull in her gut, as if one of her arteries had gone spelunking in the region of her uterus. They had walked for two hours in High Park after the third specialist gave his verdict. It was February, the temperature was sub-zero, and they had to dodge Canada geese strutting like cops along the path. They did not speak; although the words were there, their footsteps over the snow and ice told a more complete, forlorn story. They wore parkas and Thinsulate accessories, but the wind blew straight through them. Once they had circled the park four times, Paul said, "Chicken breasts for dinner?" and Beth nodded, veering toward Bloor Street.

Beth made her way closer still to the water's edge and began creeping along, stepping over boulders and small eddies of water. If she squinted she could almost envision it, and it took a whole concerted face scrunch to make it real. But the greenery here, for the most part, belonged along the edges of a golf course. And although the humidity approximated the freighted air of the jungle, it also brought with it an oppression unique to the lands that bordered Lake Ontario. She could hear Paul in the brush behind her and was flung back to Cuyabeno—that noisiness of humans pushing their way through chummy, crowded plants.

On the second Wednesday of the trip, the group had traveled in tiny, tippy, handmade canoes to the opposite shore, 300 meters downstream. On the way they witnessed pink river wraiths—dolphins cresting in the calm, fresh waters.

"We will visit one of my friends," Miguel announced cryptically.

They disembarked on a small beach where sandbugs chomped at their exposed flesh. Through it all, Miguel remained serene in his orange flip-flops, smiling as they slapped at their skin, scrambling for repellent. When they looked up, sweating, he was already waving a walking stick up ahead.

"Isn't it exciting?" Beth said to Paul. "I wonder where his friend lives. I wonder what he does in here."

"I imagine he lives his life, Beth. Just with different dining room furniture." Paul did not react well to bug bites; his legs were covered in loonie-sized pink welts. "Besides," he said, pointing up ahead, "I'm not sure Miguel knows where he's going. Perhaps he is not as canny with a compass as your coureur de bois, eh?"

Beth searched for Miguel and found him wandering over a small patch of land, stopping to make peculiar bird calls, his hands cupped up near his lips. "He's signalling," she told Paul. "We don't always have to resort to cell phones."

And sure enough, within minutes, a three-tiered whistle call came sailing back. Miguel began running over the log- and mulch-strewn ground, bounding over obstacles and jumping to high-five low-hanging palm leaves.

"He expects us to follow when he's carrying on like that?" Paul said.

But they did follow him; they had no choice. There were times when they lost sight of Miguel altogether and the two of them paused, turned to each other, fully grown Hansel and Gretel searching for signs of their own selves, the crumbs that signal a trail of existence. If not for the other members of their band, who came stumbling through the ground cover with their digital cameras outstretched, they might have believed themselves to be truly abandoned and alone.

"C'mon," Miguel finally called to them. "We're almost there."

And he was right. A small settlement presented itself in a long narrow clearing amidst a profusion of what must have been corn stalks.

"Meet my friend," said Miguel, and waved his hand toward a woman tending fire in a large pit circumscribed by stones. The woman straightened for an instant to pull her long black hair back from her face and over one shoulder. She wore grimy white shorts and a baggy red tank top over a pink camisole. No bra, Beth noticed. How wonderful not to have to worry.

Miguel sat them down on a log and told them that his friend would now demonstrate a traditional recipe. The woman bent to retrieve what looked like a turnip from a large pot near her feet and shred it into a wooden bowl. A kitten sprung from behind the log with an angry oversized rooster in hot pursuit. Then a mongrel dog roused itself from behind a post and began to chase the rooster. The assembled group watched the kitten, rooster, and dog as they circled the woman's cooking shelter. Then they sat and observed the woman shred her root vegetable. After about fifteen minutes, a fourteen-year-old girl with an infant straddling one hip came striding, barefoot, from between the corn stalks. She smiled at Beth, who smiled back. When the girl began walking away, toward the river, Beth rose to follow.

"Beth," said Paul. "No."

Beth patted Paul on the shoulder. "I'm all right," she said. "I'd just like to know her name."

Beth followed the girl into another small clearing. "Hello," she called out. "I'm Beth." She patted both hands against her chest and stepped closer to the girl, who was still smiling, her head cocked to one side coquettishly.

"Juana," said the girl. "*Me llamo* Juana."

"*Encantada*," said Beth, and for a moment the two simply stood staring. It was a moment that opened up like a hard coconut cleft in half to reveal its white tender meat.

Then Beth pointed to the baby, whose round brown eyes had pivoted toward her. "And what is the baby's name?" she said.

"No." The young girl shook her head.

She had misunderstood, or not heard correctly. Beth tried again. "*El nombre del niño?*"

"No," the girl said again.

Perhaps it was a girl? "*El nombre de la niña?*"

Again, the girl shook her head and shifted the baby to her other hip impatiently. She was bored with this. Beth was not showing her anything new. "*Nombre*," she said again. She pointed to herself and said, "Beth." Then she pointed to the girl and said, "Juana." Finally, she pointed to the baby and shrugged emphatically.

The girl stomped her foot. "She no have name," she said. "No name."

"What do you mean?" Beth cried. "She is so beautiful and new. She must have a name!"

Juana smirked. "No name."

Beth leaned up against a tree, steadying herself. If the baby had no name, then perhaps it was not . . . claimed. Perhaps it had not yet been properly tethered to this place, these people. Maybe there was a chance. In a flash, she saw it—the plump, umber-colored child tucked under a yellow fleece blanket, being ferried along Bloor Street like royalty in her sturdy stroller. If she got homesick, Beth would show her the Humber. They would gather bouquets of pale purple phlox and Queen Anne's lace and she would tell her the story of Etienne Brûlé, who learned to live among the Hurons. She would show her the CN Tower, that useless, space-age thing. Oh, there were those little pots of organic baby food in the No Frills grocery store, weren't there? And bags at the baby boutique that had compartments for *everything* . . .

Juana moved closer to her, reached out to touch Beth's cheek and hair, the silver camera that hung like a medal around her neck. Beth brightened. "Would you like me to take your picture?"

"Yes, yes," Juana said happily, bobbing up and down.

"Okay," said Beth. "You should stand over there. Maybe I should hold the baby." She held out her arms to take the child, but Juana backed away, cradling the baby's head under her stern chin.

"No," Juana said.

And then the group spilled into the clearing, muttering

and perspiring, craning their necks to see a flock of parrots winging by.

Next to the Humber, Beth could hear thunder rolling in over the lake.

"Paul," she said, "do you think we should go back, find a way to help them rebuild?"

Paul sighed heavily. Soon the sky would open, and it was possible the humidity would break.

"I mean, if we are responsible, maybe we should just take responsibility . . ." Beth knew she was whining a little, but couldn't help herself.

Paul threw up his arms, which almost made Beth laugh. "Jesus, Beth, do you even know what happened to Etienne Brûlé?"

Beth nodded. Brûlé had eventually been disowned by his countryman, Champlain, it was true. And then the Hurons decided he had betrayed them to the Iroquois, or at least this was the speculation. And those were harsher times, weren't they? "They killed him," she said quietly.

"Yes," said Paul, pleased with her accuracy, but not nearly finished with his own story. "The Hurons killed him." He paused to take a breath, then turned toward her and whispered sadly, excitedly, "Then they ate him."

And that was when Beth pushed him. If he had fallen differently, with more agility and pliability, the water might not have pulled him to the center of the flow. But within seconds, Paul was struggling in the depths of the river, carried further and further away from Beth by a wicked undertow.

For a few seconds, Paul seemed not to care; there was surrender in the position of his body. But then Beth watched as he clambered strangely toward the shallow water on the opposite shore, and she watched as the current caught him by the ankles and pulled him back into its grasp. Perhaps he would survive; it was up to the river to decide. It confused her to think about what she wanted—how rarely people's plans and yearnings find their proper, perfect form. She focused on the rushing water between them, its opaque mystery, the smell of rust, fishgut, and human effluent. She noted its very force, which was like the force of blood or cum, a liquid force that pulsed around the globe, hastening into places humans could not reach.

The evening after Beth met the nameless baby, Miguel invited her on a jungle walk. Paul had gone to bed early, blaming the bug bites and cheap wine for his fatigue.

"It is possible we will see some night animals, the nocturnals," Miguel said as they traipsed carefully along the path. "Do you have any like this in Toronto?"

Beth laughed. "Maybe raccoons," she said. "They're the cleverest creatures you've ever met, and they've adapted to us, so now we adapt to them."

"Adaptation," Miguel said. "Is that how you call it?"

The light was beginning to fade, making shapes waver, turning living tableaux into unreliable dreamscapes. Miguel placed his hand at the small of her back and invited her to take a closer look at an orchid the size of a thimble which was growing in the crook of a tree.

"Can you see?" he said. "Here." He slid a penlight from his pocket and shined it tightly on the flower. "It's precious, isn't it?"

"Yes," Beth said. And then, in a rush, "There was a child, back there, in the forest. She was maybe three months old, so sweet, and she didn't have a name. I was wondering if there might be a way, if she is not wanted or a burden of some kind, I know I—we—could provide a good home. We live in a village of sorts—clean and comfortable, with very good educational opportunities and lots of diverse friends and toys for her to play with, secondhand clothes, because we don't like to be wasteful, and love. We have love for her. We can't have kids of our own, or at least that's what we've found."

"I don't think so," Miguel replied.

"But I don't understand!" Beth began to sob, then stopped when she noticed Miguel chortling to himself, bent at the waist with the laughter that was coursing through him. He stopped for long enough to hold out a fibrous piece of bark he had pulled from the trunk of a tree. The bark was a coppery color, flecked with a darker, richer brown, and the piece he had stripped sat in the palm of his hand like a special seashell.

"Try it," Miguel said. "Rub it here." He ran his index finger across his gums. "Chew on it. It was what we used when we went to the dentist, to do the dental work. A way of freezing, of feeling no pain." He passed her the bark and she put it in her mouth like a lozenge. It was true what he said; within seconds her tongue felt clumsy and numb. She looked at him, shocked, and found she could not speak.

"Shh," he said, although she had not uttered a word. He sidled up close to her, from behind, and put his arms around her in a restrictive embrace.

I should resist, she thought, but fear was making her tingly and compliant. She wondered if there was a place where she truly belonged.

Then Miguel's fingers were down the front of her pants, his lips tender at her neck, his fingers rubbing and hooked up inside of her. "Here you go, Toronto," he said into her ear. "A souvenir." And Beth came, gasping soundlessly into the hand he had clasped firmly across her mouth. "Now," Miguel said. "Now do you understand?"

SIC TRANSIT GLORIA AT THE HUMBER LOOP

BY SEAN DIXON

Humber Loop

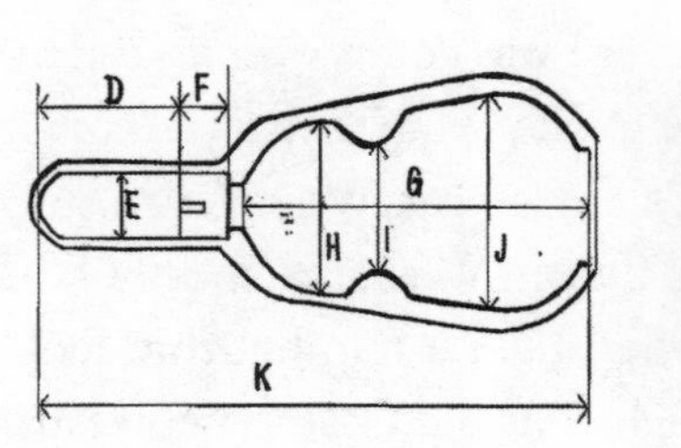

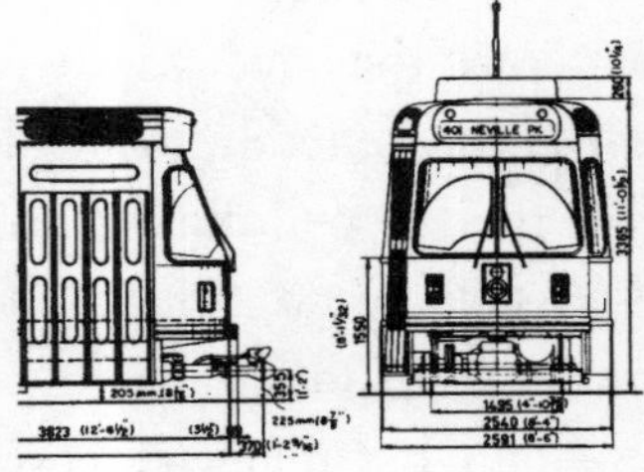

She said she wasn't married anymore. But then, about two weeks into our thing, the dude came to visit, from Ohio or Iowa or someplace like that, I don't even know. And he insisted that they sleep together, side by side in the same bed, every night for ten nights. Said she owed him that since he was her husband and she was his wife. She agreed to it, she told me, because she was afraid of him. Said she'd left a little something under my pillow to get me through. Said she'd call again in eleven days. I could hear him in the background, demanding to know who she was talking to. She told him to fuck off and then she said bye and hung up.

Reflecting on it now, it didn't sound too much like she was afraid of him.

I had three gigs lined up. Double bass players can always find a gig, even if they only know ten or twelve notes. I don't have a car, but it's not a problem. I used to have a car. A big car. Fit the soft case nicely in the backseat. But then one day I backed the car over the bass. It could not be salvaged. I kicked the car a couple of times and then sold it so I could buy myself another bass, along with a lightweight, state-of-the-art Styrofoam case, more than an inch thick, with an Oxford cloth surface. Meant for air travel. It was six and a half feet tall and weighed just over twenty pounds without the instrument. I didn't mind. The contents would not get damaged. And there were wheels. I could roll it down the street to wherever I was going, even in the rain. Means I was generally available to play. Man, I just want to play. Never tried to pull that rig onto a streetcar. Wasn't even sure it was possible. Just did gigs in the Queen West area, mostly. Walking around. And up Roncesvalles. I got a rain hat that looked like a Tilly but it wasn't, though that didn't stop people from calling me asshole.

Day after the husband showed up, it was Monday. I played the Local on Roncy, with an old-timey type group that wanted to keep things pure. Pure meant three-chords, nothing fancy. A fiddler from BC sat in that night. Changed the key in the middle of a number, tried to ramp things up a notch. Sent everyone scrambling for their capos. Afterwards I broke his nose. Wasn't myself really.

Tuesday I played with a singer-songwriter-type girl. Bar on Queen West. The flower sellers come in there. Some of them sell flowers that light up and blink. The hallway to the washrooms is pretty narrow. Her name was Harmony. Pretty sure it was a fake name. Don't know how she came up with Harmony when she sings by herself. She looked like she had kicked a bad habit and was starting over a little old. But she had talent.

Turns out she wanted to fire me. Told me after the gig I was too intense. It's true I get nervous. I take calcium supplements for that. Like beta-blockers, only cheaper. When you get nervous, your body eats up calcium, and then the depletion gives you a case of the shakes, which makes you even more nervous. It's a cycle. I tried to take glucosamine too, for arthritis. But it hurt my stomach too much so I had to stop. Anyway, I don't have arthritis.

I don't know where Harmony got this idea I was messed up, but she was pretty intense herself so it was hard to convince her of anything other than what she believed. I asked if she'd give me one more chance and she said come back in two weeks and see if she hadn't replaced me yet.

That was an early night. I went home and thought about my girl. How she told me when we first met that I made a two-dollar suit look like a million bucks. How she kept me relaxed. I was always getting paranoid. She kept me relaxed. That was her primary virtue. Guess that's what turned a little thing into love.

Wednesday I played a blues set at the 403 on Roncy. Only pops up from time to time. Singer's name was Gloria. She's Ojibway, with a blind and swollen eye and a voice like Stelco. I met her a few years ago. Up north in a tee-pee. Introduced herself while sitting on the can. Made a joke about how it was a throne and the people had to bow down before her. And they did. Then she sang some and I played on a washtub bass that someone dragged out. I hadn't played since high school. Gloria told me music was going to save my soul. She was right. Called me Plunk Henry, which I guess is who I am.

I'm Plunk Henry. How do you do.

The rest of the time was a bit of a blur.

I was living in a big warehouse building on Niagara Street.

Still am, I guess. You really live alone there. You take the freight elevator or you take the stairs. I stayed in my bed, knowing no one would come and bother me. Tried to imagine her but instead I'd see the husband with her. She'd be fulfilling her wifely duty over and over and over again. Made me a bit crazy. I'd lie there in my underwear and jerk off and cry. Or try to cry. I don't know if I cried. I never thought about anyone else. Even tried to draw a picture of her. Tried to draw her mouth. Looked more like a mustache. Tried to draw her breast. Looked more like a fried egg. Still, my doodles were better than all the porn on the Internet.

After a couple days, I was still trying to get a grip. I tried to imagine our relationship in a year or two. Maybe less than a year. Maybe six months. Not having sex anymore. Me starting to think she talked too much. She telling me what she thought of my playing.

Didn't work though.

Eleventh day she came up the freight elevator and appeared at my door. Said the husband was gone back to Iowa or Idaho. I was a bit stunned. I'd taken the mushrooms she'd left for me. When she came in, she sat down in the only chair in the room, petting the cat that got in with her, and telling him that he was a bad cat, that he shouldn't be there. I looked at her. Her skin was paisley and her eyes were burning brighter than a mirror in the sun.

She said it made her feel like a cheap whore, coming from her husband's bed to mine. I told her it wasn't her husband's bed and she wasn't a cheap whore. I told her she was my precious flower. She told me to shut my mouth. Said she felt like a cheap whore. Said she liked the feeling. Liked putting her mouth around the words.

I should have taken my cue from that, I guess.

She chastized me later. Said I burned her insides. Truth is, it burned me too. Hurt to pee for a couple of days. What comes of a girl making you so you don't know which end is up.

She seemed flattered though, she could screw me up so bad to get a bona fide chemical reaction. Like I was her little science project. And it calmed me down too. I remember getting up at dawn. Saw the sun coming in through the window. Thought, I'm normal. Wondered if I'd stay that way. Remembered how things had been a few weeks before. When I'd rehearse with fellow musicians.

Musicians are generous people, the same way that language instructors are. They know you want to communicate. Nobody wants to stab you in the back. Been told too that bass players live longer than all the others. Like elephants with their ears that grow large, encouraged by low and gentle music. I'm still waiting for that.

We holed up for a few days. I cancelled all my gigs. Was running out of money but she didn't seem to mind. Told me when we came up for air we'd figure something out. Said she knew a guy who knew a guy.

She sure knew how to make me relax.

Still, after five or six days, I realized it was the night of my second-chance gig with Harmony. The last thing I wanted to do, this stage of my career, burn my bridges.

I said I was going and she was insulted. Like, really insulted. Like a whole different person came out. I said I just wanted to play and she said I sounded like a broken record. Said her baby sister played better than me. Said if I was going to treat her like trash, she was going to treat me like something worse.

She really didn't mean it though. She was just feeling sore.

As I rolled out the door she threw an old mandolin at me. Hit the wall beside my head. I heard the crack. Reminded me how I backed the car over that bass. I lived a nightmare for a while after I lost that bass. Felt like I'd had this pact with the devil. Said he'd come to collect his pay. Only I couldn't remember any of the good parts. The upshot was any instrument I put my hand to was set to break. Even the washtub bass in Wicky. Even the one I had now. Devil promised it would make the sound of a wrecking ball going through old paneling. It was my destiny, he said. Didn't make any sense. All I did was back over a bass in a driveway. Where's the unpardonable sin in that?

There was something wrong with the freight elevator. In the end I took the stairs, lugging the rig down two floors. Awkward at the corners of the landings. Then out into the street, rolling up Niagara to Queen. Heading west. Like it was your average night.

It was hot though. Muggy. I was sweating by the time I got to that bar. With the blinking flowers and the narrow bathroom hallway. Like half the bars in Toronto, you're probably thinking. I'm sure you don't mind me keeping it vague.

From the sound of it, there were a lot of people beyond the edge of the bar, where I couldn't really see them. They didn't care too much about us. I tuned them out mostly. Toronto is a city where they welcome you with folded arms.

Couldn't tune out Harmony though. Her disapproval. She was giving me a lot of attitude right there on that little stage. Still not quite sure I deserved it. Wounded me a bit. Man, I just want to play. Anyway, nobody was really watching. Saw one pair of eyes out there, peering at me. Guess it didn't matter too much when she fired me right there onstage. Full house chattering beyond the bar.

You got to think it wasn't too good for her career either. Pulling a stunt like that.

It was still before 10. Harmony kept playing. I lumbered off, graceful as I could. Dragged my bass over to the side. Down that little hallway. Then I was in this little closet-sized dressing room type thing. Had a chair and a bunch of brooms in it. And my travel case. I moved the chair out into the hallway and propped the instrument up against it. Ducked back in and was trying to get the case to stay open so I could just slide the bass over and in. Then I was backing out into the hall again. There was a dude standing there. I'd missed him somehow. I said excuse me or whatever and was pulling the bass up away from the chair. He didn't say anything so then I stopped for a second and I turned and looked up into his face.

Next two things happened almost the same time. He brought down this bottle of Grolsch on the top of my head and the tips of my fingers went up into his windpipe.

Funny thing I noticed about the Grolsch bottle, as it rolled away. It hadn't broken and he'd resealed it before using it on my head. I think he was hoping to finish it, instead of choking from a crushed windpipe, which was what he was doing. I've got strong fingers from playing. Stronger than I think. Even if they're not as dextrous as they ought to be.

I'd let the bass fall back against the chair. He was making some kind of noise. I was holding onto him, felt like my armpits were on fire, and he was looking down into my eyes like he wanted to ask me a question. Like he wanted me to help him. Did he want me to help him? Is that the way dying works? You forgive your enemies and ask them for help? All I could think was he better hurry up and finish—the questioning, the forgiving, the dying—because somebody was bound to come around the corner of that hallway again real soon.

Harmony was still at it though. One of my faves too. She had talent. Maybe I had good taste. Maybe the song would hold them just long enough to keep their bladders. It was old blues. A cover. Rabbit Brown.

I been givin' you sugar for sugar.
Let you get salt for salt.
If you can't get along with me well it's your own fault.

I think about the way that guy looked. I do. The way he was looking before he took that swing. I see it in my head. That moment. He didn't look angry. More helpless. Anxious. He looked a lot like me. Except he was taller and fair and pretty narrow at the shoulders. So this was the husband. Fucked up like me. Didn't look like he wanted to be in this hallway any more than I did. He really was dying too. I felt bad for him.

Sometimes I think you too sweet to die.
And another time
I think you oughta be buried alive.

I didn't know what was happening. The husband had fallen against me and wasn't making any more noise. In the other room, the song was coming to an end. The door was still open and I heard voices. Nasal. Girls. Approaching the corner. I pulled him up and dragged him in. Reached forward and grabbed the knob. It was damp and nearly slipped from my hand as I closed the door.

Two grown men, one of them not breathing, and a double bass case leaning up against a pile of broomsticks in a closet. The one thing I wanted with me was still out in the hallway. Some drunken asshole was going to knock it down. Or mistake it for the wall beside a urinal and piss on it. Or steal it. I couldn't afford that.

Don't know how much time went by. A couple of minutes maybe. Felt like an hour. I heard a snippit of conversation between a pair of girls. It was about fake leather. Like in a jacket or something. And some dude having a bad trip, talking to himself about how Wednesday was zero.

Wednesday was going to be zero for me if I didn't find a way out of this.

There was only one way to go. You probably saw it coming. I didn't. Took a bit of thinking. First I had to rip the neck guard out of the case. Made me feel like I had tendinitis. Then I had to push back against the door for leverage. At one point, two or three broom handles fell across to the other wall. They made a loud noise. Insanely loud. My ears were ringing. I even heard the echo of the ringing.

Then everything stopped and I listened to my breathing. Somebody flushed a toilet and opened a door. Footsteps down the hall.

Harmony was still at it.

Things could have been worse. Case might have been too small. I might not have had a case at all. Or a soft-shell case.

There was no air left in the room. I just wanted to get out of there. Took a chance and opened the door wide. No one in the hallway. The case was facing the wrong way. By the time I was ready to go, there was a guy there, trying to get past me to the bathroom. He had to wait while I propped the case against the wall and slid the double bass from the hall into the closet. Closed the door. Then I lumbered down the hallway, past the men's. He went in and I was alone again. Standing in front of the fire exit. I banged it open and stumbled out into the alley.

Urine never smelled so much like freedom. It was starting to rain though. Thought that might do something about the heat, but it didn't. I dug into my pocket and pulled out my Tilly knockoff.

Queen Street was busier than it had a right to be west of Dufferin on a Tuesday night. Still, all that traffic would come to an end if I was willing to go far enough. West is the way to go when you've got a body in a case and time on your hands.

I started walking, trying to pretend I was just heading to a gig on a usual night in the usual way. But it wasn't a usual night. And it wasn't the usual way. Sweat was pouring off me with the rain. Still, people on the sidewalk parted to let me by. Respect for the musician. Nothing like it.

There was a streetcar coming, making its way at a snail's pace through the traffic in the street. 501. The rain started coming down harder. The sign said, *Humber*. I figured I'd take it all the way to Humber College and then I could empty out my case somewhere on campus where my cargo might be taken for a wasted student. Humber College. All those red brick buildings where the crazy people used to live, back in the old days when it was the primary mental care village for the whole province.

Getting on the car wasn't the problem I thought it'd be, though it took a couple of minutes. The driver said something I didn't understand. I'd turned and was trying to get my weight under the back to pull up the rig and he said, It's your lucky night. No pole. Air-conditioning.

He was right. There was air-conditioning. It felt good. If he was actually referring to the size of my case relative to the size of the door, I'd have to say he wasn't making himself very clear.

Car was empty. There'd been people waiting with me at the stop, but they didn't get on. Made me a bit paranoid. Like maybe I didn't look as innocent as I thought. People cut a lot of slack for musicians. But maybe they notice when your case weighs more than you do.

Still, we were headed west and nobody was stopping us. We went past the streetcar station at the bottom of Roncy. Caught a view of the lake at the left. There was a big empty patch of darkness on the right that spooked me until I realized it was Grenadier Pond. Then new town houses on the left. I thought I spotted a garbage nest under a bush.

Then something I didn't expect. We cut to the left suddenly, off the Queensway, and drove underneath the Gardner Expressway. I realized I'd never been this far west before.

Driver said, Humber Loop, last stop, and pulled into the bleakest lot I ever saw. A figure eight of track next to an abandoned snack bar with a sign on the wall that said, Don't feed the pigeons, beneath a dark wet sky, between two concrete overpasses. Last stop.

I was not going to fit out the center doors, so I rolled my rig up to the front.

Is there going to be another car? I asked.

Yup, said the driver. This car's 501 Humber. Turns around here. You want the car that says 501 Long Branch.

I hobbled down the steps with the case. He closed the doors. Then opened them again.

Oh yeah, he said. Better hope it has AC.

He closed the doors again and left. Went around the loop

and back the way he came. That was pretty funny, I thought, what he said about the air-conditioning. Except the rain was really coming down now. I was starting to get a bit of a chill.

On the upside, I was alone. Looked like I was going to be alone for a while. I leaned my load up against the building and took a look around. Every square inch of that wall had a urine trail leading away from it. Right in front of me there was an electrical tower on a big patch of grass. More streetlights than you'd expect, place like that. To my right, though, the tracks headed south into the gloom. Pulled me to it like a safe haven. There was a wide ditch full of cattails over there below the corner of an old wall. No streetlights. Another circle of tracks with weeds growing out from under them. Right in the middle, a pile of dirt and rocks. That was interesting. I walked over to have a look.

The rain tapered off a bit. I should dump the body here. I tried to think the thought again, so it would make sense. I should dump the body here. Wondered if I'd be able to get him out of the case. No, I should stick to the original plan. Farther west. The red brick buildings of Humber College.

I heard a lurch and rumble behind me, turned and saw a streetcar barreling through, back by the building. 501 Long Branch. I suppressed a surge of panic and started to trot over. Driver didn't see me and didn't stop. Didn't see anything suspicious either, I guess. He barreled around the bend, passing the loop, and moved south under the second overpass.

Next car took its time coming and was heading back around the loop. A couple of teenagers got out. A boy and a girl. Made me nervous at first, but they got preoccupied with one another around the corner of the building.

Finally, the Long Branch came through again. The kids got on, side by side, but they had to break their hand-hold to get around the bar that was inside the door. It was right in the center. Handy for the old ladies to hoist themselves up. My case was two and a half feet wide and over a foot and a half thick. The opening was just about four and a half, with a bar in the middle. There was no way I was getting around that. No way.

Sorry, guy, said the driver. You need a car with AC. He pulled away.

Who calls a guy *guy* these days?

Looked like I was going to get a cool ride whether I wanted it or not. Next car to come through was going around the loop. This dude got off looked like a sailor in an old movie. He was practically black-and-white.

Car after that had the bar. Driver opened the doors, expecting me to get on. I gestured over to my case.

Any chance of an AC car coming?

They're rolling them off the lines, he said. Account of it's cooling off. They're expensive to run. But there might be one or two of them left on the road.

He pulled away. Tell you one thing about these drivers. They're polite.

I stood for a couple of minutes. Armpits burning. Turning into a chronic condition. I felt faint. I was digging my fingers into my eyes when I heard movement to my left. Realized the sailor was still there. Just by the corner of the building. Probably the biggest fright of the night. He was looking at me. Hadn't boarded the last car. What was that about?

I eased the case up against my chest, trying to make it seem lightweight, and dragged it past the other end of the building. Pulled out my cell phone and looked at it. No calls. I glanced over at him. He was gazing up at the top of the electrical tower.

I called my land line. She answered. Baby, she said.

Baby, I said, but I didn't feel anything lower than the pit of my stomach.

I told her what I had done. She said, You did what? And I told her again. She hung up. I was starting to get anxious.

I called back. She let it ring for a bit and then answered. Don't come here, she said.

It's my place, I said. She told me it was some serious shit I'd done and she didn't want to get involved. I asked her why she didn't warn me that her husband was a psycho freak. He wasn't my husband, she said.

What? I said.

I'm not the marrying type, in case it wasn't obvious. He was just a guy I used to see. Guess we hadn't had our fill. Guess we've had it now, whether I like it or not.

A bus pulled in from a road I hadn't noticed. Down from the Queensway on the other side. The black-and-white sailor got on and it went back the way it came. I was alone again at the Humber Loop.

Don't be a drama queen, she said. He's dead and you're an asshole. Killing's wrong.

So's lying.

For an intelligent girl, she said, I sure surrounded myself with some collection of dopes. And then she hung up.

Conversation got things going though. Set me in motion. Like the kid in the TV ad who laces up the shoes and drinks the drink and climbs up behind the eight ball. With his skateboard. I dragged the case down into the ditch below the corner of the wall and opened it. I felt sorry for him. I did. But there was no time for the Catholic shit. I tried to roll him out but the top parts were stuck together. The case and the body. I walked around the other side, turned the case over on top of him, stepped on his back, and pulled. His head popped out and I fell into the cattails. Lay there for a couple of minutes. I hadn't been that close to cattails since I was a kid. Then I got up and rolled him down to the bottom of the ditch. Walked over to the rusty loop and filled my case with gravel and rocks. Dragged it back and dumped the rocks on top of him. A couple more trips and he was covered. I tried to think of a little prayer. Heard the rumble of the streetcar and dove into the weeds.

It rolled by. No idea what he saw.

After a bit, I stood up and brushed myself off. Don't think my two-dollar suit looked like it was worth much anymore. Case was a mess too. Only on the inside. Worry about it later. Closed it and latched it and dragged it behind me back up into the glare of the lights. It felt buoyant. Like a balloon. A breeze caught me in the face and woke me up. I noticed the rain had stopped.

Things were good.

Then I remembered I still couldn't get on these streetcars. Had a picture in my head of walking east along the Queensway, middle of the night. A cheap and filthy suit. Dragging an empty case with the Styrofoam impression of a human body pressed onto the inside. And the bass was still in that closet. See why I'm not telling you the name of that bar? Four grand, it cost me. Some people kill for that. I thought I might dump the case in the lake. But Styrofoam floats. And the case cost a bundle too. I tried to think of the worst case scenario: dump the case, head back to the bar, bass is gone. A ten grand debt—two instruments and a flight case—nothing to show for it. Move up to Wicky. Take up the washtub. Pretty indestructible, the washtub, no matter what the devil might say. Don't cost anything either. Not so bad. I'd be able to play. Man, I just want to play.

My phone was ringing. Missed it the first time around but it rang again a minute later. It was her. She said she was in trouble. That didn't make any sense.

She said she'd left my apartment, but there was something wrong with the freight elevator.

Take the stairs, I said.

Too late for that, she said. She'd been in a huff. Couldn't get the barrier to slide up. Finally lost patience and jumped over it. The elevator wasn't there so she fell three floors. Landed in the basement and broke her hip.

Call 911, I said. I'm stuck at the Humber Loop.

She said, You think 911 can help that the elevator's coming down right now?

I said, You think I can?

She said, Maybe you know some tricks.

I said, Don't jump over the barrier.

Then there was this horrible sound coming into my ear and I realized I wasn't holding the phone anymore. Had to go poke around the dandelions under the electrical tower till I found it. There was one message. I checked it. It was from the first call she'd made. She called me baby and told me she was sorry and she was in trouble and could I call her. Is that the way it is with people? Do they hate you until they're dying? And then they don't hate you anymore?

Do you ever find yourself wishing you could just have an aneurism? Allow the vessel in your brain to just pop and let you go? Is there some kind of higher state of concentration that would allow you to do that? Could it be learned? That's the feeling I had, right then, standing beside the snack bar with the sign on the wall that said, Don't feed the pigeons. Every square inch of wall, a urine trail leading away. Going exactly nowhere. Nowhere to go and nothing to take me and a cargo that won't fit anyway. That's how I feel, standing at the Humber Loop. Been told that bass players live a long time. Like elephants with their ears that grow large, encouraged by low and gentle music. I'm still waiting for that. I'd like to feel that.

LAB RATS

BY IBI KASLIK

Dufferin Mall

Volunteers needed for psychiatric study.
Generous compensation offered. (416) 539-4876.
Supervised by Dr. Bot.

Outside the Dovercourt 7-Eleven, K. watches police cars roll by from the nearby station. Young Portuguese gangsta impersonators with peach fuzz glance at K. in disgust from their souped-up Honda Civics as K. pops his skateboard into his hand like an ejected tape. He sips on his Blueberry Buster Slurpee, as if the life-giving fluid might suddenly be stolen away from him. K. sneers at the teens and smiles at the cops; he conducts most of his life in this territorial, animal way, though there are few things he possesses—a few good soul records, a signed copy of Paul Auster's *Moon Palace*—and only small bits of earth he inhabits. He sips and slurps until his lips are blue as a death mask and he has given himself brainfreeze.

He pulls out the wadded piece of newspaper that Christmas gave him and studies it for a moment before jamming it back into his oversized shorts. He slaps his board on the concrete and begins to roll down Dundas, past Brazilian bikini shops that look obscene and unseasonable, given the cool climate and great distance from anything resembling a beach;

past heavily stocked hardware stores and stunted middle-aged men and women sloshing their words together as if there are shells caught in their mouths. He crosses Dundas and makes a sharp left with his board, as if cutting through waves, on Gladstone. He uses the momentum of the hill to avoid Dufferin, its swath of train tracks bisect east and west; he scales up and down residential streets for an out.

K. hates Dufferin Street but is especially distressed by the Dufferin bus, which makes him feel like a homicidal dumpling. One of the most reliable ways to elicit murderous tendencies is to ride the overheated, fart-smelling bus up into the very heart of humanity: Bloor and Dufferin station, where no one believes in standing in line for anything, let alone a TTC ticket or a bus. There's nothing sadder to K. than watching immigrants climb onto the bus at the Dufferin Mall—or "The Duff," as Christmas calls it—with their crinkling Wal-Mart bags. The glorious Ethiopian queens stuffed into cheap, inadequate jeans. The baby carriages, the economy-sized flats of toilet paper and family-sized boxes of pizza-pops stuffed and the greasy stench of McDonald's fried turds on everyone's hands.

"But why do you hate The Duff? You can get anything at the Duff!" Christmas likes to remind him, when he gets all nauseous and depressed by the prospect of needing something from the inner-city excuse for a shopping center. Christmas is right, though, it's truly incredible what capitalism has made available even and especially at the Dufferin Mall: You can get your photograph taken in a booth and receive a series of stickers with your image reproduced in cartoon form, you can also get corrective contact lenses, a prepaid phone with pink kittens speaking in Japanese characters, tensor bandages made of hemp, not to mention a ten carat diamond from Peoples

Jewelers, cigarette filters in bulk, and a herb and garlic bagel the size of your head.

It would be all right by K. if he never had to step into The Duff ever again, though he knows Christmas could not live without its peopled, impoverished absurdity. Anxiety clutches at K.'s throat as he weaves his way through the well-maintained Parkdale streets to meet Christmas for lunch in Roncesvalles. They're hooking up at Christmas's favorite Polish dive, a dank, wood-paneled place called Krak where the soup specials are alternately beet or dill pickle and you can get a full schnitzel dinner for $4.99. Despite Krak's reasonable prices, K.'s funds have been nearly depleted since he left his job in advertising to go back to grad school to study pre-colonial African history.

He now understands the sour expressions his colleagues made when he made his announcement about his "life transition." At first he thought they were transmitting muted jealousy, then settled on the fact that it was the mildly dyspeptic superiority all people in advertising projected. But now he knew that their shocked faces were actually saying: *Dude, are you ready?* There would be no more Calvin Klein shoes, no more impromptu tapas lunches at Lee's, no more all-night cocaine parties on the rooftop patio of the Drake Hotel (or "The Fake," as Christmas liked to call it), no more reckless, whimsical spending of the salary he had earned, for almost a decade, by shuffling in and out of an elevator in a gentle hung-over state. There would also be no more abuse from a crisply tanned woman, whose skin bore an unmistakable resemblance to chorizo, named Marlene, who liked to accuse him of not collating pages correctly before big presentations.

As he slows his board down, he notices Christmas inside Krak, studying what appears to be the weekly newspaper with an intensity she reserves for restaurant experiences. Her ponytail is high up on her head, as if she's a very young child and an inept but well-meaning male relative has coiffed her with thick kitchen elastics. K. stares at Christmas through the dirty window; there is something wan and estranged about her: She is almost unrecognizable. Her eyes seem pulled too far in opposite directions, but this illusion ends the second she turns her head and smiles at him heartily, pointing at the menu. He's imagined it. Christmas looks as good as ever. *It's just stress*, he thinks, plunging his hand into his shallow pocket, only to find his last crumpled tenner and the same wrinkled newspaper ad Christmas has spread out onto their table.

K.'s not sure what has convinced him to submit to the study. Maybe it was Christmas's enthusiasm about the project: "It's nothing, they give you a bunch of placebos and they let you play video games all day to test your reflexes. They feed you cream cheese and cucumber sandwiches. You love cream cheese." She had beamed at him insanely. Her excitement seemed disproportionately high considering the fact that they were discussing selling his brain to science. Plus, her face still hadn't arranged itself properly. She had that kind of asymmetrical European look to begin with, all sharp curves and sunken cheeks, so it always took a minute or so to decide whether she was stunning or mannish. Today, the shocked expression didn't seem to leave her face. Also, there was borscht on her lower jaw, smudged and organic like some forgotten assassination detail.

Maybe he needed little convincing; after all, K. had blown the last of his savings on tuition, several required books for grad school, most of which had the words *Bone* and *Civilization* in their titles. Then there was the small matter of his exorbitant west end rent—why *did* he pay nearly two thousand dollars to live in a basement apartment that smelled like mothball dog and had a moldy ceiling, why? Just so he could pay seven dollars for a G-and-T and catch ageing, pseudo indie-rockers deejaying Bowie songs at the Beaconsfield? Really?

He sighed and pushed in the big institution doors of the Centre for Addiction and Mental Health. This was why he was going: because he was desperate. Desperate for cash. And there was nothing more obscene than fretting about money. According to Christmas, this study paid better than any of the other guinea pig gigs did—Christmas should know, she survived on weight-loss-ad modeling gigs (Christmas was the "After" model) and these drug-testing studies. She claimed starving herself and wearing long-sleeved shirts in the summer to cover her track marks (how else would they monitor her blood during the studies?) was a small price to pay for being a "professional nothing."

K. announced himself at the desk and was directed to the eleventh floor by a woman in scrubs with cartoons of pigs in scrubs on them. Before K. could ask her about the pigs, what internal logic or reference they signified, what insight into the mysterious world of Western medicine they hinted at, the young nurse/receptionist, who looked about twelve years old to K., said, "Wait a minute, are you involved with Dr. Bot's study?"

K. nodded as she flipped through a bunch of papers and answered the telephone in a chirpy yet business-like manner. She typed something into her computer and the printer spat out a fluorescent blue wrist-band, the kind you get at hospitals, all-inclusive hotels, stadium gigs: human-style branding. He examined it carefully and verified the spelling of his name, his date of birth, his gender, and his allergies (yes, penicillin). The brown-haired girl snapped it on his wrist eagerly, as if hungry for physical human contact with someone lucid. He gave her a floppy kind of smile and began shambling down the hall, as if he'd already ingested some Valium or other painkiller and was in the foggy world of decision-free living.

It wasn't until the elevator bell rang out, and the formaldehyde smell had been absorbed completely into the back of his throat, that K. realized he hadn't once given his name: He'd failed to fill out a single form that would alert anyone to his allergies, or his June birthday.

Dr. Bot was bald and overly friendly in the way that people are when they know others fear them. As he explained to K. what the study would consist of—two weeks of drug- and alcohol-free living, daily blood samples, and some hand-eye coordination tests ("You like Xbox, Kenny? Well, this is a little older, but the same idea.")—and handed over some documents describing the types of drugs they'd be using, K. watched the way the gloomy institutional light flounced off various parts of Dr. Bot's perfectly proportioned cranium. He wondered if its shine was accidental or purposeful and if the doctor intended his incredible globular centerpiece to be admired, or whether it served as pure distraction for his nervous subjects.

As he took blood from K., and asked him about his hobbies ("Have you heard of this rollerblading craze, Ken, or are you more the intellectual type?"), K. tried to revert the questions back to the doctor.

"So, my friend Christmas tells me this is a drug-testing study, but I see here these are tried and true oldies—clonazepam, amitriptyline—so what are you testing, effects?"

The doctor smiled at K. condescendingly but didn't answer. Bot plugged up a vial of his blood with a small black stopper, and a nurse, who looked like she'd been sucked into a vacuum from a planet of porn stars and then deposited into the orange room with K. and the doctor without any instructions, came to take his blood away. She nearly tripped on her big white platform nurse shoes that seemed to be very impractical, given her occupation.

"Dr. Bot? What effects are you testing?"

"I like Christmas," Bot said, leaning casually on the counter, which contained a large glass jar with a ridiculous amount of cotton swabs in it. "She's very spontaneous, what I call a free thinker, a truly free thinker. There really are no predictable patterns of thought going on there whatsoever, I find it fascinating. Have the two of you been dating long?"

K. sighed and studied the fold in his arm that was tightly sealed with cotton and tape, it was slowly bruising into a light green color. The doctor was obviously full of prevarications, wasn't allowed to, or wouldn't, talk.

"Everything you need to know about the study is in the forms, Ken," Bot said, as K. pulled his hoodie on carefully and tucked his skateboard under his pricked-up arm. "Okay, see you tomorrow at 8:30 a.m. sharp." Bot turned back toward the window, which displayed the varied gruesomeness and decrepitude of College and Spadina: It was the only place in the city where you could get rolled by crackheads, buy six white miniature eggplants for $1.99, and see female U of T students in Uggs rushing from their psychology classes to get hammered on vodka ice coolers at O'Grady's Irish pub, all within a six-block radius.

"Ken," Bot said, without turning around, "you didn't sign the forms."

"Oh, sorry," he said, catching the door with his foot, "I forgot."

* * *

K. had eaten three Hungry-Man TV dinners he'd gotten from the Price Chopper and was feeling a little ill. As Christmas's voice hummed along the telephone line, he thought about what a good decorator he was. *Small white, twinkly Christmas lights, it's all about the Christmas lights*. He sprawled his long body out on the floor and examined the layers of delicately latticed thumb-sized lights. As long as things stayed relatively dark—or "ambient," as his favorite show, *Decorate This, Girl!*, described it—you couldn't tell that most of his furniture came from the Ikea dumpster and Lansdowne's Value Village.

"Obsyline," Christmas said, her voice cutting through his fantasy of the triplet horse-faced decorating girls visiting his dank subterranean rooms and throwing his world into a renovating frenzy.

"K., did you hear me? The new drug is Obsyline. I Googled it, there's nothing about it, except that it's in the Valium family. You were right. Looks like that's what Bot's using on you."

"Sounds like a combination of *obvious* and *Vaseline*," he said.

Impatient, Christmas sighed, "Yeah, I guess it does."

"Well, whatever it is, I have these naps for hours, and I wake up feeling like someone's taken a shovel to my skull."

Two weeks had gone by since K. started drug testing with Dr. Bot and he'd been too exhausted to do anything with Christmas after the long afternoons of sleeping; watching women with unmovable hair negotiate badly attended fundraisers on soap operas; responding to Dr. Bot's lengthy and often nonsensical surveys ("Would you describe yourself as lethargic or woozy? How many pistons in a diesel engine? Can you think of a word that rhymes with orangutan?); eating the semi-comestible tuna fish sandwiches that tasted like fancy cat food; and flying a green video airplane through an obstacle course on what appeared to K. to be one of the first computers ever built.

"Let me come over, at least," Christmas pleaded, "I miss you, K."

"Hello, who *is* this?" K. asked officiously. "Who am I speaking to, please?"

Christmas laughed and hung up. She pulled on her itchy Guatemalan mittens. Fall had turned, suddenly it was crisply unforgiving outside. She would stop on Queen Street, on her way over, to buy a boneless chicken roti from the Roti Lady for K. to take to work tomorrow. A little Caribbean might help, that shitty institutional food was enough to make you murder someone.

To say that K.'s apartment was a disaster would have been a compliment. There was Beefaroni on the low ceilings and two weeks worth of unlaundered gitch cobbled out an enchanted trail toward the bathroom. Stacks of papers, magazines, and take-out menus were splayed across the floor in fanlike phalanxes. In the middle of the kitchen floor was a rank-smelling can of opened baked beans which even K.'s cat, Soya Sauce, eyed with outrage.

"On that decorating show I watch, they say never to sacrifice your personal mementos and sense of style for the overall aesthetic, even if—"

"Where are your skateboards?"

Christmas had opened up a closet and found it stuffed with duct tape, rolled gauze, and an enormous vacuum cleaner, which had all the technology of a NASA telescope. Boxes of Lean Cuisine and Hungry-Man fell on her head. "Where is your record collection, Ken?"

K. looked at Christmas and frowned. Who was this girl

with so much brown hair? It was everywhere. On her sweater, on her face, stuffed behind her ears. Why was she rifling through his apartment? Why was she wearing so many bangles? Bangles. Is that what they were called? What an odd word for bracelets. How very British. Only the British could have a snooty word for bracelets. What skate things was she talking about? What records?

"What records?" he asked cautiously, as if he knew her answer already and was merely testing her. Christmas turned then, from the mess, from the close, fusty food odors of the kitchen. She focused on K.'s vitreous stare.

"What the fuck?" She took a step forward and picked at something dry and scabrous just above K.'s ear. A clean strip of his curly hair had been shaved away for a series of crude incisions.

"Ow!" K. flinched, slapped away her hand. He took a step back, nearly slipping on an open *Food* magazine featuring a section on crème brûlée recipes. In a trembling voice, one that fought for patience and the concomitant emotion of understanding, K. asked her again, "Who *are* you?"

Christmas held a tiny thread in her hand, one of K.'s stitches. Attached to it was a pinkish bit of matter the size of a dust mote. Which memories had Bot taken? Which had he left? Where was the part of K. that cried to Bob Seeger songs? Where was the piece that liked the cheese on his open-faced grilled cheese sangers a little puckered? Where was the memory of K.'s drunk mother climbing onstage with a magician so that she could be sliced in two like the assistants with curler-wrought hair, wearing spangly costumes and flesh-colored tights?

K. held onto the cuff of her sweater lamely. His mouth formed a weak "o" as he breathed out his final question.

Again, he wanted to know who she was. Instead of answering him, Christmas shook him off, picked up a heavy knife from the kitchen island covered with pizza boxes, ants, and ashtrays, and stabbed her best friend: first, in the liver, then in the kidney.

He bled in her lap until morning. She sat in the dark listening to the people on the first floor shower, then make a noisy breakfast of smoothies and cereal. When she was sure they'd left, she pulled a fleece blanket over K. and left his apartment, her itchy autumn sweater soggy with blood.

She took the Queen car. It was filled with pierced and tattooed indie warriors, drunks, who reeked of urine and mouthwash, and a few finely polished high-earners who'd been too lazy to take their Beamers to the car wash. Christmas hated all of them. She got off at Spadina and walked north, up through the stench and crowds of Chinatown, toward the CAMH, clutching the thick chopping knife in one hand, a lock of K.'s curly brown hair in the other. She was going to finish this now.

Inside the Centre, on the eleventh floor, Dr. Bot unwrapped a sticky blueberry muffin and blew on his Tim Horton's double-double. He looked outside his window. He could see her, his favorite little rodent. The one who managed to scurry away from his blade, the one who'd always woken up before he could shear that beautiful hair and lacerate that fine-tuned, if lazy, brain. He watched her move into the building with determined steps. Her hair was messed, sweater soiled and lopsided.

I've killed a lot of rats to reach you, he thought, as he sat back in his ergonomic chair and waited for her.

THE EMANCIPATION OF CHRISTINE ALPERT

BY NATHAN SELLYN

Toronto Airport

Isabella Gauthier's husband Carl was still warm in the grave, and she had forgotten how to live alone. That spring was a rainy one, but those first weeks without him rolled forward so slowly that it seemed fitting they took place underwater. So she ran errands, to keep herself busy. On that day alone she had met with the lawyer, had the car's oil changed, boxed up all the books in Carl's office, and eaten dinner at the bowling club. But she still found herself home at 6 with nothing to fill the hours before she might find sleep. So she watched the hockey game with the sound off and a record on, then sat down to read her magazines in his chair by the window. At just before 11, she removed her glasses to rub at her eyes. When she put them back on, she noticed the headlights in the street. Six, on three matching black sedans.

The cars all arrived together, but could only find two parking spots, and so the last in the convoy drove on, beyond the block of town houses and out of Isabella's sight. The others parked and cut their engines, but their doors remained closed. Tinted windows made it impossible to tell who sat inside. Isabella reached over and turned off her reading light. Yet nothing happened. The sedans lay still, waiting, like a pair of polished steel crocodiles feigning sleep by the riverbank.

After several minutes, footsteps broke the silence of the

street. Isabella pressed her face against the glass, but the man to whom the footsteps belonged didn't require much effort to notice. He wore a tuxedo, and with each streetlamp he passed she gained a better view of both his solid build and the corkscrews of glossy black hair that fell toward his shoulders. His skin had an olive tone, and she guessed him to be of Middle Eastern descent, or perhaps Spanish. As he approached the two cars, their doors opened, and Isabella brought her hand to her mouth.

Four more men emerged, also wearing tuxedos. The first man, without speaking, raised his palm, and they moved toward him. As all five came together they threw their arms around one another in a mass of silent embraces. The first man went to a lawn across the street and looked up at the second-floor window, then made a gesture to the four, who immediately returned to the cars and began pulling black boxes of varying shapes and sizes from their trunks. They too then moved to the lawn. They laid the boxes on the damp grass, then kneeled to open them. When they stood up, each raised a different instrument—one a clarinet, one a violin, one a French horn, and the last a bass. The first man looked at the four, glanced at the window, then looked at the four again and said something Isabella couldn't hear. And then they began to play, and he began to sing.

Isabella had never had music in her house during childhood, and she knew nothing of opera. So she did not recognize that it was Rossini's music that quickly woke the entire block, or that it was the Count Almaviva whom the tenor hoped to emulate that evening. But she did know the music was perfect for the moment, a moment that the singer across the street was just then describing as divine. His voice soared to a climax as the window he sang to filled with light, and he dropped to one knee as a woman's silhouette came to fill it. In this way, on May 25, 1986, Pierre Alvio became engaged to Christine Alpert. Unfortunately, every mountain has a valley.

It was nearly twenty years later, to the very day, that Christine flew to Toronto. A cab arrived at 6 to take her to the airport. She had bought a new suit for the occasion, a jacket and pants set from Anne Taylor. She brought only two bags—a purse to accompany her on the plane and a larger, rolling case that she would check. Inside she had packed a change of clothes, two textbooks, nearly $50,000 in cash, and everything she would require for that evening. Her blond hair was up; an ivory chopstick pierced its bun. Nearly an hour in the bathroom had been required before she felt content with her appearance. The chopstick had finally made the difference.

The driver smiled as she slid into the backseat. He was a black man, probably in his early thirties, with a shaved head and a strange web of scars across the back of his neck. Even at this early hour, sweat poured off him, and his blue cotton dress shirt clung damply around the outline of his body.

"Good morning," he said. "To the airport?"

"That's right," Christine replied. She found herself fully alert.

"Sounds good." The cab sped through Richmond's empty morning streets. "Domestic or international?"

"Toronto," she said. "The center of the universe." He laughed—a deep, easy sound that caused his neck to bounce, like a toy, atop his shoulders.

"I hate it there," he said. "Too crazy. Too much noise, too many people. Too big. Reminds me of America, you know? You have some business there?"

"No, not this time. I'm going to meet my husband."

"Romantic surprise?" he asked.

"No," she said. "I'm going to kill him."

He laughed again. "That's very nice of you. My wife finds it easy enough to do that at home. Almost every night, I think she tries."

Christine exhaled a mock laugh in return, but didn't say anything as the car turned briefly onto the highway before beginning a long, slow loop toward the airport plaza.

"It was the first place I ever knew in Canada, Toronto," the driver said.

"Where are you from?"

"Rwanda. In Africa."

"Oh," she replied. Canadians, she thought, were so rarely from Canada. But she didn't know anything about Rwanda, except that it was an unhappy place.

"I came here a long time ago, almost ten years. And Toronto is where they took us. Me and my brother."

"Do you remember it?" Christine asked. She decided not to inquire about who "they" were—she imagined idealistic young college graduates, dressed in khaki and eager to ignore their parents' concerns over money, relationships, real life.

"Oh, yes. Maybe, I think, the best day of my life. Do you know, I had never been on an escalator before. So I remember that, my first escalator. Stairs that moved! My mind had never even thought this was possible. Now, I think it sounds ridiculous. But I remember being so scared. To time it right, that first step. My brother pushed me, I think."

Christine mock laughed again as the driver parked behind a police car, then helped her lift the rolling case from the trunk. It was heavier than it looked, and nearly toppled, but she grabbed the other end just before it crashed to the ground.

* * *

"Would you prefer a window or an aisle?" The Air Canada attendant had slender, creamy fingers, and nails that shimmered like oysters. This made Christine ashamed of her own, red-rimmed and bitten down to jagged nubs, and she drew her hands into fists after providing her passport.

"Window, if you have it, please," she said.

She spent the hour before her departure at the gate, sitting with her legs crossed and watching the wanderings of the suits and bickering families that populate an airport in the morning. A stroller designed for three children wobbled by, conducted by a weary-looking young woman. Taking a turn, it fell, and Christine stood up to help before noticing it was empty. When she sat back down, she realized that her legs were shaking. Not just that—everything below her hips was convulsing, possessed by some violent, unknown force. She pushed her heels into the carpet of the departure lounge, then counted the rapid beats of her heart until the flight began to board. Finally, at somewhere just past 3,000, it did.

But the plane itself was even worse. A mild anxiety had shadowed her for the past week, ever since she first made her discovery. Now, trapped inside the small space, it began to balloon, swelling up and contaminating the captive air. Christine tried to measure her breathing, but it seemed that—even when she opened her mouth so wide that her lips felt stretched against her teeth—her lungs would not fill. She glanced around the business class cabin, worried that someone might notice her silent terror, but no one was even looking in her direction. An attendant came by with glasses of water, and she took one, then closed her eyes and, disgustedly, allowed her mind to wander to the only memory that eased its trembling. Pierre.

She had seen him perform many times, of course. Even before they met, before the dinners of homemade pasta and weekend trips to the island and lazy Saturday mornings spent watching Italian soccer matches in bed. Before she even knew his name, she had seen him on the stage, in his debut. Her twenty-fifth birthday. She had been eager to get out and party—her boyfriend at the time, a rugby player named Eli, a grizzly bear of a man, had arranged a boat cruise in celebration. But attending the opera alongside her father was her birthday tradition, one that extended back to childhood. She loved all music, but preferred opera to concerts, which offered too much time where you were just alone with your thoughts. Without a story to follow, she often found her mind wandering to its darkest corners, spaces filled with thoughts and impulses best left buried.

Pierre was a phenomenon, even from the beginning of his career. However, that first performance was not Christine's favorite. Pierre was not yet familiar enough with the limits of his own talent. He sought to replace experience with furor, and chased opportunities before the music presented them, trampling the subtlety that would eventually form the hallmark of his style.

Nor did she imagine him as he performed now, reduced to supporting roles and celebrity appearances, obviously well into the twilight of his career. There were exceptions, of course—the odd, understated aria could still illuminate him, causing the entire audience to almost imperceptibly lean forward in their seats, straining to ensure they caught every note. But these moments only sharpened the contrast with his former self, underscoring how the ellipses of his moment in operatic history would not rival its prime.

It was nearly a decade ago, in Bologna, that he had given the performance that her memory anointed as his finest. His hometown, although he had never really lived there, having moved to Canada before beginning school. But when the Teatra Comunale invited him to lead their production of *Falstaff*, there had been no deliberation necessary. Christine was doing graduate philosophy work at the time, so her summers were open to adventure. A week later they were in Italy, at the beginning of three glorious months.

Of course, the locals hated her—they saw only a shy, mousey Canadian woman who kept a fine Italian boy locked up far away from home. But she spent most of her time in the library anyway, continuing her studies. And for Pierre, it was heaven. He slipped perfectly into the role of the foolish knight, and took the stage each evening with a sense of self-confidence that eluded him in his North American appearances. In character, he became far less troubled than in reality, when an uncontrollable European moodiness would sometimes sweep him without warning.

The performance Christine chose to remember was his penultimate one in Bologna. The opera concludes in a solo. Falstaff, who has just suffered the embarrassment of a beating at the hands of fairies, surrenders in a fugue that the whole world must surely be a farce. With each show, Christine found herself more and more desperate to hear Pierre bring the evening to its climax. She knew, even then, that he would never again be so transcendent. But that night, just as he began, there was an accident. A young oboist, well-known for his fondness for a preperformance drink, had passed out in the pit. A sound like a duck being stepped on brought the music to a halt, and the orchestra mobbed the fallen boy, swiftly bearing him up and over to an exit. The performers on stage looked at each other, suspended in the instant, unsure of how to proceed.

And then Pierre began, without accompaniment, to sing. For the rest of her life, Christine would insist that no single superlative could sufficiently describe the joy that credenza released inside her. She felt suddenly conscious of all the layers of reality around her—that of the audience, the theater, the opera, and the music itself, which seemed like it had been evolving for thousands of years toward each of those perfect notes.

Thinking of that moment—her arms wrapped around her legs, her chin buried between her knees, her feet pulled up onto the tiny seat beneath her—Christine felt herself relax. As the plane lifted above the clouds and began its journey, she closed her eyes and, for the first time in seven days, finally found her way to sleep.

Pearson was a gargantuan airport, far larger than Vancouver's, and Christine strode through it with her head down. The crowds terrified her. So many people, yet so little talking—airports were one of those places, like subway cars, where the density of solitary travelers created great moving, silent hordes. The thicker the swarm, the more isolating the experience. The baggage concourse seemed to have been built with this in mind—pillars like redwoods were spaced throughout a room the size of several gymnasiums. Christine imagined that the entire population of Toronto could likely fit inside the space. But it would somehow still feel empty. Its walls and roof were all glass and white steel, so that it felt like she had moved not only east, but also forward, through time itself, and arrived at some point in the future, inside the hangar for some monolithic spacecraft that had not yet been invented.

Christine's bag was one of the first, and she snatched it

off the ramp so suddenly that it slipped to the ground with a crack. No one paused their own searches to notice.

The hotel was connected to Terminal 3. The lobby was nearly empty when she arrived. One geriatric traveler sat sleeping at a coffee table before a bowl of green apples, that morning's paper scattered across his lap. Two young men, barely more than teenagers, stood at the front desk. Christine was only steps away before they noticed her, and thus she had to endure one describing to the other how he had been "whipping his dick like it owed him money." Red-faced, he turned to her. Ripe, moist acne covered his cheeks, and his blond hair hung in a limp swoop across his forehead.

"Good morning," he said. "Welcome to the Gateway Hotel."

"Thank you," she said. "I'm checking in, but I have a strange request." His mouth hung open in reply. "My husband is staying here tonight, and I'd like to surprise him. Would it maybe be possible for me to get into his room without you letting him know I've checked in? It's our wedding anniversary."

The boy nodded dumbly for a moment, still embarrassed. "Let me see," he said. "Can I have your name, ma'am?"

"Of course. Alvio. My husband won't be arriving until this evening." He busied himself for a moment with a computer monitor that stood below the counter, making rapid jabs at its touch screen. Christine held her breath.

"And your husband's first name?"

"Pierre."

The boy's face scrunched up for a moment, and Christine noticed that the acne extended down to his neck, its pustules thickening within the nourishment of a razor burn. He nodded.

"Looks like it won't be a problem," he said, and grabbed a print out from somewhere by his knees. "I'll give you one key, if you can sign this for me?"

"Thank you so much," she said. "I really do appreciate it. And, it won't . . . He won't know that I'm here?"

"That's right. We will, but he'll have no clue."

"Oh, that's wonderful," she said. "Thank you so much."

"Uh huh." The boy slipped her a plastic keycard. "Enjoy your anniversary, ma'am."

"I will," she said. "Thank you again. I know this is unusual."

He smiled. He had a very small head, like the ball atop a needle.

Given that it was only an airport hotel, the room was well furnished. A full desk and two brown leather club chairs surrounded an inviting queen-sized bed. Christine left her purse by the door, rolled her case to the bed, and threw it onto the duvet. She went to the window. Toronto was a distant gray bar graph upon the horizon. It shimmered in the smoggy heat. The airfield spread out below her—a sea of tarmac gradually giving way to endless, ugly squares of yellow grass. From the corner of her eye, she thought she saw something move among its tall, dying blades. Something animal, like a large rat. She imagined what kind of beasts must lurk out there, stranded in the fields between no places, surviving off nothing but insects and each other. But she couldn't find whatever she had seen again, and so turned to the case on the bed.

Inside, things were just as she'd packed them. Her clothes were wrapped around the cash, and atop them sat a hair gel container. She unscrewed its cap and sniffed—the moist mixture inside smelled like dead fish left out in the sun. Once hemlock dries, its toxicity is severely reduced. But kept damp and ground to a paste, it is lethal, choking off the nervous system like salt in a gas tank. She had discovered it in her studies—it had been used to execute Socrates after his condemnation for impiety. Plato, watching his former teacher's last moments, carefully took note of how death's grasp took hold:

> *The man . . . laid his hands on him and after a while examined his feet and legs, then pinched his foot hard and asked if he felt it. He said "No"; then after that, his thighs; and passing upwards in this way he showed us that he was growing cold and rigid. And then again he touched him and said that when it reached his heart, he would be gone. The chill had now reached the region about the groin, and uncovering his face, which had been covered, he said—and these were his last words—"Crito, we owe a cock to Asclepius. Pay it and do not neglect it." "That," said Crito, "shall be done; but see if you have anything else to say." To this question he made no reply, but after a little while he moved; the attendant uncovered him; his eyes were fixed. And Crito, when he saw it, closed his mouth and eyes.*

Afterwards, the victim and his assassin were forever bound—the red spots that cover the stem of a wild hemlock plant are referred to as the "blood of Socrates." A misnomer, of course, because there would be no blood. Only the chill, spreading through Pierre's body like syrup across a pancake.

This was the method upon which Christine had decided, but she had initially wanted something far more vulgar. In those first few days afterwards, her only solace had been the lurid scenarios she concocted in her mind. In her favorite, she has him naked, bound and gagged, with a rope tied fast around his neck. By this she leads him out into the street, where all the audiences he has ever performed for are arranged, jostling with each other for the finest views. The street is covered with the glass of a thousand bottles, and she drags him down it, the shards shredding his skin into pale, wraithlike ribbons. She had once cut her hand open dicing onions, and been amazed at the way the flesh lost all its elasticity, instantly becoming pale, almost alien. She wanted every inch of Pierre to look that way, red and white like a candy cane.

But the hemlock had seemed easier, and would allow her to be somewhere far away by the time it did its work. She opened a water bottle—there were two by the door, above the minibar—and rapped the container against its rim. Pierre would drink one before bed—he did this like a ritual, even at home—and then sleep for the last time. The paste broke off in chunks and spiraled down inside the bottle. Christine shook it until her arm hurt. Within an hour, it would dissolve completely.

She repacked her bag, left the hotel room, and returned to the lobby. The loudspeakers were playing Rush's "YYZ," and Christine wondered for a moment both how to spend the rest of her day and whether anyone else listening to the song realized it was a tribute to the building in which they stood. She decided to simply return to the terminal and wait.

After wandering for a little while, she eventually found a spot at a coffee shop in the nexus of Terminal 1. From the ceiling, five colored-glass silhouettes were suspended, their arms and legs fully outstretched, like they were dancing in space. A plaque titled the installation, *I Dreamed I Could Fly*. But to Christine the figures looked more like they were falling—as if they had tumbled downwards through the glass roof above them and, rather than shattering it, absorbed its material as their own.

Sitting down with a coffee, she began to wait. There was a magazine in her purse, but she didn't reach for it. Merely watching the crowds move back and forth before her was enough to pass the time. A few years prior, she might have hoped to spot a celebrity. But charter flights were too common these days, and airports had surrendered their status as the great equalizer. The rich and famous no longer had to wait alongside the masses as they endured the twin miseries of lost luggage and invasive security checks.

His flight was due to arrive at 4 in the afternoon, from Boston. At quarter to, Christine returned to the baggage claim. From her purse she drew a scarf and sunglasses—more than enough to disguise someone not being looked for. As she sat down for one last wait, her hands quivering in anticipation, she reached inside her jacket and withdrew the thick sheaf of letters. She had found them a week ago while cleaning his study, tucked behind the Elmore Leonard section of his bookshelf. She'd sat down on the floor and read every last one, racing through their words as if someone had dared her. Index cards, napkins, hotel stationery—the history of his adultery. And at its center a boy, just barely old enough to drink.

She'd read, in the skeletal block printing of a child's hand, how they'd met at a performance in Los Angeles. Pierre had gotten drunk, and they'd consummated things soon after. Apparently, it was neither's first time. The letters were so worshipful they were almost odes—the boy felt like he and Pierre shared something unnamable, and then he spent four pages trying to name it. He couldn't remember the last time a man had made him feel sexy the way Pierre did.

They had been meeting for nearly a year since that first

tryst—often here, at Pearson, which was halfway between Vancouver and Atlanta, where the boy lived. Thus, when the letters involuntarily reared their head in her imagination, they were dictated in a candy-sweet Southern drawl. His name was Timothy.

He didn't want to keep it a secret anymore. He wanted them to move away, to Italy, although he'd never been there. He wanted a villa where they could make love in the sunshine, in the yard, where their lips and tongues and fingers could intertwine slowly, free of the haste of secrecy. He misspelled both *definitely* and *necessary*.

But Pierre's letters were far worse. The casual way he referred to the lovers he'd had in the past—some men she knew, men who'd stayed in their home, men whom she had made dinners for, taken holidays with. The explicit way he described his desires, using words she'd never even heard him speak. And, worst of all, through forty-seven letters, she wasn't mentioned once.

So Christine knew. When he had called on Wednesday and said he needed to stop in Toronto on the way home from Boston, that there was some consulting he'd been asked to do on a children's production of the *The Magic Flute*, she knew where he was going. And she'd come to meet him.

The clock read 4:15, and the flight from Boston read, *Arrived*. On the carousel before her, bags were beginning to slip down, one after another. Cardboard boxes, bright red Samsonites, huge black rolling trunks. She waited for his, a caramel-colored duffel. But it didn't appear, and neither did he. At 4:30, the crowd around the conveyor began to thin, and she backed away, worried that she might be noticed. But by quarter to 5, she stood alone. Pierre was not coming—their plans must have changed. Perhaps he and Timothy had just met in Boston, his trip to Toronto entirely a ruse. Or he had gone to Atlanta, and even now they were locked in some squalid bachelor apartment, soaping each other in its phone-booth shower.

The luggage for the next flight, from Minnesota, had begun to descend. Christine paced, unsure what to do next. The bags were identical to those that had come before—the same boxes, the same Samsonites, the same trunks. Each was a different life, she realized—each had a separate owner, with its own history, all moving independently of one another. And this made her feel very small, as if she was nothing more than a bag herself—inside an airport, inside a city, inside the civilization that must have cities. Exhaustion swept over her. Stumbling, she made her way back to the hotel.

In the elevator up to the room, Christine slumped against the mirror. She could go anywhere in the world from here—the cash was in her bag at her feet. All futures were only a ticket away. But she felt sapped of direction—the Christine before her in the mirror looked old. Unwanted. Impotent. On the fourteenth floor, the doors opened. Dragging a hand along the wall and her tiny case behind her, her eyes half closed, she stumbled to the room.

A hanger dangled around the knob, something she didn't remember having put there herself. She picked it up—*Ne Pas Deranger*, it read. French. She took a step back. Men's voices came from inside the room. Laughter. Deep inside her, a rage awoke. This was not enough—it was too passive. She wanted him to know. She wanted the boy to die, to leave him stranded and alone. She wanted to fly him to the middle of the desert and then abandon him, with nothing but the knowledge of his own infidelity to wait with him for death. Socrates's death was far more than he deserved. Fist clenched, she raised her hand, ready to knock. But something stayed her hand, forced it down, to the hanger. She flipped it to its English side. *Do Not Disturb*. And then she left.

On her way back through the lobby, she stopped at the front desk. A new, more handsome boy had replaced the one from that afternoon. Smiling, she asked him to send a bottle of champagne to her husband's room. And then she flew away.

PART III

Road to Nowhere

A BOUT OF REGRET

BY MICHAEL REDHILL

Distillery District

It's bad news whenever a policeman walks into your bar, but it's worse when you've been having an affair with his wife. Katherine and I had been seeing each other for so long that I didn't really ever think about her husband anymore. He was in the background, like a great-uncle, and for the last couple of years we'd stopped being careful, he was that regular in his work and in his habits. To listen to Katherine, all they had left in common was the marital home. He probably had affairs too, was how she saw it, and she believed a series of unspoken arrangements kept the balance in all of our lives. But if that was true, then what was Leonard Albrecht doing at the back of my bar, squinting at one of the old photographs behind glass, like he was thinking of sitting down for a plate of calamari and a beer?

The Canteen was the name of my bar, a name I borrowed from the original saloon that stood on this spot, more than 150 years ago. I'm down a side street in the Distillery District, one of Toronto's oldest unwrecked neighborhoods. For a lot of years in this city, all the most interesting neighborhoods—at least the ones with a story to tell—have been taken over to build condos, but this corner of the city was so unpopular, so out of the way, that they left it alone. It stands at an angle to the shore of Lake Ontario, close enough to drink its waters, but far enough away from the city's old wharfs that the only business done from its docks was its own. Until fifteen years ago, the distillery was a miniature city unto itself (complete with its Victorian cobblestones and cramped walkways) that churned out whiskey, rum, and during WWII, acetone. I'd never met anyone who'd been behind its locked gates, and tucked in behind the monstrosity of the Gardiner Expressway, it was all but inaccessible. But it was industrious for an invisible, unloved corner of the city: It was still putting out rum when it closed in 1990.

Some smart business types thought it might make a decent tourist destination and started cleaning it up a few years after it shut its doors. I got in on the ground floor for what was a lot of money five years ago, though now I couldn't buy a chunk of cobblestone to paint my name on for that kind of cash. I've since made back what this place cost me and I've parlayed its status as the original distillery bar into a couple of lucrative sidelines. In general, I've been lucky in business. And up until now, it seemed, in love too.

Albrecht was meandering toward the bar where I was polishing glasses, getting ready for the lunch rush. It was 10 in the morning on an overcast September day. Bartenders are supposed to be good people-readers, but the truth is, you don't need any skills to read a person who's come into a bar to drink alone, and those are the people who like to talk. The movie cliché is wrong, though: Most of the people—men, usually—who sidle up to a bar to unburden themselves aren't suffering from heartache. Half the conversational openers I hear are some variation on, "Fucking Leafs, eh?" and I can tell you that, after a while, all those suckers pining over the Stanley Cup or the World Series trophy make you hungry for a story about love. Just once I'd like some stubbled broken heart to sit down at my bar and say, "The day she walked into my life was the day my life ended." Or something like that.

My point here is that I had no idea what Albrecht was thinking, although I'm pretty sure he knew what I was thinking, since he was giving me time to notice him. I don't know the first thing about cops, but I gather from watching movies that they can figure out a lot from your body language. I just stood there trying to polish glasses in as unguilty a way as possible, but for all I knew, the angle of my arm was telling him I'd been sleeping with his wife for nine years.

He gave me a smile and a little wave when he saw me looking at him. "Nice place," he said.

"It'll do."

"Mainly tourists?"

I stared at him for a second. The small talk was supposed to show me he was in complete control. "It used to be," I said finally, "but the locals have found it." The sweat from my palm smeared the glass I was cleaning and I had to start over. "It's about fifty-fifty now."

He nodded appreciatively, looking around a little more. "I live over by Queen and Bathurst," he said. "I go into the Wheat Sheaf sometimes. But I work out of 51 Division, five hundred meters from here. You'd think I'd have had cause to come in before now."

"I guess we keep our noses clean," I said.

"I usually work nights, so you must. Or we would have met by now." He pulled out a stool and sat, ran his fingertips over the old, burnished wood on the bar. He had massive, thick hands. I knew what he looked like from the pictures in his house, and I knew he was a big man, but in person he was considerably more imposing. There were a couple other surprising things about him too: His face was warm and his eyes soulful. He had a huge gourmand's nose. If I hadn't been on guard, I might have taken an instant liking to him. "This bar and the Wheat Sheaf," he said, "they must be about the same vintage, eh?"

"About that. 1830s or thereabout."

"I just love these old places," he said. "Nobody really cares about them, though. If they're in the way, down they come. Lucky this spot wasn't of interest to anyone."

I had to smile. He was playing me perfectly. I put the glass into the overhead rack and took another one out of the rotary washer. I decided it was time for him to make his point. If I had any say in the matter, I wanted this over before there were customers to deal with. "Listen, officer," I said, "the lunch rush is coming in soon. Is there anything I can help you with?"

He seemed to shake the cobwebs out, like he just remembered he was on business, and drew a wallet out of his inside jacket pocket. He flipped his ID open to me. "Sorry, I slip into reveries I guess. Detective Inspector Leonard Albrecht," he said. "Don't worry, I'm not here on licensing business."

"I figured as much," I replied, keeping my eye on him.

"You're Terry McEwan?" I nodded. "You got any unhappy ex-employees?" I thought about that for a minute. What the hell could one of my ex-employees have told Leonard Albrecht about where I went in my off hours? I said that there were none I was aware of. He opened his notebook. "Do you remember a Deborah Cooper?"

"Yeah. She served tables here this summer. She was seasonal, you know? I hire them in June and cut them loose after Labor Day." A glimmer of something began to surface in the back of my mind. "What did she say?"

"Well, she came in last week to complain you were running an illegal after-hours club here."

"Yeah?"

"Is it true?"

I tried not to show my pleasure at his line of questioning. *How do you like that?* I thought. Leonard Albrecht shows up in my bar *not* to blacken my eye for having an affair with his wife, but because he's pulled duty to look into my underground activities. Someone up there had a very black sense of humor. "It depends what part you're asking me about. The 'illegal' or the 'after-hours.'"

He tilted his head at me minutely, like a huge parrot. "From that I take it's a yes to the after-hours part, but you're of the opinion that you're not doing anything wrong."

"It's a private club, detective."

"You charge money?"

"It pays the servers for their time."

"I see. And there's nothing leftover for you. So you're basically volunteering your time, right?"

He had me there, but I couldn't come up with something to counter him with. I was thinking of how I was going to tell Katherine all of this. *You're not going to fucking believe who walked into my bar this morning*, was what I was already saying to her in my mind. I could see the dread and curiosity in her eyes, the way she'd say, *NO!* when I told her, like there wasn't a chance I could be telling the truth. We'd be sitting on the couch, two glasses of wine on the coffee table in front of us, and I'd tell her and she'd slap me on the arm, her eyes wide—*Get out!*—and then she'd be laughing hysterically with her hand over her mouth. I heard her in my mind as if she were standing right there at the bar in front of me. *Oh, how awful!* Her mouth pursed in delighted horror. *You poor, poor thing!* I was almost of a mind to draw this out as long as I could.

Except I had a problem now. Leonard Albrecht was real.

"You still with me?" he said.

"Sorry," I replied. "Am I going to need a lawyer?"

"It depends."

"On what?"

"On whether you're straight with me or not."

I processed that for a moment and it dawned on me that if the man was as much a student of history as he'd said he was, he might be interested in what was below my bar for more than just procedural reasons. "This was a worker's bar," I said. "Mainly Irish. They opened it and ran it, but management told them what hours they could keep, what activities were allowed. I guess running a bar on the grounds of a distillery has its challenges." Albrecht smiled. "Anyway, I guess some of them didn't like being told their business. They secretly dug themselves a basement and they did what they liked down there."

"Which was what?" asked Albrecht.

"Music, dancing. The occasional cockfight. And there was a boxing ring."

"That's what she said." He looked down at his notes. "Cooper. She said there was fighting."

"Is that the illegal part?"

"Oh no, it's *all* illegal. Selling liquor in an unlicensed room, holding a sports contest. Both are pretty bad, but the two of them together are really bad. You sell tickets to the bouts?"

I saw Gillian and Henry, my lunch staff, come in through the side door. They shot me looks and disappeared into the kitchen. "We only have three or four fights a year."

"You sell tickets?"

"Yeah," I said, starting to think maybe I shouldn't have felt so smug about Albrecht's reason for visiting me. Maybe an accusation and a fat lip wouldn't have been as bad as this was starting to look. "Listen, I didn't really know—"

"You knew," he said. "Let's not go down that road." He stood up. "Show me."

"Is there any way we could do this when the bar's a little quieter?"

"Your people can handle the first rush. You've got other business. Let's go."

When Alan Kravitz handed me the keys to the place, he held one of them up, a rusty, old-fashioned one. "There's a little storage space under the bar, might be useful to you. Be careful, though, the floors are rotting and I don't know how strong the beams are."

The first time I went down there, I brought my cook with me to see if he thought it would be a good place for a fridge. "Christ," he'd said. "You could dry salami down here."

We'd walked through the small, dark, dusty room with two flashlights and a pair of long sticks, pushing crates aside with them. There was a disgusting stained cloth lining one of the walls, and I guess Kravitz hadn't brought a stick with him when he first investigated because I used mine to pull the cloth away and found a door behind it. It lead in to an enormous room with a broken-down piano in it, a bar, a stage, and a tattered old boxing ring. There were some forty chairs arranged around the room. We'd shone our beams into the cold, lightless place and looked on it with genuine wonder. Under the bar was a log with a record of bar sales and admission fees and the like, and we saw that there hadn't been a soul in that place for eighty years. "You thinking what I'm thinking?" I asked the cook.

"You'll need another license," he'd said.

"Or not."

It took two years of secretly refurbishing the place to get it up to scratch. I tried to keep as much of the old grandeur as I could, but the piano had to be replaced and the boxing ring recovered, although the ropes had survived and so had two of the turnbuckles. If I could find anyone to fight in the place, they'd have the chance to get knocked silly against a turnbuckle that had dimmed the lights on some Irishman a hundred years earlier. Katherine had been the first person outside of the bar I'd shown the finished room to. "Wow," she'd said. "I'm not the only thing you're doing on the side."

I poured her a Scotch and we toasted the future. She'd been at almost every one of the bar's traditional music nights and boxing matches since we opened. Now her husband was standing in the middle of the room.

"Cooper didn't do it justice," he said.

"She was only down here once. She told me she wasn't comfortable working off hours, even for the money I was paying."

"Expensive to keep a secret?"

"Obviously not expensive enough."

He walked into the room, turning slowly to take in all the details. "Looks pretty authentic."

"I had pictures of nineteenth-century saloons to guide me. I did a lot of research. This wasn't the only speakeasy in Toronto in 1850."

"But it's the only remaining one."

"I think it must be."

He walked among the round zinc tables toward the stage. "There're wings?"

"Dressing rooms too."

"Wow," he said. "These the original floors?"

"No. They were a mess. We did these ourselves. We kept as many of the old nails as we could salvage, though. Some of it's original."

He walked across the front of the stage to the corner of the room where the boxing ring was. For matches, I had four men simply lift the ring and bring it into the middle of the room, where we'd arrange the chairs around it. You could break it down and put it away, but I liked the look of it, menacing and lonesome, in the corner of the room under a single light. He stood beside it, wiping his hand over the canvas. "You got a champ?" he asked me.

"Ernie Paschtenko. Russian kid. He fights out of the Cabbagetown Club, but someone brought him down to us and he's been fighting friendlies here for a couple of years. His record is ten and one."

"You do some training here too?"

"A little."

"And who judges the bouts?"

"I do, with a couple of the regulars."

"Nice," said Albrecht. "A whole secret world, huh?"

"Until now."

"You fight?"

"I spar once in a while, but no. I don't got much of a chin."

Albrecht pushed one of the ropes up and threaded himself under it onto the canvas. For a big man, he was lithe. He stood in the ring, testing the platform. "I tell you what," he said. "I know a good thing when I see it. I'll write this up back at the station house and say everything's in order. But you got to promise that you'll get a license for down here. I can't help it if someone less inclined to see the charm of this place stumbles onto it."

You have to do a certain amount of diminishing the missing corner of the triangle to feel in your right mind when you're cuckolding a man. Leonard Albrecht hadn't deserved an atom of it. He was good people, but it shouldn't have surprised me. He'd once loved Katherine. I wondered if there was a way I could make it up to him without his knowing what I was doing. "I'll get a license then," I said.

"That'll mean inspections, McEwan. So you have to put this ring away when it's not in use. And you can't charge admission anymore."

"Okay."

"You got any kind of records for your sales?"

"Somewhere."

"Get rid of them. The day you get your license is the day this place officially opens."

I crossed the room to the ring. "I'm grateful for this," I said to him. "I'd be happy to put you on the list. You know, for matches and other things."

He was pretending to fence with an invisible opponent, dodging blows, feinting left and right. "That'd be great," he said. "I could slip in if I get a quiet shift some night."

"You ever box?" I asked him.

"Naw, just a student of the sport. I don't understand people who say it's all brutality, though. It's the most basic contest there is. Man against man, a duel of honor. My wife hates it."

No she doesn't, I thought. If Leonard Albrecht was planning on coming to matches, though, she wouldn't be seeing any more fights in the basement of The Canteen.

I watched him up there shadowboxing, and my heart went out to him. He had no idea what his wife was made of. And he was so lonely in his work that he was willing to let a complete stranger off the hook if it meant being a part of something. I went to the cabinet behind the ring and got out two pairs of gloves and headgear and held them up. "You want to see what it feels like?"

He came over and leaned on the ropes. "And let you knock my block off? How do I explain that back at division?"

"We'll take it easy. You'll like it."

He thought about it for a moment, then smiled and took off his jacket, tossing it over the corner as I stepped into the ring. I laced him up, but he waved off the headgear. "If I wear that, you'll feel free to hit me."

"It's safer with it. Just in case." I didn't want to clock him accidentally, but he didn't want to wear the gear. I tossed both protectors over the ropes. "Rule one: Keep your chin down. Tuck it into your lead shoulder, since you're going to turn a little on an angle to me, give me less body to punch at. It's natural to want to lift your head, but it's the worst thing you can do. You got to protect both your throat and the button." I touched the point of my chin with my glove. "And keep your hands up," I told him, as we faced off. "Protect yourself and stay outside, you know what that means?"

"Keep back from you."

"That's right. Because you're the bigger man here, you want some range. You want to keep me out from where I can work under your defenses, you understand?" He nodded. "And keep your eyes loose, like you're trying *not* to look at me, but see my eyes and my chest and shoulders all at the same time."

He nodded again, and we started circling each other, moving around the ring. He kept his hands up pretty tight to his face, but I could see him watching me between his gloves. There's a lot you can learn from watching the fights, and he'd gotten it down pretty good, feinting away from me, keeping his head moving. I threw a couple of light jabs at him and he dodged them, returning punches when I was out of position and even connecting a couple of times, light jabs to my hairline. "That's good," I said, "you've got some ring sense."

"You're moving pretty slow."

I started circling a little more aggressively, coming in when I sensed an opening, but he knew when to step out, break away. It was enjoyable. I'd sparred with Paschtenko, but that kid could knock me upstairs if he wanted to, and most of the time I spent in the ring with him, I just stayed away as much as I could. This was different, and in an odd way, it was a little intimate, like the beginning of a friendship. It was strange to have the man's body in front of me, that body I had betrayed indirectly, at both a physical and emotional remove. This body so well known to Katherine. I suddenly felt grateful that he was not shirtless, that there was no more of the raw animal in front of me. I let us go a couple more minutes, connecting a few times, taking a semi-solid punch or two to the kidneys from him. If he got into shape, he might have something, I thought.

I stepped back. "Well, officer, I should probably get back upstairs." I'd lowered my gloves, but he was still moving toward me. I was completely open for the punch he threw, but I managed to slide away from it; he would have tagged me right on the chin. I batted his glove away. "Whoa," I said. "There's the bell."

"Sorry," he said, dropping his hands.

"Good instincts, though. Get yourself a trainer, you could put some tiger in that tank of yours."

He picked his jacket off the turnbuckle, folded it over his arm. I stepped out and tossed the equipment back into the cabinet. "When's the next bout?" he asked.

"Two weeks. You got a card?" He reached into his wallet and handed me one. He was sweating lightly. "So this is all going to stay on the QT?" I asked.

"Yeah, as long as you do what I say."

"License, no ticket sales."

"Get rid of your records."

"Right," I said.

"And one more thing."

I snapped the light off over the ring. "You were never here, right?"

"Yeah, that. And stay away from my wife."

I had my back to him and I froze, waiting for the blow, but it never came. "What did you say?"

"You heard me, Terry. We're giving it another try and I want you to keep your distance. I'll let you know if it doesn't work out between us."

I turned slowly to face him. "Jesus Christ," I said.

"I know." He slipped an arm into his jacket. "You seem like a nice guy and I'll be happy for her if we can't get our act together. As long as you go semi-legal here, you should both be fine. But for now . . . you know." He offered me his hand. After a second I took it.

"Look, I'm . . ."

"I'll be seeing you, Terry."

He released my hand. I felt it drop, dead, to my side. "See me where?"

"Here," he said. "That Cooper girl really did swear a complaint. I'm glad she did. This is the coolest thing I've stumbled across in fifteen years."

He went out the door without another word.

I turned off the rest of the lights and locked the doors. Upstairs the first wave was being seated in the bar. Gillian came over as soon as she saw me. The look on my face, I guess. "Jesus . . . was that guy from the commission?"

"No. He was a cop."

"Oh fuck," she said. "Is everything okay?"

"For now. But he warned me I could lose everything if I don't clean up."

She breathed out heavily. "Anything I can do?"

"Serve lunch," I said. "What else is there to do?"

We did forty covers for lunch and another seventy-five at night. An average day in The Canteen. I looked him up online once I got home. He'd been an Ontario Golden Glove between the ages of sixteen and twenty-five. A heavyweight. He hadn't won a single belt, but my guess is he didn't want one bad enough.

I never heard from Katherine again, but after a few months, he started to show up at the fights. I said hello, but I let someone else serve him. Life is full of TKOs. You might think you're still standing, but there's the third man, waving his arms, and it's all over.

For Steven Heighton and Michael Winter

BRIANNA SOUTH

BY RM VAUGHAN

Yorkville

BRI BLACKOUT! WHAT HAPPENED TO HOLLYWOOD'S "BABY GIRL"?

—*Toronto Sun*, September 12, 2008

The following excerpt from Brianna South's diary was obtained by the Sun *from unnamed sources, three days after her shocking disappearance. South, the controversial seventeen-year-old star of last summer's breakout comedy,* All the Nice Girls, *and the upcoming live adaptation of the '80s cartoon series* Pulsar Girl, *set to close the Toronto International Film Festival on Friday, left her room at the Four Seasons Hotel in Yorkville on Wednesday evening for an unscheduled outing. South's family have arrived from Fort Worth, Texas, and will make a statement later today. Police have released no further information.*

September 4

Ugly. Okay, not the nicest thing to say, I know, but who said, "It's not mean if it's true"?

Probably somebody who came to Toronto and stayed a whole week in a room my grandmother would like, with thirty-six French TV stations and no hot towel rack and the worst warm walnut salad I've ever had, that's who.

I've been outside exactly three times—from my hotel

room to the service elevator to a town car to a raw food restaurant, then back, then to a TV station in an old factory that smelled like a hot dog cart, then back, then to a *boring* movie from Mongolia they showed in an opera theater.

Jayson said I should see it, or just be seen seeing it, or at least walk into the theater. Like I understood any of it anyway, like I understand Mongolian funeral rituals and polo. I hate polo. Then it was back to the car, back up the service elevator, back here. It's so ugly. The view is of a museum that looks like another old factory, but with a bunch of bent aluminum siding sticking out of it, like a giant *ugly* metal rock. I think it's supposed to be art. I *hate* my life.

Later

Nobody likes my film. I can tell, because they won't shut up about it. If it was good, they'd be all calm and quiet.

I don't even remember the Pulsar Girl cartoon, and I'm in the "target market" for the movie. Newsflash, idiots: *Girls don't go to comic book movies*.

But you can't tell them anything, they're all fags. Only fags would make that movie. Everything is so funny to fags, stuff nobody else thinks is funny. Jayson said, "It's already a camp classic" in the restaurant—he thought I wasn't listening—and that is the fucking kiss of fucking death. You can't make a cult movie. It just happens. Even I know that, but you can't tell fags anything.

I *hate* Jayson. He leads me around like a dog. It's his job to get me the best interviews and the best articles and so far all he's done is drag me in front of people for show, not to talk. *Nobody* talks to me. They talk around me. I'm beginning to figure out that the whole point of this film festival is to just show up. I could be dead and they could drag my body from party to party and I'd still be the biggest news in town.

I mean, even Melanie Griffith got a newspaper cover, just for doing her own grocery shopping. She hasn't made a movie in years, but the whole stupid city freaks out because she can pay for a braised chicken all by herself without a helper.

Okay, that was mean. I'm hanging around Jayson too much. I sound like a fag. I really, really need someone to talk to. I could be dead and nobody would notice.

September 5

He called again, just ten minutes ago. I'm too excited. I shouldn't be this excited. I don't know how he got my room number. Everything is supposed to be secret—where I go, where I stay, where I eat, where I shit (especially where I shit). But he found me. Hotels are cleaned by ex-cons, like Mom says, so it's no surprise. What's a few fifties up here—like, eleven dollars at home?

He is so smart, it scares me. He says he found forty-six minutes of Pulsar Girl on YouTube. He says it's good, the flying looks real. I feel a little better.

[The remainder of the page is covered in drawings of hearts, vines, and what appears to be the same word, perhaps a name, repeated nineteen times. The word or name has been scratched out. Forensic textile experts hired by the Sun *were unable to read the word.]*

2:30 p.m.

I told Jayson to fuck off ten minutes ago. Fuck, that felt good. I should have done it before, like on Day One.

He wants me to go to this party in a science museum, a fundraiser for stem cell research. I told him I don't believe in using unborn babies to cure varicose veins. So he said I didn't have to pay to go, they only want me there for PR, so I wouldn't really be supporting anything I didn't believe in if I wasn't paying. That's Jayson logic.

I mean, I know I don't act all Christian, but I do love Jesus and babies. And my parents would kill me. So Jayson says, "SharLynn Kashante Jefferson is going," like that is supposed to make me all jealous or nervous or scared. SharLynn is okay. She's nice and, okay, she is pretty, but come on—she's on a stupid hospital show, with, like, four other black girls. And, I mean, really, only my father watches hospital shows.

So I told Jayson to fuck off. It just came out. Fuck. Off. Now he probably thinks I hate SharLynn, or that I'm racist. I don't care, I don't care, I don't care. I mean, I don't think they even get her show on TV up here.

He will be so proud of me when I tell him what I did. He says I have depths inside me, strengths and energies and powers I don't even know about yet. He says I am all diamonds inside.

September 6

Worst breakfast press conference of my life.

I felt like this tree, this skinny, dry tree, like the kind that used to grow in the back of our first house, behind the gravel pile. Garbage trees, skunk wood, Dad used to call them. You just cut that kind of tree down because it's no use. It's a weed with pretensions, Dad said. So you cut it down.

That's the way they treated me. Cut, cut, cut, cut, cut. One guy from France asked me about Iraq, if Pulsar Girl could stop the war (!!!!). Like I've been to Iraq, or even Europe. So that's all I could think to say: "Never been there." They laughed, mean laughs. Jayson just sat there. He said his microphone wasn't working. He fucking lies so much. Every word.

I lit all the foxglove-scented candles he sent and turned on Canadian MTV—which is, of course, in French, but at least the music is American—and I got in the bathtub and filled it really slow. He says foxglove is a medicine flower and the Irish call it Dead Man's Thimbles. Doesn't sound all that healthy to me, but he's the expert.

We connect over things like that. I mean, he's an expert in old things, in legends and stories, and I'm an expert in acting. The first time he wrote to me, I have to admit my Creepy Guy Radar went off a bit, because his handwriting was so girly. But I kept reading (because, okay, I was bored on the set), and he wrote that he thought All the Nice Girls was really a remake of the Story of Rachel and Leah, who are sisters in the Jewish part of the Bible. I looked it up.

I really am a lot like Leah, the "barren" woman, which I think means she was deaf. I mean, I'm not deaf, but I do sort of drift off a lot, and I am "tender-eyed" too, like the Bible calls Leah. I have a good heart, and I'm way, way too nice. And I've been overlooked all my life.

He's coming.

[The remainder of the paragraph is illegible. Forensic textile experts hired by the Sun *believe the page was scraped with a nail file or the blade of a sewing scissor.]*

Now it's 7:30 and Jayson was supposed to be here at 7 to pick me up. Another hospital party, for kids with bone cancer, or inside-out organs or bugs in their blood—something gross, it's always something gross.

I will *not* hug the really messed-up ones. I told Jayson—no hugging and wipes, bring sterile wipes. He never listens.

This afternoon he was in here, going over my dresses for tonight, and I turned away to look out the window because A) I didn't want to look at him because I *hate* him, and B) because there was this beautiful red bird on the window ledge. Bright red, and big, big as a cat.

Jayson said it was a Pope bird or a Thorny Cross bird, or another churchy name, like he knows anything, and after it flew away (actually, it really just sort of fell off the ledge, *I hope it's okay!!!*), I caught Jayson fucking around with my phone, my private phone with all my addresses and numbers.

I said, "What are you doing?" and he clicked it shut like it was nothing to invade my privacy. He said he thought it was *his* phone, no bigs. But his phone is blue, and mine is tangerine. Jayson wonders why I don't trust him.

I've decided I don't care that I don't know what *he* looks like.

Well, okay, I care a little, and I have an imagination, because I'm an actor—but if he's really ugly or old I really don't care.

I've met every good-looking man in the world in the last year and the big secret is *all good-looking men are exactly the same*. They're like men's dress-up shoes: They come in black or they come in brown, they have pointy ends or they have square ends, and that's that for choices.

I'm so bored with "beauty." I can look at any big actor now and I can tell you in ten seconds which trainer he uses, which diet he's on, where he gets his facials, who fills his pecs with saline, or his dick. It's like math, like algebra—squats plus tensor bar plus Nevada mud bath plus coffee enema three times a week equals one shower scene in your next movie. Do the same math five times and eat raw lamb for twelve days and you get a sex scene too.

I mean, if I can figure this out after two movies and one season on 7th Heaven, when I was like nine, why can't the public figure it out? It's amazing that people don't just start shooting celebrities, just for fun, just to see how quickly the producers can grow a new one, like starfish legs.

I don't think I'm unreplaceable. I don't think I'm special, or like a part of history. No fucking way am I doing "art."

Maybe college would be fun. I'd like to get drunk and throw up all over myself on a cute guy's front lawn, like my friends back home do every weekend. Nobody worries that they're "out of control." It's totally expected, totally acceptable behavior. I mean, Jayson even took the mini-bar key. "It looks better," he said.

Better to who? The maid? Jayson is so controlling. And I pay him for it. That's fucked.

He told me his name today.

Okay, it can't be his real name, probably, but it's still a name.

Azrael.

He said it was Jewish for, "He who makes the lasting peace."

It's beautiful, even if it is fake. Fake and beautiful are the same thing anyway.

Twenty-nine hours till he arrives. I'm excited, more than I should be. I should be excited about, like, one hundred other things in my life, but he's the only mystery I have left. Once you've spent seventeen hours hanging from a green wire pretending to be scared of the end of a mop that's supposed to be a giant lizard alien head, most of the surprises are gone out of life.

I mean, I could get pregnant, that would be new. That would be news too. Brianna and Azrael. What would the tabloids call us? Braz? Anra? Briel? Brianna and Azrael. Brianna and Azrael.

Please, God. Please, God, let him be cute. At least cute.

No, forget it. Sorry, God, scratch that. I am such a C-U-Next-Tuesday. I don't care. Azrael can have three heads and a harelip on all three mouths. He's a listener. My listener.

"He who makes the lasting peace."

Ten minutes would be enough for me.

Fuck, Jayson's here, at ten to 8:00. Nice and late. Off we go to pet the zombie kids. I wish I had some gloves—those long kind, up to the elbows. I could pretend it's part of my outfit.

September 7

Needy—people are so needy.

If I had terminal cancer I would just want to be left alone.

I wouldn't want balloons, or slides I couldn't slide on, or an ice cream cake I couldn't eat anyway—and especially no fucking thank you would I want fucking Mr. ET Canada Ben Mulroney signing my IV bag!!!

I mean, Jesus Christ!!! Why didn't he just sign the kids' foreheads so they can all be buried with his autograph? That guy is like an animatronic dinosaur at the Tar Pits—he moves his head, he opens his mouth, he moves his head in the other direction.

Best moment: Mulroney corners me while this girl who can't stop moving her head is getting her face painted like Spider-Man (because he figures nobody can hear him over the girl going umma umma umma) and he asks me, all "real" and sweet and concerned, if I want to talk about Pulsar Girl and why I'm fighting with the director.

Please, why would I fight with a director after the movie is done? What's the point?

I smell Jayson's stale CK One all over this. Maybe that's the new sell talk for the movie—Brianna's tantrum. Somebody has to be blamed, and it's never the director because here's another big secret: Directors are pure profit. You can work a director till he's like ninety-five, as long as he can point at the actors and mumble.

The sad part is, the kids were really excited to see me. I don't get it. Maybe one of them, maybe two, has ever even seen me in anything. But Somebody Special was there, and that's all that mattered.

I kind of think that if I only had a few weeks to live, I would consider myself the most Special person on earth, as a survival strategy. I would let all my animal instincts take over, become totally selfish and full of self-love, even self-worship. I would save every breath for me.

September 8

Azrael sent me the most beautiful plant. I wonder if I can take it back on the plane?

It's an orchid, I think. There's no real roots, just a ball of hard wood underneath this cloud of green spongy stuff that looks like a pot scrubber. The flower is navy-blue, or purple, I can't tell. It's huge, the size of two grapefruits, and it smells like dish soap, but salty. That part I'm not liking so much.

His note says the flower represents "purity risen from offal" and that the flower has "cleansing powers." That explains the smell.

I asked Jayson what "offal" meant, but he just went all faggy on me and waved his hands around like I just farted. He says the flower looks like something you put on a coffin. He would know.

September 9

Another fight with Jayson.

He wants me to do a breakfast television show tomorrow, at 6 a.m. It's a total waste. People who watch television at 6 a.m. don't go to the movies, because either they are senile and stuck in a home, or because they have to go to bed at 5 p.m. to get up for 5 a.m.

It's a total waste of time. I mean, maybe I'd do it for Good Morning America or Today, but Canadian breakfast television? Why don't we just set up a webcam in my room and beam pictures of me to Yakistan, or wherever? It would amount to the same at the box office.

So, I said no. I am allowed to say no.

Jayson freaked, really freaked. He screamed crazy stuff at me like, "I know more about you than you know," and, "I'm the reason you're here." Over and over. I walked into the bathroom and shut the door. So he stood there, right outside the bathroom door, close enough to hear me piss, and I think he was crying!!!

I came out after, like, twenty minutes (because I was bored and that bathroom is beyond ugly), and he was standing by the window, perfectly still. Calm as a sunflower, like my grandmother used to say.

"What have you got to wear if it rains?" he says. What a psycho.

I sent him to get me some new makeup, which I do not need, to get rid of him. I think I'll "forget" to pay him back.

* * *

I hope you can get Google Maps in Canada. I have to find out where *Leslie Spit* is (I know, *eewww*, gross name).

Azrael says it's the most private place in Toronto—a beach with trails and tall grass and flowers and, I guess, the ocean.

That tells me two things: One, he is from here, which is too bad because I hate long-distance relationships, and two, he is not interested in publicity, he doesn't want to be Mr. South.

He just wants to meet me, like a *person*, the way people are supposed to meet—without some Jayson or whoever in the middle, some fixer or arranger or scout or manager or protector.

I am so *bored* with being protected. It's not natural.

I mean, if I can't figure out who my friends are on my own, how am I going to make it to, like, twenty-five?

I'll get eaten alive.

MIDNIGHT SHIFT

BY RAYWAT DEONANDAN
University of Toronto

"Over here," Meera said, taking Yanni by the hand and dragging him down a freshly mopped corridor. It stank of ammonia, an antiseptic nasal assault that held a warped erotic appeal for some among the stethoscope and lab coat set. Meera drew Yanni's mouth to hers and tasted his youth, inhaling his masculine scents and flavors.

"Slow down," Yanni whispered. "And be quiet. Someone will hear!"

"Wimp," Meera chastized, running her dark hands under Yanni's loosened shirt. "There are only two nurses on this floor, and they're both at the station." Yanni still hesitated. "Besides," Meera continued, "maybe you *want* to get caught?" She grinned in her devilish way and pinched his nipple, pushing Yanni against the sterile white wall.

He was yielding to her touch, soft clay beneath her willful hands. Meera pressed him against the sign that read, *2nd Floor, Rheumatology*. The irony was not lost on her, as they strived to express an act of guileless youth in a place of broken agedness. The odors of imposed sterility, the colors of bureaucratic lifelessness and joyless dull lights—these were tokens of a philosophy that pushed aside the ardor of youth, the mystic charms of sex, and dirty, musical physicality. It was as if she and Yanni were consecrating the lifeless drywall with their hot, staccato breaths, all the time mildly aware of the clicking heels of the midnight nursing shift a hallway away, and of the almost imperceptible groans of the elderly patients swimming in their beds, wracked by dreams impossible for naïve, young medical residents to comprehend.

They clutched each other in that particularly desperate way, with each muscle seemingly both shocked and delighted that it had been recruited to such a pleasant purpose, and melted into the slow rhythm of human intimacy. The barren hospital corridor seemed less foreboding now that their eyes became accustomed to the darkness. At the end of the hall, a small window was open, letting in dull sounds from University Avenue below: a rushing stream of honking taxis, whooshing motorcycles, traffic lights hooting and chirping for the blind, and the chatter of the occasional passersby.

"Come on," Yanni said, spinning from the wall and dragging Meera by her stethoscope. He pulled her into one of the empty patient rooms and onto a bed. The tightly tucked hospital sheets were a cliché, one that made them both chuckle as they gave up trying to get under them. Then they heard a noise.

"Who's there?" It was a man's voice, weak and desperate.

Yanni sprung to his feet, letting his open shirt fall back into place. "I'm Dr. Rostoff. This is Dr. Rai. Who are you?" Meera clicked on the room light, revealing an elderly man in the room's secondary bed. "This room is supposed to be empty."

"Manoj Persaud," the man said, looking pleadingly at Meera, perhaps finding solace in a face as brown as his own. Yanni snatched the man's chart, flipping through the long paper sheets with guilty annoyance.

Yanni frowned. "Meera, he's supposed to be in the Latner Centre." He whispered: "Palliative care."

"I know I dyin'," Manoj Persaud said weakly in a slight Caribbean accent. "Na need fo' whisper." He pulled himself to a sitting position on the bed, revealing striped pajamas and furry pink slippers with bunny ears. Meera smiled at the sight. "One a dem volunteer give dem to me," Persaud said, gesturing to the slippers. "When I dead, you can tek 'em."

Meera sat next to the strange man and started with the usual doctor routine: the pulse check, the penlight in the pupils, an examination of the mouth and tongue. Persaud pushed her away. "What you doin', child?" He coughed blackishly. "I said I dyin'. You go find somethin' new fo' kill me faster?"

Yanni dropped the file onto the bed and sighed. "Mr. Persaud, you are eighty-eight years old and suffering from several very serious medical conditions. I don't know how you got to this floor or this room, but we have to get you back to the Latner Centre right away. They can take care of you better. We just don't have the facilities . . ."

"Boy," Persaud coughed, "I come down here because he comin' for me. He go get me sometime soon, but he cyaan do it now. Na now. He got fo' wait till me ready. I got fo' hide, just fo' tonight. Just until me can tell somebody m'story."

"Who?" Meera implored, stroking the old man's face and feeling cold, wet fatigue. "Who's coming for you?"

Persaud's eyes widened and his jaw dropped. He leaned forward and beckoned her closer. The room seemed to darken then, with the hum of the old ceiling fan fading into the ether, and a taste of slightly stale honey upon the air. "Yahhhm," Persaud said, in all solemnity. "Yahhhm come fo' me."

Yanni frowned, but Meera motioned him back. "Yama," she explained. "The Hindu god of death."

"Yes, Mr. Persaud," Yanni said. "I'm sorry, but death is

coming. For all of us. For you sooner, though. I'm sorry. Which is why it's important—"

"Shut up, boy," Persaud said sharply to Yanni, then turned to Meera, cupping her heart-shaped face in his spotted hands. "You undahstand, right? Yahhhm come fo' me, fo' tek m'soul. And dat's all right, child. Dat's all right. Is okay. But na now! Na right now! Not before me can tell you why Yahhhm come fo' me personally."

Yanni pushed his hand through his thick blond hair and sighed again. Typically, rheumatology rotation didn't involve psychiatric consults, but the midnight shift was famous for its many exceptions. And psychiatric issues were certainly not unknown to downtown Toronto hospitals. He reached for the phone by the bed, but Persaud intercepted with his skeletal hand.

"Boy. Please listen." Persaud's eyes were those of a doomed beast, pleading upward from the abattoir floor. "Yahhhm is comin' here. Tonight. Right now." His eyes slowly drifted to the hallway, to the open window at the end. Instantly, from the street below, there was a loud smashing noise, followed immediately by the sickly sound of bending metal and the unmistakable screams of humans in distress.

Yanni and Meera raced to the window. From the other end of the hallway, the shift nurses were also running to windows, so loud was the noise. Down below, like a report from the evening news of any unnamed metropolitan center, a scene of traffic horror unfolded. Two delivery trucks had collided and were blocking traffic on all six lanes of University Avenue, sprawling across the pedestrian median and had even knocked down one of the ghastly statues that usually stood watch. One truck was on fire, and police and fire engines were miraculously already on the scene. No casualties could be seen through the press of onlookers, who continued to stream in from nearby Queen Street, likely drawn by the sounds of disaster; but no doubt the emergency room below would soon be pressed into duty. It was an excellent ER, Meera knew; one of the best in the country. Still, a part of her wondered if she should rush down to help.

Persaud coughed loudly and beckoned them to the bed. Meera came back to his side. "Yahhhm," he said, as if in explanation. "Death comin'. Na got too much time. Got fo' tell you m'story first!"

"Look at all the people down there!" Yanni called from the window, amazed by the flow of late-night disaster voyeurs descending on this otherwise unpopular street. "I know it's a horrible thing, and I hope everyone's all right, but what a show it must be on the ground!"

Persaud stroked Meera's face then fondled her stethoscope. "You so young to be among we so old. And dis," he indicated the end of the stethoscope, "dis does give you comfort? You med'cine cyaan stop Yahhhm when Yahhhm want fo' come." He grinned an awful toothless grin that slitted his yellowing eyes and widened his gaping nostrils. But there was nonetheless something attractive and familiar about him. "How old you be, child?"

Meera said nothing.

"Is okay," Persaud said. "No need fo' answer. You daddy dead, right?" She nodded, almost zombie-like in her silence. "Is okay," he soothed. "We all got fo' dead. Is okay." Meera's face hardened. Whatever slight spell the strange old man had cast on her was now fading, chased off by the invocation of her father's sacred memory.

"Dr. Rostoff is right," Meera said. "We have to get you back to your room. Then we'd better go to Emergency to see if we're needed."

Persaud's lips tightened and he studied her carefully. He turned to Yanni, who was still bewitched by the scene of carnage on the street. "You, boy! Tell me you see Yahhhm."

"What?" Yanni, annoyed, waved Persaud away. He kept looking through the throngs on the street. To a man, each was enthralled with the heroic acts of firefighters hosing down flaming trucks and pulling bodies from crushed vehicles. But there was one . . .

Persaud called to Yanni. "You see him, na? Tell me!"

Yanni was silent. But he kept his eye on this one special man on the street, this one man who was not watching the carnage. Instead, he was looking up, directly at the window from which Yanni now peered.

"Describe he!" Persaud ordered. But Yanni remained silent. The watcher continued to stand apart from the crowd, his hands in his jacket pockets, locking eyes with Yanni. Yanni's fingers yellowed as they gripped the windowsill more tightly than was comfortable, but he snorted dismissively at the watcher.

Meera gazed over at her friend and colleague, and was at a loss. She was torn in many directions, ripped apart like one of the vehicles in the street. Competing responsibilities and desires jockeyed for priority. Yet the balance of her focus remained on the strange old man in the bed next to her.

"You is Indian," Persaud said. "You go undahstand. Dat is why you been sent fo' hear m'story."

Meera shook her head slowly. "Mr. Persaud . . ." She paused, knowing that further appeals to him to return to Palliative Care would be met with stolid refusal. And with the emergency outside, it was unlikely she would find sufficient help to move him against his will; not without sedating him.

She fell into his gaze, so sad yet intense. His yellow fishlike eyes bent into that sad configuration, and the spotted skin on the sides of his face drooped in its losing struggle against time and gravity. He looked so familiar, so sadly familiar. "I'm not Indian," she said. "Well, I'm of Indian descent; but I was born in Kenya and grew up here in Toronto . . ."

"Doesn't mattah," Persaud said, shaking his head forcefully. "You is Indian. Like me. I was born in Guyana. Never been to India." His accent seemed to be thickening as the evening progressed. But Meera had no trouble following. His gravitas commanded complete focus and understanding. "Never been to India," he said again. "Don't know m'caste or m'daddy's caste. But I is a pandit just the same. One priest of God!"

Meera reflected, was tempted to smile. Her own father, whom this man so wished to resemble, had hated religion. He had refused to raise his children with religion, had thrown his wife's idols from the home, and had famously quipped, "When things go well, we thank the gods. But when things go to hell, we blame everybody but the gods! What bullshit is this?" Yet in the end, even he had asked for a priest.

"You were a pandit in Guyana?" she asked him.

"Yes," Persaud said. His face darkened and his eyes deepened. The sounds of the street seemed to retreat then, isolating Meera alone with the old man, cushioned from Yanni, the window, and the rest of the world. "I is a pandit now, and I was a pandit then." He paused and stared at her meaningfully. "I was a pandit of Kali." He spat the last word.

Again Meera smiled. "I didn't know Kali was so popular outside India."

"Kali be another face of the same God," Persaud said, screwing up his own wizened face in mock dismissal of her seeming ignorance. "Goddess of blood, she. Goddess of glorious bittah red wine that pump in we veins. She scare the white people, na. But we know: She be a mama just like any lady. We respect Mama. We respect Daddy. And when you is a slave or servant in the cane fields of Guyana—back when the white man tek all you history, all you possessions, all you beliefs, and give you Jesus Christ instead—when you is a slave or a servant, you need cling to you mama and you daddy with greater force!" His gaze intensified, as did his hold on Meera's hand. "Because dat is all you got, in the end. Dat is all you got."

It was then that Meera noticed Yanni was being uncharacteristically quiet. She looked to him and saw only his back, with his untucked plaid shirt whipping in the wind from the window. "Yanni," she asked, "are you all right?"

"He's just staring up at me," Yanni replied. He continued to look down into the mêlée below, red and yellow flashing sirens reflecting off his expressionless face.

"Yahhhm," Persaud intoned. "Tell dis old man, please, boy. How the god of death look? He tall? He old or he young? How black is he face? When he come, I not go see he. He go tek m'soul and I not go see he face."

Yanni replied without intonation, only fact. "He's about twenty-one, five foot eight, but quite heavyset, wearing a white-and-blue University of Toronto jacket. And he's blond . . . and white." Persaud jerked at the last. "Maybe he's just catatonic. Or in shock. All he does is stare up at me; at this window. Maybe he needs a doctor."

Meera squeezed Persaud's hand, then stood up. "Yanni," she said, "it's time we went to work. Let's send for a wheelchair to take Mr. Persaud back to Palliative, then you and I had better report to Emergency. You think?"

Yanni detached himself from the window and scratched his head. "Sure, M. Let's go."

"Wait!" Persaud bellowed. "Listen! All me need is ten minute. Just listen a m'story fo' ten minute, then you can do what the hell you want fo' do. Yahhhm go come before ten minute. Just listen a m'story, na. I got fo' tell somebody before me dead, or Kali go cuss m'soul." He stared at the two of them for a good long couple of heartbeats. "You want she fo' cuss m'soul? No? Good. Come listen, na."

Yanni made an odd dismissive noise and returned to his post by the window, voyeuristically surveying the crowd. Sheepishly, Meera moved back to Persaud's side, an imploring look in her eyes. "Okay," she said. "Tell me. But then we have to take you back to your own room."

And Manoj Persaud launched into his tale . . .

It was years before Guyana had obtained its political independence from Britain. The decades that had passed of slavery for the blacks, of near genocide for the natives, and of indentured service for the Indians had bred a thirst for release from the chains of colonial rule. With each layer of Europeanness painted atop this weather-beaten Asian and African tapestry came a strengthening of its foreign matte, a calling for connections to lives and philosophies left centuries and fathoms away. African animism, sporadic puddles of voodoo, the naturalistic magics of the scattered native tribes, and the myriad faiths smuggled from India all found fertile soil in this wet chasm of discontent. Amongst the Indian immigrants, the cult of Kali was revived and flourished.

In the telling of the tale, Persaud gurgled and his words took on a distant tenor. "Goddess Kali," he whispered. "Omnipotent power absolute. She be the origin of cosmos and spirit. Deity of time, eternity and source of all energies. Kali bless us and we triumph over evil, destroy rogues and knaves, expel inauspicious souls, and repel demons." He focused on Meera again, slowly intoning, "She be knowledge. She be bliss."

Meera felt the dying man's pulse again, worried for his stress. She opened her mouth to speak, but Persaud covered it with his quivering hand. "Let me finish, na. You got fo' undahstand. The white man, he afeared o' Kali. He think she be demonic, wit' blood and scariness. But dat is fo' he. Kali is we mama. She be the female face of God, the angry mama who does protect she pickney, she children. We is she children. It is—what you say?—a metaphor. We weak before the white man, so we need one strong image of we mama fo' protection. You see?"

Meera nodded. And Persaud continued his narration . . .

Manoj Persaud had been a priest at the temple of Kali, where scores of devotees came weekly, sometimes daily, to offer obeisance to the mother goddess. In exchange, they received stable employment, healthy children, enough food to last the month, or whatever else it was they prayed for. It was Persaud who interpreted the omens and prodigies, who interceded between mortals and goddess. It was Persaud who interpreted the lost ways of obscure India to the subcontinent's forgotten and wretched Caribbean progency.

But tensions were mounting as demands for political independence grew louder on the streets, in the newspapers, the rum shops, and even within the temples. "And one day," Persaud said, "dem came fo' talk wit' me." Six men they were, regular devotees of Kali, some even Persaud's relatives. They abased themselves before the priest and asked for a special *puja*, a divine way or ceremony, for Kali to guarantee and accelerate Guyana's impending independence.

"I tell dem fo' pray and fo' make sacrifice to Kali, like dem always do, wit' coins, food, and fasting," Persaud said, a sense of both sadness and horror growing behind his eyes. "But dem say dem want something extra. Something more. Fo' Kali. Fo' big big magic."

The younger Persaud had watched his devotees with growing unease, as the full extent of their petition came to be understood. For a boon of this magnitude, one affecting a whole nation of people, the old ways would have required a human sacrifice. But modern times employed modern methods, with pumpkins standing in for human heads; or the use of human effigies constructed of flour and mud, slashed with razor-sharp machetes. Persaud presented these tamer options to his petitioners.

"But dem know the magic," he said with growing weariness. "Dem know the sacrifice, how the sacrifice must be aware. It must know it own fate and not be acting to stop the cutlass." Only then would the magic work, when the ultimate unseemly price had been paid. Only then would Kali grant them their wish.

Meera grew pale with the unfolding of the tale. Like a journey taken on a cloudy morning, its horrifying destination was rapidly becoming clearer as more steps were taken. Persaud's face was pleading, almost desperate with apology. "No," he said. "I not want fo' do dat! I tell dem. Dis pandit does not hold wit' dem old ways!"

But he had to tell them something. If he just sent them away, who knew what atrocity they would enact? Perhaps they would kidnap some poor fool and murder him sloppily in their own homemade Kali *puja*, accomplishing nothing except creating misery for all involved—and offending God in every way possible.

"So I tell dem," Persaud said. "I tell dem: It must be a white child. Dem must kill one white child." He sat back against the wall, grinding his gums, waiting for Meera to react. But there was only silence.

Meera regarded him with a strange detachment, struggling to balance horror with pity and disgust. She felt herself slide backwards, her hands near her face.

Persaud leaned forward again. "Undahstand! You got fo' undahstand! Where dem stupid boys go find one white child? We never see no white pickney. Only white *man* wit' he gun, he whip, and he stick. Where dem skinny brown village boys go get one white child? I been tryin' fo' save dem, see? I been tryin' fo' prevent dem doin' some damn stupidness!"

Persaud's eyes exploded into tears. They rushed like torrents down his cheeks and into the sides of his huffing mouth. His breathing was shallow and forced, wheezing at times between bouts of fitful, pathetic wailing.

"I been tryin' fo' mek dem task impossible," he whispered into the tissues Meera was using to wipe his face.

"But it wasn't impossible," Meera asked cautiously. "Was it?"

At that, Persaud reached into the front pocket of his pajama pants and pulled out a crumpled, yellowed piece of newsprint. Meera took it and unfolded it. On the top it read, *Stabroek News, Georgetown, Guyana*. The date was 1961. It was a story about the disappearance of the baby daughter of the overseer of a sugar cane plantation in rural Guyana. Her name was Helen and her surname was seemingly Dutch. There was no photo, but Meera assumed the girl was white.

"My God," she said aloud. "They found one." Persaud nodded and sobbed. "But how can you be sure they killed her? Or that they were the ones who killed her?"

Persaud laid back against the headboard of the bed, spent. His face glistened with tears and sweat and his head now resembled a desiccated brown skull. He seemed to be aging before Meera's very eyes. Unexpectedly, he smiled in that dejected but resigned way that the elderly sometimes do. "I know," he said, "because dem bring me she body. Dem wanted fo' know if it been done right, according to the old ways." He breathed sporadically now. "And I told dem yes. Yes, it been done good, according to dem damn old ways. Yes."

Meera stared at the pathetic old man, suddenly aware that she was watching death creep over him, consume him cell by cell. It was an oddly emotionless observation, one that shamed her and pushed her back into her professional demeanor. Only then did she notice that Yanni was standing behind her, his hand on her shoulder. "You heard?" she asked him.

"Yes," Yanni said. "It's a city of immigrants, you know. Everyone's got secrets and stories from some faraway place. We're supposed to start fresh when we get here, no? Let's take him back now, okay?"

But Persaud was not done yet. "Boy," he said weakly to Yanni, "Yahhhm comin' now. Go and see."

Yanni slitted his eyes in annoyance, but returned to the window nonetheless. He rushed back to report to Meera: "It's true. The fellow who was watching me is gone. I think he might have come into the hospital!"

Persaud's face contorted then. With surprising strength, he locked his hand onto Meera's arm, hurting her slightly. "Yahhhm comin'!" he gasped. Meera could sense the otherworldly terror that possessed Persaud, but could do nothing for him. She tore his grip away and began sifting through the room's supplies, searching for a sedative.

From the empty hallway came the unmistakable sound of approaching footsteps. These were not the steps of the nurses, who wore sneakers or delicate high heels, but of a large man in boots. Meera's eyes met Yanni's and the young man leapt to his feet and to the door, just in time to intercept a blond youth in a blue-and-white University of Toronto jacket. "You!" Yanni barked at him. "Visiting hours are over. You're not supposed to be here."

"Sorry," said the young man, looking about the room sheepishly. "I'm with the student paper. I saw the light coming from the window and thought it would be a good place to get an aerial photo of the accident." He pulled a camera from his jacket pocket and showed them.

"You'll have to leave. Sorry." Yanni pushed him back into the hallway and toward the exit. "See?" Yanni called back to Persaud. "Not the bloody god of death!"

But, of course, Persaud had already expired. His lifeless body lay sprawled atop the bed, like a grotesque skeletal clown bedecked in striped pajamas and pink slippers. His final expression was not that of an old man placidly accepting his final rest, nor that of a holy man content to meet his god. Rather, it was a pose of profound terror and worry, with crevices of skin radiating around his open mouth and his gaping yellowish eyes. Thankfully, Meera was not reminded of her father. He had had the good grace to slip from mortality with silent dignity, his worldly tasks completed, and with no important words left unsaid. But, she judged, not so for Manoj Persaud.

"I thought telling his story was supposed to bring him peace," Yanni said.

"I don't think he told us the whole story," Meera explained. "He said they brought the girl's body to him. But he didn't tell us that she was still alive at the time."

Yanni slipped his hand into hers. Meera stretched up and kissed him on the cheek.

"Hey," she whispered. "Midnight shift is over."

CAN'T BUY ME LOVE

BY CHRISTINE MURRAY

Union Station

Union station. 6 o'clock. Commuter-throng in the basement concourse. Head-numbing fluorescent lights, the terminal as garish as a 1950s office space. I breathe in the odorific confluence of fast food and rubber-soled shoes and scan the room for a free bucket seat, preferably one with a view of the overhead screen. Train's not up there yet, so I've plenty of time.

I locate a seat between two average-looking drones. The lady to my right ruffles her newspaper back and forth like a perturbed swan beating its wings. She gives me a peripheral going-over and crosses her legs purposefully, cinching her ankles together. To my left, a mid-forties businessman reads from a men's magazine with a semi-naked brunette on the cover. I recognize her—young actress, former child star. She's on her knees, legs apart, back arched, blouse open above the navel.

There's something attractive about Union's retro décor. Its generic quality makes it easy to ignore. You can see the people for the trees, so to speak. Not like new terminals, where you can't see the people for the gleam off all that stainless steel. Different story here, from the dude engrossed in "Real-Life Sex Injuries 101"; to the lady now methodically folding her newspaper into accordion-style strips; to the platinum blonde with long silver nails standing at the bay of pay phones dead ahead. She's wearing a neon-green mini-dress, rollerblades over her shoulder. Cradled by her neck, the phone seems too large for her childlike head, the black receiver as oversized as a clown's shoe—a clown's phone.

I'm not a perv, but let's face it, I've nothing better to do than to watch neon roller girl over there. I've already visited the magazine store, bought a cinnamon bun. I have a coffee in my hand that's so Ibiza-hot I could spill it on my crotch and sue for damages. It was sunny on the walk from the office, but the smell of autumn left my nose lightly frosted. I'd bought the coffee to keep my hands warm. I hadn't decided whether to drink it or not, but now, out of boredom, I flip the sip-lid, snap it into place.

The talk went well today—better than expected. "We like what you're up to, Chris," Darrin had said. "Want the whole team to follow your lead. Show them how you're doing it. Get them to reinvent the fucking wheel."

The wheel was ad copy. I'd come up with a new approach I liked to call *ad absurdum*. Only, I didn't come up with it; loads of writers were doing it already:

"Say a product is new and improved," I'd explained today, clicking through slides. "So, you write *New and improved* on the packaging, right? Trouble is, there is nothing more dusty and hum-drummy than writing *New* on a new product. What to do? . . . What you need is to make up a new word. Trick is, you've got to make it sound like other words, using known prefixes and suffixes, so that your audience understands it right off the bat. No sense speaking a language they don't understand, see? It can be as easy as adding *-tastic* to the end of word, as in *Tastetastic!* Or as tricky as launching a frying pan around Halloween with the words, *Terrifry your food!*

"Think about it," I'd concluded, leaning over them. "*Edutainment* might be a word in the dictionary now, but it didn't used to be. We need to harness the power of hybrid words. If we trademark them, we could actually own our own language—and just think of how *advert-ageous* that would be!"

That was the kicker: the big finale. Then it was handshakes and nervous laughter all around, and a lot of, "Ad absurdum, eh? I like it, I like it."

Roller girl leans forward, her breasts perform a tandem sunrise over her low-cut dress. They suggest a shape not unlike two small champagne glasses—the kind designed after the bosoms of Marie Antoinette. *Aristocra-tits.*

I don't mind small breasts. My rack is small too, and they've served me well with the ladies, although I usually wind up with larger-breasted girls.

Roller girl looks over. Probably felt me staring.

No. Her eyes are glassed over, seeing through me. She curls her tiny nose up and wrinkles her chin, as if suppressing a sneeze. Her nostrils grow wider, as though she's stopped breathing. Then she gives a tiny snort and pulls her lips back, revealing a pair of sharp incisors. She doesn't want to cry, but two droplets spill over. Oh, she sees me now. Her black pupils swell into focus. She sees me and glares, spinning around to face the bay of phones.

Must be a telephone breakup. Crap boyfriend. He's probably cheating on her too, or at least she suspects it. Although maybe not. Girls being cheated on usually go for the jugular, play the hysterical card. They don't even try not to cry.

She hangs up the phone and half turns her head. Funny, I don't remember hearing her say boo into the phone. It's like she just took it, whatever it was.

The lady and the businessman stand up. Two trains boarding, mine included. Roller girl's sitting down, legs tucked underneath her, crying a little more obviously now. Platform 3B, ten minutes to departure. Oh what the hell, I guess I have time.

"You okay?" I say to the top of her head.

"Please," she says, pushing her hair back, looking up. Her makeup is smudged from here to last night. "What?" Her words are heavily accented.

"Do you need help?"

She shakes her head.

"Should I leave you alone?"

She squints her face up. Her eyes are light brown, baby-poo brown.

"Do you have a problem?" I say slowly, idiotically. "Do . . . you . . . need . . . help?" I make a futile gesture with my hands.

She looks down, wipes her nose childishly, and then starts, as though she has an idea. Craning her neck to see behind me, she leans out, taking in the concourse from left to right. I check the time. Seven minutes to go. *The train on track 3B is westbound to Oakville . . .*

"If you're okay, I have to go catch the train now, it's just, you seemed upset . . ."

"I go train," she says quickly. "You go?"

"Mississauga," I say. "Clarkson. You?"

She nods her head. "Yes!" she says, smiling with a mouthful of tiny white teeth, all crooked, but sweetly arranged. "Take me?"

"Train is going now," I say. "You live in Mississauga, going there?"

"Yes, train. Sauga."

"I go now," I say, adopting her caveman speak. "You want come?"

She swings her knees around, tight skirt clinging to her thighs, and stands up awkwardly. Flash of black panties, porcelain skin. The rollerblades come off the floor with a clatter.

We hurry across the room to the escalator. I step aside to let roller girl go up first. She keeps glancing back, as though she's trying to catch me at something. Maybe she's realized I'm gay. Some women are like that, as though you'll automatically find them irresistible. She must think I'm watching her ass the whole way up. As it happens, she wouldn't be half wrong.

We get to the platform, the hulking green double-decker in view. She hesitates.

"You're sure you want the GO train?" I ask. "Not subway? Underground? Metro?"

She shakes her head emphatically.

"Clark-son," she replies, smiling a little.

"This is the one," I say, stepping past her into the train. The doors have started beeping. She scoots in behind me. I lead the way upstairs and locate two window seats on the half-level. We interrupt the pair sitting on the aisle. I don't get train-sick, so I let roller girl have the forward-facing side. She pulls her skirt down as far as it will go and sits, offloading her purse and rollerblades between our feet.

The train starts up, slow and clunking. I lean my head on the window frame and close my eyes. I'm about to settle into my commuter-nap, when I hear roller girl gasp. She pushes her body back into her seat, away from the glass. I look out onto the platform, but there's just some guy there, overweight and wearing a too-small suit buttoned over his paunch. He's out of breath, brown comb-over flapping in the breeze like a question mark above his head. He gives the train a hard stare, heads back downstairs. I look over at roller girl, but her eyes are closed now, lips thin, as though she's holding her breath.

How old is she? I wonder. With a body like that, could she be a day over eighteen?

We roll out of Union Station, past the CN Tower, heading west along the highway. I never would have moved to the burbs, but when my parents gave me their condo by the tracks, it seemed stupid to look that gift horse in the mouth. My folks had planned on retiring there, so it's fully loaded: two bedrooms, two bathrooms, huge closets, and walking distance to everything. It's so convenient that when they decided to retire to B.C., to be closer to the grandkids (knowing full well they weren't getting any munchkins out of me), I couldn't think of how I could say no.

Roller girl's head lolls forward, her legs slightly splayed. I take off my jacket and lay it across her lap. I don't know why I'm protecting the modesty of a girl who chooses to wear a dress like that, but I feel a whole lot better after she's covered up. She doesn't stir, and I don't think she's faking. Her hands are half-open, limp. Hands don't lie.

I wake up around Port Credit. Roller girl smiles. She's pulled my jacket up to her chin and curled her arms behind it. My mouth is dry. I fish an old bottle of Evian out of my briefcase, peel my tongue off the back of my teeth, and take a swig, swishing the lukewarm water around like mouthwash.

"Next stop," I say. I rotate my finger once forward to make sure she understands.

"What name?" roller girl says, furrowing her eyebrows. "What. Is. Your. Name," she says with the emphatic diction of an ESL class.

"Chris," I say, trying to look pleased. I'm still asleep. "Yours?"

"Magda."

"Nice to meet you, Magda," I say, speaking slowly. I reach out to shake her hand. She smiles.

"Yes," she says. Her hand is small, but not soft. She must work, I think, although how she can do anything with those nails is beyond me. Maybe they're acrylic. "Nice you," she says, to the rhythm of a gentle shake. "Nice. To. Meet. You."

We let go and look to the window. After a minute, I stand up and Magda hands me my jacket. She scoops her blades and bag off the floor and shimmies down the stairs behind me. Magda holds onto the passenger pole, swaying. I wonder who her friends are—maybe cousins? I imagine a gaggle of leggy blondes on the platform, waiting for Magda. *Meet friend, Chris?* I should be so lucky. No, it'll be a short walk back to the condo, followed by a half-hearted root around the freezer. I wonder if there's still some lemon sole in there. *Fishtastic,* I think.

The train pulls into the station.

"This is it!" I smile at Magda, pointing ridiculously.

We wait for the doors to open and step out. Magda keeps pace with me along the platform. Too bad, I was sort of hoping to lose her in the crowd. I walk to the edge of the Kiss-n-Ride, then turn to say goodbye. Cars wait expectantly like so many famished pigeons, edging forward to collect their passengers before moving away.

"Goodbye, Magda. Nice meeting you. You wait here, yes? For your friends?"

"No friends," she says.

"Don't worry, your friends will come."

"No friends," she says again. "You friend. I go with you."

"Whoa, Magda, what are you talking about?"

"Go with you, Clark-son." She's not smiling anymore, she's holding onto my arm. "Chris, friend."

"You can't just come with me."

"Please!" she says, eyes wide, tugging at my arm. A couple walk past and pause, looking on.

"Aw shit, Magda, no. You can't come with me. No," I say, untangling my arm. "Sorry. No."

She edges her lower lip forward, eyes even wider.

"Sorry, Magda. Goodbye." I turn around. Don't look back, Chris, keep walking. But I hear the clattering of her roller-blades as she follows along behind me.

"No friends, Chris," she says. "No house."

I turn around. "Why did you take the train, then?"

"Go with you!"

I turn and keep walking, but I only manage two steps before looking back. She's got her hand on her head, face crinkled up in panic. I feel like such a prick.

"Fine!" I shout to her. "Okay? Fine. My house."

"Yes," she says, "Please, yes. Thank you!"

"But anything funny and I call the police, all right? You know, police?" Yeah, call the police and say what, exactly?

Magda nods, wipes her face, and pushes her hair behind her ears. We set off. As we exit the parking lot and turn onto the sidewalk, a red minivan leads the pack. It inches by, then speeds up and turns a corner.

Magda keeps her mouth shut, probably sensing that I'm pissed off. I'd already done my bit. Now she's on her way to my house? We turn down the nondescript drive that leads to my condo. I enter the punch code, unlock the lobby door, and hold it open while Magda wriggles past. She waits for me at the elevator. We don't meet anyone in the corridor. I'm glad. With an average age of seventy-five-plus, Magda's outfit could set off a string of heart attacks on my floor.

I leave her standing in my living room and go to the bathroom, locking myself in. Just calm down, I think, this isn't a crisis. All you have to do is feed her, put her to bed, and then find some charity hole on the Internet you can deliver her to in the morning. She's just a kid. It's one night. Whoever she's running away from, she probably just needs to think things over before going back. I take a few deep breaths; watch my face in the mirror. My skin looks tough, wrinkled. How the hell did I get to be thirty-eight?

I've calmed down and am up to my elbows in the freezer, trying to decide between salmon steaks or lemon sole, when the switchboard buzzer rings. I pick up the line. I can hear the shower going—Magda must be getting clean.

"Hello?"

"Hello, I'm sorry to disturb you, but I'm wondering if you could help me?"

"That depends."

"Look, my car won't start, and wouldntchaknowit, my cell phone's dead too. I need to borrow someone's phone to call my wife and the CAA. I've rung a whole bunch of buzzers. Would you mind coming down to help me out? Bring your cell phone, if you've got one, and we can make this quick."

"Has anyone else picked up yet? I'm sort of in the middle of cooking and—"

"Thanks, I'd really appreciate it. You won't believe the kind of day I'm having."

Click.

Well thanks a lot, buddy; you wouldn't believe the sonofabitchofaday I'm having too.

I wash my hands, grab my cell, and call the elevator. I don't bother to tell Magda—she's still in the shower, and at this point I don't want to see any more of her than I have to. The elevator picks up two college students from the second floor, and Carl and Jenny are already in the lobby downstairs. Geez, this guy really did push all the buzzers.

I see Mrs. Fitzgerald from 3G outside, babbling beside a red minivan. She waves and I go to join her, but my hand freezes on the door release. It's the comb-over man from the train platform, coming around the minivan. He points at me and smiles, saying something to old lady Fitzgerald that I can't hear. The sweet thing laughs with one hand over her mouth, looks back at me, and then continues muttering away.

Comb-over waves at me to come outside. I raise my hand to decline, and back away. I tell Carl and Jenny that I've left something cooking on the stove. This is too weird. I take the stairs to the second floor. I can see the red van from the stairwell window. Comb-over has climbed into the driver's seat. He tries the ignition and, when the van starts up, raises his hands in a dumbfounded expression. Fitzgerald laughs. Comb-over shakes his head for a minute, then waves goodbye. He gives the building a final once-over, and drives away.

I'm pretty shaken up. Could this guy have followed us all the way from Union? He would have had to go to every station and watch the passengers unload. And why the broken-down car—if he were looking for Magda, couldn't he just ring all the buzzers and ask if she were home?

Not if Magda didn't want to be found.

When I get back upstairs, Magda's changed into one of my old T-shirts: a smiley face with a bullet hole through the forehead. She must have rooted through the bathroom chest of drawers. She smiles and slides onto one of the stools by the breakfast bar. She's beautiful without makeup, a real Barbie doll. Damn. I clear my throat and leave the room, fish my old bathrobe out of the closet, and hand it over. If I'm going to figure this out, I need to be able to concentrate. She puts the robe on and I start getting down to the business of cooking dinner. I always think best when my hands are busy.

Okay, so if this comb-over guy showing up here is just a random coincidence, then there's nothing to worry about, right? But if he followed us from Union and saw Magda come in here with me, and if, let's say, he's used this prank to find out my name, he'll be back. Either way, I've got to figure out what's going on, and fast.

Sorting this out would be easy enough if Magda could actually talk to me, but with her English . . . ?

"Magda, are you in trouble?"

"Thank you, Chris," she says, indicating the bathrobe.

"Where are you from?"

She shakes her head. She doesn't understand.

"Polish? Hungarian? . . . Romanian? Russian?" Nothing.

I go into the bedroom, find my laptop, and bring it to the kitchen. I connect to the wireless and search for free online Polish translation.

"Magda, *Polski*?"

She laughs, nods her head. "Yes, *Polski*."

Oh god, lucky break.

I start typing. *There was a man here looking for you*. I click on *Translate* and show her the screen. Her smile dies on her face.

"Type," I say to her. "Type in *Polski*."

I gesture at the keyboard. She two-finger types and pushes it back at me. I click *Translate*.

—He (it) is a bad man.

I take a deep breath.

—Why is he a bad man? I write.

—He (it) produce I make bad thing with people.

—Why did you get on the train?

—It ran away from bad person.

—Should we phone the police?

—If I call police, he (it) will kill me. He (it) will kill my family. He (it) say that owe money. I must pay. If sufficient amount pay him (it) money; he (it) will leave me sole. I make bad thing with people to produce sufficient money.

—How much money does he want?

She shrugs her shoulders. She's hugging her knees up on the stool, rocking back and forth.

—What should we do? I type.

She shakes her head. "Don't know," she says out loud. She types something and clicks the mouse.

—Hide away?

Oh crap.

I get up and turn off the rice burner and pull the fish out of the oven. It looks and smells like fish, so it'll do. I empty a bag of pre-washed mixed greens into a bowl with some cherry tomatoes and pour out a half-finished bottle of white wine into two glasses. Liquid courage. We might even be able to manage a little dinner conversation.

By the time I sit down at the table, Magda has typed another message for me.

—I understand you like girls.

I look up at her. She runs a finger along her lips. Then types again.

—I like girls too.

I smile awkwardly and give her a thumbs-up sign. Then I hand her a fork and a plate of fish. I'm not going anywhere with those thoughts right now.

After dinner, we settle on the sofa with bowls of ice cream and I switch on the TV. I bring the laptop in there too, in case there's something we want to say to each other. I give Magda the remote. She settles on one of those stations that play nonstop makeover shows. It seems not much is lost in the translation—she cackles right on cue with the purchase of an ugly shirt and tie.

It's after midnight and Magda is doing the last of the dishes when the phone rings.

"This won't take very long," says the voice on the line, "if you listen carefully."

"Hello?" I say. "Who is this?"

"I know Magda is there, and I don't want this conversation to be even a second longer than need be." Comb-over?

"I don't know what you're talking about," I say, buying time.

"Cut the crap. There are these things called phone books, and once some old bitty gives you a name and you have an address, it's easy-peasy to look a number up. I know you're in there, and I know Magda is in there too."

Easy-peasy. I want to laugh. His scratchy voice sounds exactly like a pimp, or at least a bad dramatization of a pimp. Magda looks over anxiously.

"What do you want?" I say.

"I want my employee back, or I want you to pay for her time."

"I didn't ask her to come here."

"That's of little concern to me. Right now, whether you choose to accept it or not, you are in possession of my property, and you are not paying for its use. So, if you would like to keep her there, you either hand over her rate in cash, or you hand Magda over, understand?"

"And what if I don't? What if I call the cops instead?"

"Well, then you have made some pretty powerful enemies;

enemies who know where you live. And don't think you'll be doing Magda any favors either, calling the police. We'll just recruit her twelve-year-old little sister back in Poland. I can't wait to ripen that tender ass. Plus, once Maggie's deported back to Poland, we'll just pick her up and put her right back into harness."

Magda finishes the dishes and lays the dishcloth over the tap to dry. She walks over and puts her arms around me from behind. I'm not expecting it, and I shiver a little. She holds me closer and rests her head on the back of my neck. I start to pull away, but then I wonder if she's trying to hear the phone. I don't move.

"Look," I say. "I'm tired. What do I need to do to make you go away so I can think this through?"

"Pay for her. $400 for tonight, and $200 every night after that."

"Fine."

"You're a smart dyke."

"Yeah. So how would you like the money? I don't suppose you take PayPal?"

"You'll be passing through Union Station in the morning?"

"Uh-huh."

"Go to the pay phones nearest the digital platform sign at 8:30 a.m., all right? Bring the cash in a plain envelope and leave it underneath the third phone, then just walk away. I'll be watching you. If it's not the right amount, I'll drive straight to your place and wait for you to come home. Got it?"

"Yeah."

"Nice doing business with you, Chris. Enjoy Magda tonight. Just pay extra in the envelope if you're not through with her. If you misplace the merchandise and she goes AWOL, though, you're responsible for the full price of the goods, got it?"

"And how much is that?"

"Ten thousand dollars, at least, and that's if I give you a discount."

I hang up. Magda unwraps her arms and looks at me, a question in her eyes. I get the laptop and tell her that it's okay, but just for tonight. She reads the translation, eyes bright. She pulls on my hands and giggles. I tell her that I'm tired and need to go to bed. She puts her hands on my waist and pulls me into a long hug. Then I go to my room with the laptop and shut the door. I plan on researching a place that will help Magda, but I'm too tired to think. I scrunch the duvet up around my ears and fall asleep.

I pick up the cash and do the drop, just as comb-over said. Then I pretend to leave the station, but do a U-turn on Front Street and come back down. I watch the pay phone from behind one of the pillars. A redhead in a Hooters T-shirt and jeans is on the phone. One hand on the receiver, she reaches under the box and slips the envelope into her purse. Is that what Magda was up to yesterday? I shake the thought out of my head. If that were the case, why should she run away?

I'd put $600 in the envelope, to buy us time. I had the savings, and it wouldn't even pinch. She was still asleep when I left the house this morning. I poked my head into the guestroom. Her full lips were parted, eyelids soft, her hair arranged in spokes, like rays of the sun, over her pillow. I left a loaf of bread on the counter, an econo-sized jar of peanut butter and my phone number at work scribbled on a pad, just in case.

After work, I unlock the door and find her sprawled on the sofa with a bag of nacho chips and the remote. More makeover shows. She's wearing another oversized T-shirt of mine from the '80s. *Relax*, it says, in bold caps. She stands up and gives me a kiss on the cheek.

"Hi, Chris!" she says cheerily. "Laptop?"

I take it out of my briefcase and open it up. She writes,

—*How was your day?*

After dinner, we curl up on the sofa again, Mag at one end, me on the other. We've hit on black gold—a marathon of home improvement shows. Mag giggles when they take a sledgehammer to the walls. During a commercial break, she says my name. I look over. She splits her legs apart, lifting her T-shirt. No panties. My face goes hot. I stand up and walk into the kitchen. She follows behind. The laptop is on the counter. I type,

—*I am very tired. I am going to bed.*

—*I arrive to your bed too?*

I shake my head.

The phone rings at midnight again. "I hope you enjoyed yourself," comb-over sneers. "Now you know the drill. You want her for another night? Just leave the money there, same time, same place. If not, I expect Magda to be standing there instead. Got it?"

"And what if I need to phone you?" I say. "If there's some kind of problem?"

"Don't call me, I'll call you."

"Hello?"

I turn out the light and settle into my pillow. This whole charade could cost me a fair wad of cash. I'm drifting off again, when I hear the latch to my bedroom door click. I reach for the light. It's Magda. She's leaning up against the doorframe, her blond hair tussled.

"You need something?" I say. "You okay?"

She walks over to the bed and climbs in.

"Fine," I say, "But no funny stuff."

I put out the light. I'm too tired to argue anyway. I turn my back to her and fall asleep.

I drop the money off and walk the same loop as before. It's picked up by the same girl, same shtick with the telephone. I wonder what Magda is doing in my apartment. I should get another set of keys made if she's going to be staying awhile. At least then she could go out. I explained to her yesterday how the auto-lock works. If she leaves, she won't be able to get back in. She didn't seem to mind. She's probably sleeping the day away. I imagine she has a lot of zeds to catch up on.

The phone rings at my desk at noon. "So, you want her until Friday, but what about the weekend?" says comb-over. "I'll need a bigger wad tomorrow, in that case. It's Thursday today, you dig?"

"How did you get this number?"

"You must think I'm a bloody nincompoop. So, what's your deal?"

"How much for the weekend?"

"A grand."

"What?"

"You heard me."

"And how much for Magda, you know, outright?"

"Fifteen grand."

"It was ten grand before."

"You don't qualify for the discount."

"Call me back," I say. "In an hour. I need to think."

I hang up the phone and put my head on my desk.

It's not the money. I have the money. I have over forty grand saved up for the condo I didn't have to buy. And hell, I could probably get her for ten, if I haggle. Maybe that's what I should do. I'll just haggle for ten, and then comb-over will be out of my hair and I can think about this properly. I'm out a grand this week already, so it's not like the price isn't fair. What's a few grand for a person's freedom? If I buy Magda then I can do what I like. I can get her a key made, and we can just move on with our lives.

I practice my lines until comb-over calls back. I deliver them quickly, in a tough-girl voice: "I'll give you ten for her, not a penny more, and then you gotta leave us alone."

"Make it twelve and you've got a deal."

"Fine, twelve," I say. "How and where do you want it?"

"Same time, same place. Stand there with a briefcase full of cash and a phone in your ear. When my girl comes and picks up the receiver next to yours, you put the briefcase down by her feet. She'll pick it up straight away, then you say goodbye into the phone and fuck off."

"Done."

"Nice doing business with you, Chris," comb-over coos. "You're a filthy dyke, but I like you."

I'm still shivering when I get home. She must see the look on my face, because she turns off the tube and comes right over. The bank asked some pretty awkward questions, but I explained that I owed my parents some cash. It was a convoluted story, but the young thing behind the till handed it over.

"It's gonna be all right now," I say, putting a hand on her shoulder. She points to the laptop. I write that I'm buying her from the bad man. I click *Translate*. She shakes her head, types:

—*Again?*

I guess the translation isn't going through right, so I try another wording. She seems to get me this time, because she puts her arms around me and buries her face in my neck. I start to shiver more violently and she grips me tightly. Then she pulls away and kisses me on the mouth, but I can hardly feel it. My lips are dry and there's a fever of blood in my ears. She takes my hand and leads me to the bedroom. I sit down on the edge of the bed. Magda kneels on the floor. She lifts my left foot, slipping off my shoe. I lie back on the bed. She pulls off my sock and runs a finger along the sole of my foot. I quiver. Then she starts massaging my ankle. Her hands run up and down my legs, under my trousers. She stops and I look up in time to see her pull off her T-shirt. Her body is thicker than I'd imagined, but perfect. By the time she unbuttons my fly, I have no will to resist her. All I can do is let go.

I wake up happy, Magda breathing deeply beside me. I kiss her forehead and slip out of bed without waking her. My laptop under one arm, briefcase of cash in my hand, I'm actually whistling as I board the train. Whistling! The drop is easy. I start shivering when I get to the pay phone, but then I revisit last night, and that settles it. I set the briefcase down next to the redhead. She picks it up, and I say goodbye to the dial tone and hang up the phone. I don't bother doing the U-turn today.

Comb-over rings at noon. "This is just a courtesy call," he says. "She's yours. Enjoy the merchandise."

"Don't call here ever again," I say, relishing the hard shape of the words. I hang up first this time.

After the call, I swing by Darrin's desk. "You've been quiet since the presentation, Chris," he says. "Thought you'd be ass-pompous with success. Everything all right?"

"Little under the weather," I say. "Keep shivering. Think I've caught a fever-flu. Mind if I duck out early?"

"Knock yourself out. We can live without you today."

"Thanks, man," I say, pulling a listless face. "Appreciate it."

"No sweat. Just be in shape by Monday, all right?"

"You bet."

I get to the station in time for the 1:43. The pay phone kiosk is empty. A kid walks by and checks all the change slots with his finger.

On the train, I think about Magda. Maybe I should take her shopping for some new clothes. We could go to the grocery store too. I've never asked her what she likes to eat, just cooked her what I had in the fridge. What if she hates fish?

I reach the condo by 2:30. I call the elevator, but I can't wait, so I take the stairs. I think of what to type into the laptop.

You're free, I'll type. *I've set you free! What do you want to do now?*

I unlock the door, already picturing her on the sofa, an oversized T-shirt cinched high on her thighs. What will we do tonight?

But she's not there. I look for a note, but there's no sign of one.

I should have known better.

PART IV

Flatland Flatline

TOM

BY ANDREW PYPER

Queen West

She moved to Toronto from one of the smaller cities a couple hours west along the 401, a place with a borrowed, European name that embarrassed her, so that now when people ask where she's from she shrinks it in her mind until it's only a country crossroads, a pair of stop signs with white crosses in the ditch to tally the fatal car accidents, and answers, "It's so tiny. You wouldn't have heard of it."

The only thing she's ever done for money is serve men drinks in bars. Just men, because the bars have always been strip bars. "It's easier," she explains whenever it is suggested she wait tables in a proper restaurant instead. By easier she means there are rules in strip bars she has come to depend on. The men keep their eyes on the dancers, their hands to themselves, and tip foolishly well. No description of the chef's special features, no flirty walk through the wine list recommendations. No female, diamond-necklaced customers giving her looks meant to remind her that what she is doing now is all she is. Will ever be.

She is twenty-six years old.

In moving to the city, she'd planned on doing something else. She wasn't sure what. They shot a lot of movies in Toronto. Could there be a job for her on set? Wardrobe? Makeup? Fetching the director's cappuccino? Whenever she walked by a movie shoot on her way to work, most of the people seemed to be standing around drinking coffee, or mumbling into walkie-talkies, or stifling yawns against the backs of their hands. That was moviemaking? She could do *that*.

But what *was* she doing? What employment was she walking to as she passed these boring yet still somehow glamorous location shoots? She was on her way to serve men drinks in a strip bar.

Her five nights a week at For Your Eyes Only is temporary. A cash grab to pay for the time required to settle in, make some connections. Soon she'll quit. Soon, her real Toronto life will begin. This is what she told herself, and what she mostly believed.

In those moments when doubt crept in—when she felt she might as well be back in that smaller city with the name she was too embarrassed to say aloud—she had one consolation to return to. She may be a strip bar waitress, but *she wasn't a stripper*. She'd been asked many times and always refused. This was her sustaining source of pride, of identity. She wasn't a woman who showed her body for money. Not looked at. Not an object.

When she delivered trays of beer and rye-and-gingers to men in the places she worked in, they rarely made eye contact. Sometimes this was because they were absorbed in the entertainments on offer, but mostly because, for them, she wasn't there. It was skin they wanted, the uninterrupted study of hidden parts, and in that room—windowless, overpriced, smelling of baby oil—they were freely allowed to watch. It made her feel invisible.

But what if you started feeling invisible all the time? Not just in strip bars, but on the street, standing before the bathroom mirror? Her answer was to move to Toronto, rent a studio apartment on Queen West with a back alley entrance, join the millions of others pursuing fame, breakthroughs, love, matters of real importance.

So far it hadn't helped. If anything, the city had only perfected her invisibility. There were so many more people not to notice her. So many more shared looks or *Good mornings* or acknowledging smiles that didn't occur.

It's because of this that, when his face appeared at her window, she thinks he is someone she knows. After only three weeks in Toronto she's learned that strangers keep their eyes to themselves.

Her apartment—just a room, really, with a fridge-sized toilet and kitchenette peppered with mouse turds—has only one window. She kids herself that she chose the place for the view. A brick wall, ten feet away on the other side of the alley, plastered with graffiti tags and a pleading, unheeded homeowner's message: *Hobos! Please don't poo here!* This is the small square of world she can see from her mattress on the floor. It is ugly. But she's always thought the truly big cities, the real ones, are meant to be ugly. It is the sort of apartment and the sort of view that, down the line, she will look back on as Where She Started From. She reminds herself not to replace "shit" for "poo" in the retelling.

It is lying on this mattress, staring through this window after a slow Tuesday at For Your Eyes Only, that she sees him. The top of his head at first. And then, as he rises higher, the whole of his face. Because she is almost asleep, she spends some moments trying to fix him in her mind as an introduction to a dream. The pause allows her to get a good look at him. And for him to see her too. Only later will she realize that he would have noticed that her eyes were open, her hand inches from her phone, and that this hadn't stopped him from looking.

Of the different kinds of men who visit strip clubs, she would guess the man at the window belonged to the Ones Who Don't Want to Be Here. Men forced to entertain visiting business associates, a shy friend dragged along to a stag party. These men watch the dancers too, but in the way the visitors to the AGO studied the Rothkos and Moores and Carrs. They are art appreciators, not perverts. This was what they intend to convey with their thoughtful squints, their chins held in their palms.

Yet here this man is, staring at her in her bed. And *she* isn't art. She is a woman wearing nothing but bikini underwear (it is hot, the room is *always* hot). And he is invading her privacy. He is breaking the law. He is a creep.

Even as she sits straight and pulls the sheet up to cover her breasts, she takes note of his features for the composite sketch the police will ask her to help make of him when she calls this in. White. Thirties. Prematurely gray hair cut preppily short. A face belonging to someone who, if he were to open the door for her or lend a hand lugging her groceries onto the streetcar, she'd think, *There goes the last of the good guys*. Good with kids, dependable, few vices, if any. A little sexy, but not dangerously so, not someone who'd have to hurt you to excite you. A man to marry if you were lucky.

And money. His *face* says money. Born with it, educated to make more of it, would always have it. She'd never gone out with anyone for whom these things weren't an issue. She'd never gone out with anyone like him.

She picks up the phone. Starts dialing 911. The face falls away.

Leaning out the window, she hears him round the corner of her building, but doesn't catch sight of him. Just the pebbly scrape of his leather-soled steps. And below her window the three-legged chair he'd pulled out of the garbage to stand on.

She doesn't press the last digit that would bring this moment to official attention. Instead she turns the phone off, puts on a T-shirt, and returns to lie on her mattress. She's scared. But there is a prickling sweat on her forehead and neck that has nothing to do with fear. The man at the window reminded her that she is not actually invisible. And with visibility has come a rush of blood to her extremities, a lead weight in her limbs. She's so heavily, uncomfortably alive-feeling that, for a time, she's not sure she can move.

She doesn't call the police that night, or the next morning, or at any other of the hundred points over the twenty-four hours that follow the Peeping Tom's visit when she's told herself, *I have to do something*. Because it runs against what she regards as her plucky, take-no-shit nature, she wonders why she doesn't. The theory she tries to situate at the top of possibilities is that she has deemed the guy as nonthreatening, a corporate frat boy she can easily handle if he ever returns. He hadn't *looked* like a rapist (though she knows better than to judge these things on looks alone). But this isn't the reason she doesn't call the police. Nor is it because she is curious about him, or suspects her physical description wouldn't be enough to go on, or that his watching her turned her on. It's because she thought this was the sort of incident one experienced in the city. Complaint wasn't part of the bargain. A cheap apartment off a crack-pipe-and-needle alley, a neighborhood known for its human stew of drugs and punks and artists and out-patients off their meds: A face at her window is the *least* she should expect living here.

He doesn't return to her window that night. Or the next. But on Thursday, waking with a *People* still bent between her fingers, he's there.

This time she screams. A bubbly, uncertain utterance that takes a moment to find itself, before coming out as a full-throated horror movie declaration. It makes him disappear. Yet when she goes to the window, expecting to catch him in hasty retreat, he is merely backstepping down the alley, facing her, taking his time. A kid being called away from joining the line for a roller coaster.

Over the next week, she catches him twice. Which means that he has come more often than this and she has slept through it. Or perhaps not. She believes she is able to detect his presence no matter how deep in slumber he might find her. They are connected, the two of them. Not romantically, nothing like that. In fact, he comes pretty close to disgusting her. His unmet need. The passivity. The lies he must be telling someone. Maybe it's all her experience being around watchers and the watched. Whatever it is, without liking him, he's become hers.

She calls him Tom.

It's only when she spots him that she realizes that she was looking for him. Walking ahead of her along King Street near Bay. A suit among suits. She knows it's him from the shape of the back of his head, his swimmer's shoulders, the ambling steps that carry him faster than would appear possible: the parts of him she sees each time he makes his back alley getaway.

He hasn't seen her. She had been making her way along the opposite side of the street. Her ostensible purpose was a time-killing wander that would lead her down into the underground malls for a bit of shopping (a new bra) and maybe lunch in the food court (nasty Chinese) before her shift at For Your Eyes Only. But she knows she has no reason to be down here with the traders and lawyers and bankers, other than to see if Tom is one of them. For *her* to see *him* for a change.

So you've got a thing for street meat, do you? she thinks, trailing him after he buys a hot dog from a vendor on the corner. *Maybe that's what I am to you. Street meat.*

Tom stops to wave to some others at the far side of the Toronto-Dominion building's broad concourse. A group of men and women laughing at some shared joke that Tom's appearance has reminded them of. Friends. They're just office pals, she feels, but he would have plenty of others. University drinking buddies, childhood mates, close siblings. His long list of associations tests the memory of his BlackBerry's address book. It makes her wonder about her own friend count, who she would call first if she had to confess something terrible or share lottery-winning news. Soon this question becomes who she would call at all.

He moves on, wiping the mustard off his hands, tossing the soiled napkin into a trash container in a graceful, basketball free throw. He joins the others funneling into the building, people moving purposefully toward their places on the sixty floors above built slim and black as a domino tile.

A truck passes on the street between them. When she can see into the glass-walled lobby again, Tom is gone.

That could have been it. A "chance sighting" that provided her with some small measure of private revenge, a turning of tables. But instead of letting go of Tom, she starts to follow him. Even after several days pass without catching him at her window, she spends her free afternoons and days off shadowing his movements, noting what he eats for lunch, the routines and schedules that make up his life. He's a lawyer. Married (a gold band), with a family (a baby seat in the back of his Mercedes). He golfs, but she suspects this is mainly in a client-entertaining capacity. A big tipper. As far as she can tell, hers is the only bedroom he peeps into. Then again, because she works most nights, she couldn't say this for sure.

It's just a game she's playing, a tit-for-tat, which prevents her hobby from being a violation or strange or sad, though she can't help wondering if it is some or all of these things. She's getting to know him. Somehow the anonymity of their relationship only makes it more intimate, in the way that all shames are intimate.

She continues to wait for him to appear at her window. Yet over the days—and then the weeks—of her surveillance, he doesn't return. It's ridiculous, she knows, but she can't help feeling a rejection every night she stays up late, her eyes on the wall across the alley, waiting for him to break the spell of invisibility that's been cast upon her. She's angry with him, but her anger is not for his perversity, but his rudeness. She's been twice wronged. Once for peeping on her, and twice for not keeping his promise to return.

On her day off, she waits in an idling taxi on King Street, and when his car emerges from the underground parking lot, she instructs the driver to follow him.

She'd expected this part—the car chase through the late rush hour traffic—to feel like a movie. Instead, it makes her wonder if she's going to throw up out her open window. It's sick, and it makes her feel sick. But she can't stop. Can't, meaning won't. Can't, meaning something portentous and life-altering has been deemed to hinge on where Tom's journey ends, and what happens when he arrives there.

They head north up Bathurst. Past the gaggle of squeegee kids skipping suicidally through the lanes like filthy elves at Queen, the bleary-eyed hospital workers in their scrubs at Dundas, and up beyond Honest Ed's, where downtown gives way to leafy, residential blocks in which, when she was first looking for a place to live, she'd viewed a dozen basement apartments she couldn't afford.

The Mercedes takes a right. She tells the cab driver to make the same turn. A couple blocks on, across from the park on Albany that borders a huge, seemingly half-finished stone church, Tom parks at the curb. She tells the driver to stop.

"Are you, like, a detective or something?" the driver asks her. What she's doing suddenly gives her a thrill. This isn't some lonely, pointless quest after all. It's a *job*.

"Yes," she says. "A private investigator, actually."

She watches as Tom gets out of his car and walks up to the front door of his house. One of the stately, renovated Victorians that tend to be featured in the Real Estate section of the *Globe*, the only pages she looks through sitting at For Your Eyes Only's bar as she finishes a coffee before her shift. A tasteful home with historical quirks: original stained glass, tin ceilings. Located in the Annex, a neighborhood she has been told was once a ghetto for students and immigrants and hippies, but is now an enclave of million-plus properties for those professionals not quite ready for their graduation to Rosedale or Forest Hill. The sort of house she has literally dreamed of. And in these dreams, a man like Tom has been there with her, kissing the back of her neck as she tends to the fresh-cut flowers he has brought home for her.

Once he's gone inside, she waits for the taxi to leave and then, as though the idea has only just occurred to her, she walks to the parked Mercedes. She is alone on the shady street. A dog yips in a neighbor's yard. More distant, a child practices piano scales.

She bends at the waist and trots across Tom's lawn, arms swinging closely at her sides, as if a soldier making a smaller target of herself in the midst of cross fire. The grass under her feet has been recently mowed. After her weeks of breathing Queen Street alley flavors—rank garbage, hobo poo—the smell is lush, exotic.

Around the side of Tom's house she lowers herself to her knees. Crawls into the flowerbed beneath the living room's bay window. It strikes her that her fear of turning around, of not seeing what she's come here to see, is greater than her fear of being discovered. She *is* a private investigator. But somehow it is her own privacy, not Tom's, that she is investigating.

Slowly, inch by inch, she raises her head. Holds her breath.

An empty room. Traditionally furnished, ancient rugs on the hardwood. But this oldness is offset by the abstract canvases on the walls, a pair of cubist nudes. A room that speaks of a family's generational hand-me-downs—the slightly frayed sofa and chairs—as well as the sensual vitality of the current inhabitants. She hadn't seen the living room precisely this way in her dreams, but now that she has seen it, she knows this is how she will start dreaming of it.

A child totters into the room. Followed by her mother, laughing after her. The child is Pampers-ad cute, the mother clear-skinned, treadmilled. Tom's wife. A woman she would like to study further if it weren't for the arrival of Tom himself.

He is laughing too. His daughter is at the age of still learning to walk but believing she already can, so that her movements are a comical series of lurches and grabs. He comes to stand in the middle of the room. His wife chasing after the little girl, both circling the coffee table.

Happiness. This is what she'd title this picture, if it was a picture. For if these people aren't happy, if what they have and share and can look forward to doesn't make them happy, then who is?

Tom turns. And sees her.

Neither of them move. Neither speak. Tom's wife and daughter continue to swirl around him like an eddying tide upon a rock. He's not surprised to see her there looking in his window. It's as though he's been expecting her for some time.

She will debate this point later, when she remembers this moment and stretches it out, mining its details. It may only be her imagination, but her vision is good, her view unobscured. There is only a sheet of glass and fifteen feet of air-conditioned space between them, which just makes her more certain. He smiles at her.

He is rich. And she is poor.

She realizes this only now, her feet sinking in the pungent mulch of his flowerbed. Of course she's always been aware that she doesn't have money, but looking into Tom's home, she sees that she will likely never have it. And not just money, but all the tailored, meaningful, identity-making things she's dreamed of one day acquiring. Opportunities, epiphanies. An escalation of jobs on one of the movie sets where Toronto is made to look like New York. All the good things that aren't destined for her.

She stares at Tom, and he at her. His eyes tell her something. How moving to Toronto from wherever she came from could open up a world, but just as easily expose her existing world as the limited, luckless thing she sometimes fears it is. She thought the two of them were connected, but she was wrong. They are strangers. As it is for the patrons at For Your Eyes Only, the one rule of living here, in a real city, is that she can look at the lives of others, but not touch.

A TASTE OF HONEY

BY KIM MORITSUGU

St. Lawrence Market

I thought about calling in sick today because of the big-whoop movie shoot that's going on, the shoot that everyone in the South Market Building, the whole neighborhood it seems, is so stoked about. But if I avoided every person, casting director, film production outfit, or theater company that has ever rejected me for a part, I'd never go anywhere or see anyone. And if I stayed home, I'd have that shitty not-invited-to-the-cool-party feeling, even though the shoot won't be cool, or a party. I'd just spend the day writing angry thoughts in my journal anyway, and listening to my stomach acid churn, and the self-help books say I should accept the successes of others in the face of my defeats, not obsess about or dwell on them, so fine, I'll go to work.

This way, I can hear the banal and inane comments live—from Karen, my boss at The Honey Hut, and Nick from the cheese shop across the way, and Nadia from the butcher counter—about how they saw Denzel and Scarlett in person and how short they are and how there's an awful lot of waiting around in the moviemaking business, isn't there? They'll say: But you know that already, don't you, Jen, because of that movie you were in. With Mark Wahlberg, wasn't it? When you were listed in the credits as "*Girl in Disco?*" That was funny. You were good in it, though too bad about the makeup job they did on you. And that leather bikini top you had to wear. How come you aren't in this movie, didn't you audition for it?

I might as well sooner rather than later give them a bullshit line about how I guess I didn't get the part because I wasn't right for it. Rather than because I'm a big motherfucking loser who, when I heard that the call was for an "office receptionist with attitude," thought the role was so right for me, would be so easy to play, that I made the mistake of getting my hopes up, when how many times have I sworn never to hope again, never to go into an audition expecting anything at all? N-to-the-fucking-power-of-n times is how many.

I ride my bike downtown like always, and coast along Market Street, past the lineup of camera trucks and movie trailers staked out by a row of orange pylons. When I park the bike at my usual stand and lock it up between two big rigs, I kind of hope some crew guy will emerge and tell me I can't leave it there, so I can get testy with him, and maybe start a yelling match, but no such luck. I light up my prework cigarette, step over the stream of electrical cables winding across the sidewalk, settle into my smoking spot under an overhang, and hear a squeaky young voice say, "Jen? Is that you?"

Coming at me is a short, thin girl in a floaty top and tight jeans tucked into stiletto-heeled boots. Her too-long-to-be-real curly hair extensions coil and loop over and around her pert tits. What is she . . . eighteen? And how the hell does she know me?

"It's me, Honey Cooper," she says. She has a pretty face, all blue eyes and cute upturned nose and glowing skin and curly eyelashes. "From the Ryerson theater program? We met when you came out to speak to my acting class last year, and you said it was funny my name was Honey because you worked at a honey place at St. Lawrence Market? Hey, that's where we are now. Small world or what?"

Christ, I met her when my old drama prof invited me to speak to the naïve little undergrads on "Hard Truths about the Acting Life." The topic was the prof's idea, not mine, though I had no trouble spinning cautionary tales about the profession based on my own bitter experience. This kid must be one of the suck-ups who approached me after my talk and claimed to be a fan of my work, which consisted, ten years post-graduation, of twenty measly acting credits. Still consists of twenty measly credits a year later, fuck me.

I say, "Is Honey your real name?"

"No, it's a nickname that my grandma gave me. When I was two years old, she thought I was so sweet that—"

"Did you graduate from the Ryerson program yet?"

"Um, yeah, last spring. And I've been auditioning like crazy for anything and everything ever since, like you said people have to do when they're starting out. I want to thank you for giving that talk, by the way. It made such a difference to get the inside story on the acting life, to know what to expect, how hard it would be to break through." She tilts her head and smiles. Fetchingly. "You were so inspiring!"

This is hard to believe, considering that I'd ended my talk by telling the class that if I'd known when I was at their age and stage what I knew ten years later, I would have given up on acting, and set my sights instead on marrying some rich guy who could bankroll a comfortable lifestyle. I was dead serious, but the class laughed as if I were joking.

I muster up some fake interest in Honey's career. "And how's it going? Have you done any commercials yet? My first job was in a commercial. For tampons."

"I remember that one! Where you wore little white shorts

and rode a bicycle? That was a classic! But hey, I'm doing better than that, because this is my first job, today, here. Is that wild or what?"

The dreadful meaning of her words seeps into my brain and clogs it up so that I can only repeat, "Today? Here?"

"In the movie that's shooting up the street! It's such a great story how I got the part: I auditioned to be a receptionist, and I was mad too young for it, but they liked me so much they created a character in the movie, just for me!" Her eyes dance while she tells this story. The Macarena, it looks like, but still.

A vein in my forehead starts to throb, and I say, dully, "Just for you."

"Isn't that amazing? I play a babysitter who looks after Denzel's kids. The scene we're doing today is where I take the kids downtown to meet their dad at his office and we witness a shooting on the street that leads to the whole home invasion thing that happens later when I get caught in the cross fire and die."

"You die? That's great." Her eyes stop dancing and I say, "For the acting opportunity, I mean. Death scenes can be real career-makers."

"I know! But I have to get through this week's scenes first, and I'm so nervous! What if I sweat all over Denzel when I meet him today? Or faint on him. Wouldn't that be the worst?" She emits merry peals of laughter at this point, I'm not sure why—because she's a merry young soul, maybe. I, meanwhile, struggle to swallow the anti-merriment bile that has surged into my mouth.

I can still taste it when an assistant dude comes out of a trailer and calls to Honey that she's needed inside.

"Hey, break a leg," I say, in all sincerity.

"Thanks. I'm so glad I ran into you. You're, like, my role model or whatever. Come visit me on-set when you have a lunch break?"

I'm in no mood for improv, but I feign regret. "I don't know if I'll get a break. The Honey Hut gets busy at this time of day."

"Please? You could coach me. Give me some more of your wise advice."

"Tell you what: I'll try." Sure, I could coach her a little. Or I could cut the bitch. Either one.

My boss Karen is all agog when I go inside and tell her I ran into someone I know who has a part in the movie. She says, "Could she introduce us to Denzel, do you think?"

"I wouldn't ask her to."

"Because it would be uncool, you mean?"

"Beyond uncool."

"Oh. I'm sorry."

"Never mind. What do you say we put out the lavender honey to sample?"

She touches my arm with her bony hand. "I meant that I'm sorry I wasn't sensitive to how awkward it might be for you to work today, with the shoot going on outside."

Awkward? Before Honey popped up, the situation was awkward. Now, it's mortifying, enraging, soul-destroying. I try to breathe deeply and evenly, which is difficult when my forehead vein is throbbing to the beat of a goddamned rock band. When I can speak without spitting, I say, "So, lavender honey, then?"

Karen shakes her head. "I don't know how you can stand a life in show business."

Me either.

She says, "It must be so difficult, what with the constant rejection and being passed over in favor of people who are probably no more talented than you are."

Probably? What the fuck's with probably?

I spend the next few hours minding the hut, serving customers, and thinking of ways to harm Honey, remove her from the local talent pool. The butter knives we use to spread honey on crackers don't have sharp edges, but applied with force at the right angle, they could draw blood. The honey walnut cake that we serve could do damage if Honey has an allergy to nuts, but what are the odds of that? I'm picturing taking the end of one of her hair extensions, winding it around the electric juicer we use to squeeze the lemons for honey lemonade, and turning the power to high, when Honey herself shows up at the stand, in full makeup.

She says, "They don't need me on the set for at least another hour, so I thought I'd come over and visit. Hey, this place is cute!"

Karen begs to be introduced, asks Honey a flurry of questions about Denzel, and gives her a free jar of our finest orange-blossom honey. Honey proclaims delight at this gift, the two of them chat away, and Karen doesn't read my eyes when I use them to communicate volumes—or even a haiku—about how I want Honey to go away, not linger. "Take a break with Honey, go outside, get some fresh air," Karen says. "I'll be fine here."

I take Honey out to the second-floor veranda on the south side of the building, a picnic tabled area with a less-than-enchanting view of the Gardiner Expressway, an affordable housing complex, and the occasional homeless person shambling by with a shopping buggy. She refuses my offer of a cigarette, I light mine up anyway, and I let the wind blow my exhaled smoke in her direction, but she doesn't flinch, only retrieves a few pages of script from her bag and says, "Would you mind running lines with me? Pretty please?"

Maybe I can hold up the train of her gown when she goes onstage at the Academy Awards to collect her first Oscar too.

The scene she wants to rehearse calls for her to walk along the shop-lined street, hand-in-hand with two adorable children, singing "The Wheels on the Bus" (Is this cloying and cliché enough, this setup for violence? I can already hear how the scene will be scored, with pingy piano music in a minor key), when a street thug with a gun pops out of a picturesque doorway and, right before the traumatized eyes of the kids and babysitter, shoots dead a gangster who is getting into a limo.

To entertain myself and help Honey get a feel for the material, I could do the voices of the characters in the scene, alternate my pitch and cadence between those of the kids and the adults. But reading the lines in a flat, uninflected tone, like casting directors do whenever I audition, is *way* more fun. Especially if doing so might freak Honey out or throw her off.

She does better than I thought she would reciting her lines opposite my monotone. She's not stellar, but not terrible either. The consolation is that she's not as confident in her line readings as someone in her charmed position could be.

After we've run through the scene, she bites her lip and says, "What do you think? Am I underplaying it too much? Should I go bigger?"

I'm stubbing out my cigarette when she says this—not on her arm, because a cigarette burn would not render her unemployable or even unconscious, and scars can be covered with makeup, so why bother?—but on the tarmac floor of the veranda. I grind out the butt, and realize there's more than one way to end her career before it starts.

I say, "Now that you mention it, I think you could go bigger. In fact, you should. Definitely. Good idea."

"Really?"

"Yeah. I'll let you in on a trade secret: You know that crap about how in the theater you have to play to the upper balcony, but in the movies you're supposed to be low-key in close-up?"

She blanches under the heavy makeup. "That's crap?"

"I'm afraid so. Especially for someone like you who's petite to begin with—what height are you without heels, four-foot-eleven?"

"I'm five-three!"

"Same thing. And you're so young too. If you underplay your part, you'll be invisible. Which is great if you want no one to notice you in the role, if you want to let the scene be about the other actors and the stunts and the special effects."

"I don't want that. This is supposed to be my big break!"

"Then make yourself memorable."

"Let's try the scene again," she says, "and I'll play it up."

She's such an easy mark, I almost feel bad about what I'm doing to her. Almost.

Karen slips out during the afternoon to watch what she can of the shoot from behind a barricade on the street, and reports back that multiple takes were done of a scene that involved Honey. When I press her for details, like were Honey's reactions the focus of the retakes, and did Honey seem to be overacting, she says she doesn't know, the whole setup was a little confusing. Also disappointing, because boo-hoo, she didn't see Denzel.

I force myself to saunter outside rather than run when I emerge from the Market Building after 6, after we've closed up shop. Dusk has fallen, Front Street rumbles with rush hour traffic, and on the side streets, crew people are packing and loading up equipment. The day's shooting is done then, but is Honey also finished? As in fired? I'm starting to think she's skipped off without saying goodbye, when she comes out of a trailer in her street clothes, her bag over her shoulder, a tissue in her hand. Could she be wiping her eyes? She *is* wiping them. Fucking A.

I erase the diabolical smile that has come out to play on my face, replace it with a picture of innocent concern, wave, and say, "Hey. How'd the day go? You still alive?"

In answer, she hugs me. Right there on the sidewalk, in the middle of the evening foot traffic, in front of random strangers rushing by on their way home from work or going out to dinner and the theater. She hugs me, and she laughs her annoying merry laugh, peals and all. "It went well, thanks to you! The director loved my energy and passion—he said my performance was perfect for the high drama of the scene. He liked it so much he got the kids to ramp up their reactions to match mine and did lots of takes. And get this: Denzel said that he'd never seen anyone act so well in their first movie role, that I was a natural!"

Her energy and passion? Please. My chest feels tight and my eyes ache. How much good luck—how much of my goddamned share of all the goddamned available luck in the universe—does this little twat have? I'm about to start sobbing, that or stabbing, but all I can say, stupidly, is, "I thought you were crying just now. You were wiping your eyes."

"I was trying to remove some of the makeup they used to cover my freckles. But who cares if I look pancakey? I'm a real movie actress now, woo-hoo! Want to come for a drink with me and celebrate? I'm meeting some friends at a pub around the corner." She steps over to the curb, then turns back to where I stand, stunned, behind her. "Come," she says. "Join us. Come and be happy for me."

A flower truck, high and wide and white, accelerates along the street behind her, gunning to make the green light. I don't have to shove her. A good nudge—like a hurrying pedestrian could give her by accident—is enough to topple her, in her silly high-heeled boots, over the curb, onto the road, into the path of the oncoming truck, all five tons of it.

She died instantly—I know, because I stuck around long enough to watch some guy who'd seen too many medical shows on television run over and feel for a pulse on the neck of her mangled body after the truck driver had slammed on his brakes (and dragged Honey another ten yards) and jumped out of the cab and freaked out big-time. "Call 911!" the guy directed an onlooker, and he bent down to listen for breathing, to see if her chest was moving. A minute later, when he stepped back from her corpse, he said, "Does anyone know this girl? Was anyone with her? Who saw what happened?" People spoke all at once, no one noticed me, the truck driver wailed on, and I walked away, unlocked my bike, plugged in my headphones, and rode home, let music drown out the sounds of the crash that still reverberated in my ears: the screech of the brakes, the dull thud of the impact, the crunch and squeal of metal bending.

Tomorrow I'll go to work and Karen will be all teary—she's boring that way. She'll ramble on in a quavery voice about how she can't believe such a tragic accident happened to someone so young and sweet whose life was so full of promise and isn't it horrible? And I'll say yeah, I heard it on the local news this morning, what a shock: It *is* horrible.

What I won't say is how horribly unfair it was for Honey

to make it without paying her dues, without suffering for her art, without living, every night and day, for years and years, with self-doubt and self-loathing and shame. I won't say that for Honey to do so well, so easily, was not just undeserved, but not right. Not right at all.

I'll let Karen pat me on the arm in the way she does that makes my flesh crawl, and I'll change the subject, talk about Denzel. Later, when I take my smoke break, I'll call my agent and tell her enough with sending me out for the ingenue gigs or to play young moms, I'd like to start reading for character roles, for parts that are a bit more meaty and complex and nuanced. I don't want to get my hopes up—and I won't, because I know better than to be optimistic, after all this time, after everything I've been through—but I think I could do justice to that kind of shit. I really do.

STALLING

BY EMILY SCHULTZ
Parkdale

Apparently, Bonnie Brown-Switzel couldn't shop for an affair. One week away from their third anniversary, she kissed Mr. Switzel (as she affectionately called him) goodbye as they both left the loft. She set off through the city to do her errands—grocery list neatly tucked inside an angora mitten. As she headed west, each step her Camper boots took felt extra long. The February street smelled like wet newspaper. The wind carried a rancid whiff from the tucked-away abattoir that kept their condo affordable. Bonnie felt like she was carrying the idea of the affair inside her mouth—words she couldn't say. She bit her lips to keep it inside, in case it should fall out onto the snow, only to get picked up by the wrong person.

The boy at the Price Chopper who helped her get the olive oil from the top shelf—"No, the virgin"—had long pink fingers that limped across the labels self-consciously. Two distinct spots of red blazed on his cheeks. His blush was endearing, as were the pale thick lashes that fused above his large eyes. The bone nubs in the back of his pants as he stretched for the proper brand and bottle were irksome. Bonnie urged the dizzy-wheeled cart away.

She would have to take more decisive action. The last flirtation she'd had was five years ago, with an actor, genteel and passionate, the type who noticed everything, the type who wooed. On her way out of the store, she passed by the karaoke bar where they had met, the black and silver *Applause* sign still propped up in the front window beside the stage. Five years. Post-marriage, it seemed seven times as long. Not that she had anything to complain about. As marriages went, hers was supine. They were only three years in, but they had passed without quarrel. The memory of the long-past flirtation nibbled at her mind.

Drawn out again, after ten minutes of walking—farther into the worn-down and newly built-up neighborhood of Parkdale—she turned onto the street where *he* lived. She didn't know which house the actor lived in, only the street. It had been so long, and she had never been inside; declined his offer coyly when they'd shared a cab, he stumbling out, she traveling on to the safety of Roncesvalles and High Park. Now, she pulled a tube of Mac from her pocket and coated her mouth without stopping. Her boots punched semi-circular tracks into the snow. Today she enjoyed the *tap-tap-tap* sounds. Today she wanted to be noticed.

What would she say if they met? There was plenty of likelihood, after all—this was *his* street, and he was not the type to hold a day job. She stopped in front of an old Skylark, the color of sky. This was his car, she was sure of it, it must be. He hadn't had one then, but time had passed. If he had a car, it would be this one. She peered in its windows for hints of its owner—only a snow-scraper and a portable stainless-steel coffee mug—and glanced at the houses on either side. She recalled the strength of the limbs beneath his pressed shirt, his muttony chest, the tab of fur that showed between his clavicles, the rosemary-wine smell of him through cotton-wool. Her heart accelerated. She was almost at the end of his street. If she were to meet him, it must happen now.

A woman was coming toward her along the same sidewalk, a black Paris-style shawl around her shoulders. Could she have an affair with a woman?

They shared a look and the woman smiled as they passed one another. Bonnie had no idea the woman was actually his sister-in-law, that she was, at that moment, taking him cough syrup and throat lozenges, that he stood behind one of the tall glaring windows, not recognizing the swaying tendrils of Bonnie's hair, seeing her only as a man sees two pretty women together on the street, that he watched the exchange with one hand in a striped flannel pocket and the other reaching suddenly to grope himself—in spite of his sickness—quickly, without release.

Before Volker Gruber arrived in North America, he had imagined a never-ending party: women who were easy and sophisticated, men who would share their drugs, their musical equipment, their couches. Instead, he had to work all week just to afford going to one of the few meager parties. The women never said hello and the beer was weak. He quickly learned that in Canada anything before 1979 was irrelevant; in a way, it was one of the things that had attracted him, the newness. But since his arrival, he found himself missing Germany more and more. He felt it most under the fluorescent glare of grocery aisles, trying unsuccessfully to find words he knew.

Volker watched the stock boy strain upward for a bottle of oil, jerkily deliver it to the woman with the dark hair and even darker halos around her eyes. The movements of the people accompanied a strange rhythm in Volker's ears, pumped from headphones. He left his sweatshirt hood up, the headphones like a secret antenna connecting him to the outside world though a constant pulse. Volker pushed his cart up aisle three to Kruder and Dorfmeister, scooped out several bags of oatmeal and sugar, visited the meat counter, lifted potatoes and onions from produce. The cheeses were atrocious, he wouldn't even go near them. That required a special trip to Kensington Market.

On the streetcar, a young blonde sat in the single scoop seat across from him. She was wearing a dark-blue hoodie, the cuffs punctured with holes through which her thumbs looped. Her silver fingernails keyed a rhythm on her knees. She had good pants, good shoes. A short choppy haircut framed her head and she wore purplish-pearl lipstick. She looked like the girl in the Internet service advertisement overhead. He smiled through the music at her pale sleepy eyes. She didn't look at him. Blondes never did. For some reason he got the brunettes, the tall leggy ones who hid in baggy pants and hunched over to surprise him with their height and grace. Not unattractive, but brunette nonetheless, they loved him. It was because he was dark too.

It was different with guys, easier to make friends with them. They stood together and nodded their heads, watched whoever was playing or spinning. They shuffled alongside one another, faces saying everything: *It's good, it's good*. He could do that. Volker spoke in a different dialect with this group—one of drum machines, sequencers, oscillators, filters, brands. E-MU Emulator, Roland TR-909, Korg MS-20, ARP 2600. Women required more language. Sometimes Volker knew he could get by with a head nod, a smile, could hook up if it were a friend of a friend, if there were someone who knew him to introduce him, vouch for him. But in the morning, the drugs were gone and the girls always seemed to hang around, uncertain, their movements—with the headphones off—composed of snapping, Volker's words stilted and loud, saying not much of anything.

Toronto was very sluggish when it wasn't dancing. During the day it was an ugly smear of fried foods and snow, people with their hands out, the buildings only a few heads taller than the people. During the day he bussed dishes in a restaurant on Queen Street West. At night he changed his clothes and went clubbing. It was the one thing the city was good for. Six months of this. He played the first Thursday of every month. Familiar and unfamiliar faces in front of him, a flurry of cute girls with pierced tongues bopped under his hands. He moved over his gear like a magician, the sound in his head finding its exit. Between each set, thirty days of penned ricocheting, lifting dishes and glasses in and out of the machine.

The streetcar rattled up an incline on its tracks like an automatic hospital bed. He felt it but didn't hear it.

The amount Cynthia Staines ate diminished in direct relation to the things she bought. These days, she ate almost nothing at all. She skipped lunch because she was working; it was an excellent excuse, no one could argue with it. Anyway, she did not have time to chew the fat with a bunch of do-nothings at The Muddy Duck.

Today she was savoring a tuna wrap one of her coworkers had brought back for her. Cynthia had already made up her mind: She would eat half and that was all. The other woman had already gnawed her way through a southwestern chicken sub, all tomatoes and orange sauce, balled up the napkin in her little fist, her pin-striped lap littered with crumbs, a plump polyester pair of Old Navy's passing for office wear. It had smelled like heaven, and disappeared like it was a mirage.

"Listen," Cynthia said into the black slots in the mouthpiece. The telephone was the most efficient way of both delaying and prolonging the devine glut of mayonnaise crucial to the supposed low-fat wrap. "I know you can help me. I want you to wave your magic wand and find me a driver by Friday."

The coworker gingerly deposited her lunch things in the garbage and reached for her Day-Timer. Cynthia turned away from her, leaned back in the swivel chair, propped a square-toed black shoe dangerously close to the sandwich, and eyed it with contempt.

"Friday," Cynthia said again, louder, "I know it's close, but you'd be such a dear . . . I would definitely owe you lunch."

She hung up.

"Idiot." Cynthia ground the word between her teeth and the woman looked up with surprise. "He wouldn't lift his finger; take his wife's pulse if she were dying." Cynthia laughed loudly, the chords of it straining through the office wall out into the village of cubicles. She shook her head in feigned affection. "He's going to do me this favor; he doesn't even know he's getting the boot. *You didn't know?* Well, it's not like I'm asking for anything out of the ordinary, nothing that isn't in his job description. You have to cut the dead wood. Really, nice enough guy, that Jackson, but rocks for brains. Andy came in here the one night, laid it all on me, told me about Jackson at the last conference. He did this performance you wouldn't believe—you just don't talk out of line like that, ever. I can't believe I didn't tell you this. Andy came in one night, said, 'We've got to lose senior staff. If not Jackson, then who? I hate to do it to him, I just need one reason to keep him on, something solid, help me think of it, one thing I can take to the board.'" She held out her arms emptily.

The smell of the sandwich crept into Cynthia's nostrils. She grabbed it off the desk, took six small bites, the medicinal fish taste oozing through her wisdoms. She chewed until the pita slid down her palate without struggle.

"But that's business, it's all balance." She stared down at the nub of sandwich. "In the long run it's better for the company. Jackson will do me this last favor and then we'll be even."

A few rings of green onion lay on the wax paper, an inside-out company logo showing through from the other side. Out of the bottom, a thin milky trail leaked. Cynthia balled the half-sandwich inside the paper and let it fall into the waste-paper basket. Her coworker offered her a piece of chewing gum, the silver foil crackling. She chewed it hard and fast, pushed it with her tongue against the roof of her mouth where it would stick without looking unprofessional. It deposited a burning twiggy taste of mint.

Bonnie Brown-Switzel stood outside the pharmacy beside battered newspaper boxes that had been ransacked, neon flyers for burlesque shows and ESL tutors rubbing paper shoulders. She fumbled through the white plastic bag, searching for her purchase. Her fingers clamped around the tube and she experienced a youthful thrill. She rummaged in her black leather shoulder bag for her compact. The oval of her mouth was powdered, her lips slightly chapped from walking all day.

This was her prize. The classic vixen's tool. The tip of its perfect red tongue met her bottom lip where she let it linger before climbing up to accentuate the peaks. It was, if not the same color that the woman on the actor's street had worn, very similar. Bonnie usually steered clear of bold colors. She was feeling reckless. She peered into the handheld mirror, very pleased.

"Can you lend me thirty-one cents?"

She hadn't heard him. He was right at her elbow. When she looked up, his eyes burned into her.

"Just thirty-one cents. All I need is thirty—"

It was growing dark already. Bonnie shook her head and bolted a few feet, stopped by a youth on his bicycle.

"Yo, watch it," he called, swerving, the bike dropping down from the sidewalk to the curb into oncoming traffic, spraying thick black slush.

When she looked down she saw that she had crushed the head of the lipstick into the tube, damaging its shape. It was not broken, but its newness was gone. She pulled a tissue from her purse and wiped the lid, pushed the compact and the recapped tube into the depths of a side pocket in the purse as she walked, even though she knew they would lose themselves between empty gum packages, business cards, and store circulars.

"Hooor!" the homeless man called after her. "Bitch!" A wave of heat knocked against her forehead, and she sped up a few steps. When she glanced back over her shoulder, she saw he was already engaged with someone else, a thin man in dirty flannel and a pair of bedroom slippers. "I'm not a man!" her original fellow was yelling, his head turning between the new arrival and a couple of passersby. "I'm not a man!"

Bonnie ducked into the doorway of a bar she had passed many times before. Its entrance was littered with weekly newspapers. She would pop in and catch her breath, flip through a paper in the foyer, pretend to look for a movie time or an address, and then duck out again when the street had quieted. Between the two doors it was light, she could hear a familiar swell of music, the tinkling of glasses from inside, see the white-shirted man sliding them into the rack above the counter carefully, as if he were dabbing paint on a canvas. His eyes penetrated the door and connected with Bonnie standing there. Before she could pick up the club mag, she was grasping the handle and she was inside the second door.

Volker Gruber watched nothing with interest. His movements were slow and precise like one who is waiting, saving all his energy for something greater. Noon to 8, he told himself, another two hours, another thirteen dollars. Ten would pay his way in. Five for his first drink. Another two hours and he was already in debt to his plans.

He stared absently, trying to make sense of his losses, as an older woman stood between the doors of the establishment, disoriented, bobbing back and forth to some kind of internal flutter, apparently deciding whether or not to come in. The sound system overhead bleated something utterly offensive, the same line quadruple-repeat. A chorus in another language was no more interesting than in one's own. Without focusing, Volker could feel his eyes burn dark with annoyance.

He could have no idea that this would be his last night in Canada, no idea that 6,197 kilometers away, Herr Gruber had clutched a hand to his fatal heart. Volker stilled, unsure if he should greet the woman or go back to the kitchen. In moments of indecision, his head filled with great handclaps of static.

The woman maneuvered her way past empty tables up to the bar and perched pertly on the stool. She had thirtyish thighs and moved off-cadence, like a skeptical cat. Had he seen her before? She seemed like so many of their customers—styled exactly so, but still the uncertain type, with thick dark hair. She liked him, he could already tell. The dark ones always did. He smiled at her. The bartender, Vincent, was in the back.

Volker placed his hands on the counter, elbows out, like he owned the place. People were so gullible. She would be gullible too.

The woman licked her lips, the color on them reducing ever so slightly. She gazed up at a chalkboard above Volker's head. He gave her the eyes. She looked at him, glanced up, looked at him again.

"I'll have a . . . a . . . maybe a . . ."

He reached behind himself and fumbled for a bottle. He hated to waste a rock glass with two hours to go. He always ran out of the short rock glasses first. A bottle of red wine raised, Merlot. "Mer-lot," Volker stated, letting the words fill his mouth, thick and red. "Mer-lot?" He lifted his eyebrows. Their eyes met. She nodded. "Mer-lot." The long-stemmed base plinked against the counter.

She fumbled in her purse. How much? Neither of them knew. She pulled out seven dollars and set it on the bar. He looked at the money. She added another dollar. He set the sky-blue five atop the cash register for Vincent to ring in. Three made their way into Volker's pocket, where they jangled together, crisp and sweet. He grinned at the woman, nodded, and made his way back to the kitchen, his hips already stepping to the rhythm to come. He could feel her admiring eyes beating a soft steady path between his shoulder blades on down.

Cynthia Staines put her turn signal on and edged over toward the snow-gray Jameson exit. She checked her blind spot at the last second, just in time to avoid the front end of a hurtling red Malibu. The old muscle car hit the gas and the horn simultaneously, surging dangerously near as it burst ahead of her with a penile display of pride.

Cynthia swore loudly. She edged over tentatively and then sped up to ride his bumper. He slowed, and she slammed her foot on her brake. He was on and off the brake lights like he was playing the drums. A vicious urge to smash right into the inane license plate—*BRADCAR*—forced Cynthia to lay on the horn until the guy sped off down Lakeshore Drive where the exit merged with the street.

Cynthia turned, cruised a few blocks, cursing, until the need to pull over stopped her. She was shaking. She snatched a tissue from the box and held it against her eyes for a second. Then she folded it neatly and tucked it into her blazer pocket. Her fingers still trembled and she grabbed hold of one hand with the other. She dug into the skin with her thumbnail, held it there, a small crescent appearing. She glanced up into the driver's mirror. She had to eat.

Slamming the car door, she clattered across the sidewalk. An Italian restaurant blaring teen pop normally would have given Cynthia reason to doubt the quality of food. But she was not concerned with quality. She ushered herself in quickly, did not wait to be seated. "Scotch and water and a menu," she said when her server appeared.

"What type of Scotch would you like, ma'am? We have—"

"Your best. And I'll have some bread right away, focaccia or garlic bread, whatever you have . . . and a garden salad."

"Shall I still bring a menu?"

"Yes," she snapped.

The food was over-seasoned but warm. When she got this way, it didn't matter. Forkfuls went in without acknowledgement. Her mouth and eyes filled with steam. If she noticed the server watching her from the back, she didn't bat an eyelash. She was all gnocci, all bread and olive oil. She was swallowing, swallowing, swallowing. The brown swirl of vinegar adorned the plate three times, and Cynthia felt herself melt into its shapeless whirl.

A woman at the counter was acting very coy with the busboy. From where she sat, Cynthia could see the servers through the small rectangular window. One wall of the dining room was mirrored and, though she doubted anyone else could see, their positions were reflected to her. They were standing at the back of the kitchen, their hands traveling back and forth with a skinny white spliff, on which they both took turns. Cynthia piled her plates at the corner of the table so the busboy would come and take them. She glared at the dark-haired woman, whose small rump, upon the red bar stool, made a pinpoint like an exclamation mark out of her tight composed body.

The busboy was on his way back to the kitchen when Cynthia flagged him in the same mirror she had used to watch his coworkers. Cynthia saw the woman on the barstool observe their interaction, still coyly sipping from her wineglass through lips that left a dainty colored smudge.

The boy, who was perhaps twenty-four or twenty-five, tall and dark and wiry, approached the table. His thumb knuckle grazed her plate. She put her hand on his arm, waylaying him.

"What do I owe you?" she asked, her purse snapping open, a wad of bills there, appearing instantly in her lap.

He looked down at the money, sheathed from anyone's sight inside the open mouth of the black silk change purse inside the black leather bag.

"Server . . ." he replied. He had an accent. She liked that.

She smiled, lopsidedly, a quivering finger going to her hair, which she wrapped around it, the long blond strand falling forward in a manner he would surely understand. "Where is your bathroom?" she queried him with an openly sexual smirk.

He gestured helplessly, his face a blank slate.

When Bonnie Brown-Switzel entered the ladies' room, her ears filled with the sound of panting and shaking. The metal walls of the cubicles resonated with a strange savage music. The quiet grunting came from the third stall, bumping firmly against her ears. She had been about to let the door fall closed, but reached behind her and caught it, shutting it softly.

Without looking at the shoes beneath the pink partitions, she knew that it was the busboy and the blonde: a short, sharp woman with a Roman nose, pin-straight yellow hair, and powerful watery eyes, the kind of woman who held herself very upright in spite of her height and made Bonnie feel as if she should do the same. Bonnie had seen him go down to the basement after the blonde, a couple of rolls of toilet paper under one arm and a plastic gray key taped to a wrist-thick stick with *Don't Lose* written on it in black marker. One of them was moaning—him, Bonnie thought—the other grunting. As they pitched against the side of the cubicle, the toilet paper dispenser mouse-squeaked a repetition of hips and tin, and Bonnie stood motionless in the doorway.

Slowly, she made her way along the wall, toward their hideout and into the stall next to them. The cubicle door closed of its own accord. As she set one foot upon the toilet seat, it wiggled. She paused—her heart hammering louder than any other noise she made—and then lifted the other foot up. The sound of grated breathing filled her ears. She held her breath. Crouching, she put her hand flat against the partition, and could feel the vibration of the two bodies on the other side. The exact spot behind where one of them was pressed naked.

Then the woman whispered urgently, "Not like that. Do it hard. Make it . . . make it hurt."

"I can't," he replied, his voice thick.

Bonnie felt a heaviness welling low in her stomach, as it did when she had drunk too much coffee. She felt her head duck inside the feeling. She pulled her hand across her belly and leaned sideways, bracing her cheek against the thin makeshift wall that thrummed with them. Under the other hand, a heart was etched into the cubicle's wall. *Michael,* it said inside it, though "Michael" would obviously never enter the ladies' room to read it.

In another moment, the room filled with squealing, which was stifled, perhaps by a hand. It turned to a soft mewl, and what the man said was rough, in another language. She had no idea if it was vulgar, or if an "I love you" had fallen deafly between strangers. The scent of spring rose in Bonnie's nostrils, the acrid airing out of things from winter. Over the soapy rose smell of the bathroom came a pungent, earthy aroma. Their bodies in motion. She imagined the places from which the smell seeped—from the boy's pits, from his balls, from between the legs of the pin-straight blonde. Bonnie moved carefully to find a better position, leaned her forehead against the spot where she could feel them most, curled her fingers through her hair, and pulled it to keep herself silent.

Soon they stopped. He exhaled. Bonnie could hear the saliva in their mouths, ticking. There was the sound of shuffling. Buttoning. A belt buckle. A clasping of snaps, or was it purse lips? Then the woman said simply, "Thank you."

The cubicle door opened and the skeletal wall shook beneath Bonnie's cheek. She pulled her hair harder. The wooden door to the restroom opened and closed. He was gone.

In a moment, palms slapped the floor and the woman in

the next stall began to wretch, vomiting violently. Bonnie shifted quickly, the squeak of the toilet seat concealed by the moist unpleasant wash of things going down the drain next door. The unzipping of a bag, and the woman had straightened. Bonnie could feel the weight as the woman leaned again against the wall nearest her.

A moment of cold-tile silence followed. The fluorescents crackled.

Then the woman on the other side began to cry, her sobs small and controlled, like stones thrown into a basin.

Bonnie waited until the door had opened and closed again and stillness stretched past 8 p.m. Then she tentatively left the cubicle, her face, in the mirror as she passed it, much as it had been that morning. She stopped to wash her hands, though she didn't know why.

At home that night, as she lay in bed, her back pressed to Mr. Switzel's ample stomach, his great arms wrapped plainly around her, thin rivers ran from the corners of her eyes. She wondered where the boy had gone when he finished, what waited for him, what words he had said, and whether he would remember them later. She wondered if the woman lived alone. Mr. Switzel shifted, patted her thigh solidly, as if it were a cocker spaniel. Outside, she could hear the wind bubbling through the thin, decorative tree below their balcony. Three years, she thought, the length of time they had been married. Forty-seven years still ahead. It will all disappear, she thought. I will ruin it all.

SICK DAY

BY MARK SINNETT

CN Tower

Donny Freemont was just too damn disappointed to go on. It was as if floors had fallen on the inside. He lowered his head and thrust his chair away from his desk, then leaned all the way back to stare fixedly at the stippled ceiling. It was ridiculous, he knew that, but there was no denying it had taken firm hold. He put the call through to his receptionist.

"But Mrs. Sanjit is already here," Tina protested.

Donny squinted at the door, as if he might see through the bird's-eye maple laminate that had impressed him so much when he signed on at the clinic two years ago. Then he concentrated on the hiss in the receiver, tried to match it to the space beyond the door, to Tina wriggling at her desk, and the line of molded cobalt chairs out there that he considered a grave mistake because they were flimsy and uncomfortable.

"Does she know I'm in here?"

Tina huffed. "She's not an idiot, is she? She's been here half an hour. You *know* how she is." She lowered her voice. "She saw Mrs. Lawford come in and then leave. And I think she might even have been here when your one-fifteen left. Shit, you're going to want me to cancel all those for you too, right, Donny? You have a full slate of appointments this afternoon. And you know I'm not going to be able to reach most of them, and they're going to show up and I'm going to have to *talk* to them."

"Do you think she can hear you, Tina?"

"Oh, now you think *I'm* the idiot."

He stood at the window and waited for the all-clear. A half-mile away, a glass-fronted elevator climbed the CN Tower. Below him, a woman scurried diagonally across the intersection. Another woman shook out a yellow Shopsy's umbrella and inserted it roughly into the bracket on the side of her hot dog cart. A light snow began. He tried (and failed dismally) to track the first flakes all the way to the ground.

He had glanced at the day's appointments when he arrived. In addition to Mrs. Sanjit, he could look forward to Howard Desai and his grossly swollen prostate. And Timmy something-or-other, who needed twelve sutures removed from his forehead. There was Anne Davies, chronic, non-responsive depression, and ancient Hetta Jamieson experiencing another flare-up of her gout. Flu shots, blood work, and sore throats. Hardened lymph nodes that frightened the hell out of everybody. Well too bad, Donny thought. Today there was nothing he could do for any of them.

Safely out of the building, he headed north and then west along Queen. Turned up the collar of his wool jacket and burrowed into the afternoon's cold shadows. He slowed a little beyond Spadina. He liked this stretch. The halogen-drenched tattoo parlors and used CD shops, the YMCA mission and thrift shop, the all-white design stores and so many restaurants: The Left Bank. La Hacienda. Citron. The Paddock, a few doors south on Bathurst. The last time he was in there—was it Thursday? Friday?—they had been playing the new Radiohead CD and Grandaddy's *The Sophtware Slump*. He was pleased to recognize both those albums, particularly Grandaddy.

It had made him feel relevant, it had made him feel young. His noting the way it made him feel was, he suspected, a sign that he was, in fact, not young at all, and was just clinging to the illusion of hipness because he haunted once in a while the "alternative" aisle at HMV. But he was mostly at ease with that. He believed that in all the important ways he could still pass for a man in his late twenties.

He ducked into the Stephen Bulger gallery. He wanted to warm up. A small vee of snow had gathered in the neck of his coat. He shook himself out, stamped on the welcome mat. The woman in the back room looked up from her work and smiled. They knew each other. Eleni had been at his wedding. She and Maria, his wife, had graduated from Queen's University at the same time, both of them coming away with a degree in English literature. And now Eleni worked in this gallery and struggled with a first novel, while Maria worked at least half the year (or so it felt) in northern Ontario, scouting land for a reforestation company, each spring supervising a team of tree planters, setting up bush camps, keeping in touch with her husband via radio phone, meeting him in Thunder Bay occasionally for a rushed and never completely satisfactory twelve hours before he flew back south and she lit out once more for the logging roads.

"You missed the opening," Eleni said. She indicated the walls. A husband and wife team had photographed human embryos preserved in formaldehyde, snakes curled in thick-walled beakers; fish crammed together and stacked heads up, like . . . well, like sardines. He saw at once that the colors involved were brilliant, alive; the work hummed. One of the fetuses seemed perfect, viable, and wore what was described in small black type as *a Turkish cap*. Next to it were another baby's feet, severed at the shin, the cuts ragged and amateurish, the plump toes webbed. The photographs were mounted on sheets of half-inch acrylic which, Donny supposed, was intended to approximate the experience of viewing the original containers. "They were here," Eleni continued. "The artists. Do you like them?"

He stood before huddled pre-infant polar bears, three of them, floating, with oversized velvet paws and hooked ivory nails, golden fur. But all he could think about was the damn music. The reason for his having fled the office and scurried like a rat along Queen Street. For his standing beside Eleni when he should be listening to the irregular heartbeat of Janice Wolcyk, while his wife, the adult, fulfilled her obligations and slept under a thin floral duvet at Thunder Bay's Lakehead Motel.

"Who knows," he said. And then he confided in her.

She took him to her desk, set him up with a glass of Pinot Gris left over from the weekend opening. She pushed aside assorted slides, black-and-white proofs of Italian industrial sites, a pizza box from Terroni's a few doors down, and then sat on the edge of the work surface. She crossed one leg over the other and tugged at the thick, soft hem of her black leather skirt. She's the doctor here, he thought bitterly. And I'm the patient. I am Sunil Desai with his strange rash. I am Angel Caddis with his night blindness.

"A new CD did this to you?" She seemed amused more than anything. It wasn't very professional of her.

"I know. I know."

"A bad song has you running away from your responsibilities. You have to be kidding. Are you?"

"Well, obviously it's not really that. It can't be."

"What is it, then?"

"I don't know," he admitted. "I only know what triggered it."

"A song," she repeated.

"Right."

"Jesus." Eleni stared into the gallery as if ghosts were waltzing at its center. Finally she said, "I remember one of their songs." She sounded wistful. She looked at him. "Well, I remember a lot of them, of course. But they were never really my thing. Too *boy* for me."

"Which one?"

"In the video, he's sitting in a bar, moving a glass of whiskey around gently. Singing. It's really quite moving."

Donny nodded. "'One,'" he said.

Eleni reached out and touched Donny's shoulder. She laughed lightly. "You're right. That's it." She took back her hand. "And at one point he doesn't sing along with the song. He just stares mournfully, as the words go on without him."

Donny nodded again and she poured him more wine. She thinks I'm a sad case, he thought. Perhaps even that I need to be medicated. He held her gaze until she looked away awkwardly, into the gallery. She asked after Maria.

"She's fine. *We're* fine. It's not that."

He remembered the phone call he had made to Maria last night. It was late, past 11. The polls had closed hours before in the American presidential election, and the result was too close to call, he thought, but the networks had just called it anyway. There was a one hour time difference between him and her. It was enough that she might still be awake.

He was right because she answered quickly. She'd been doing paperwork, she said, and was glad to hear his voice, but asked if she could put him on hold. Before he could answer she was gone, and some quirk in the Lakehead's wiring left him able to hear everything happening at the front desk. The receptionist fought off the drunken advances of two men on their way from the bar to their rooms. "When did she get off?" one of them asked. "Shortly after she comes up to see us," the other one slurred, and the two of them cackled, thumped at the counter. When Maria came back on the line she apologized; she had been in the middle of a massive calculation: trees and hectares, hectares and trees. He told her what he'd heard.

"I know those guys," she said. "They're fucking assholes." They were hunters, and in their orange coveralls you could at least see them coming, she said.

"Too bad the moose can't," he said morosely, and they shared a sad, distant-from-each-other laugh. "How much longer will you be?" he asked.

She didn't know. "It depends. Whenever it snows, and if that snow stays on the ground, we'll call it a day." The TV flickered across the room and he told her it looked like the Americans were stuck with Bush, and she produced a sound that suggested to him a wince.

By the time he woke up this morning, CNN had retracted their initial election result forecast, and Al Gore had similarly retracted his concession. It was a shock. The future of the world had changed while he slept. Thrown, he beheaded two soft-boiled eggs and sat with them in the kitchen. Cholesterol be damned. He unfolded the *Globe and Mail* and began to read. Then it came to him. He had bought the CD and hadn't heard it yet. It was still in his briefcase. He found the bag in the front hall and wrestled with the wrapper. He slid the new disc into the player. The neighbors in the condominium below wouldn't appreciate this at 8 in the morning, but he turned up the volume anyway, stopped at six and then nudged it past seven. This was his home. He could do that.

It began. *The heart is a bloom, shoots up through the stony ground*. He liked it.

He recounted this series of events for Eleni in the gallery. She had moved from the desktop into her chair. Poured herself some wine. She sat across from him and swivelled back and forth. It was good of her to indulge him like this. Since he arrived three people had come in and looked around. One of them, a woman in shin-high green suede boots, had looked over the price list and hung around expectantly, but Eleni had ignored her, which must have been hard. These photographs cost three thousand bucks each; it didn't matter how good they were, they wouldn't sell themselves.

"And then what happened?" Eleni said.

Donny rubbed his face vigorously. He knew he should extrapolate from what had happened rather than giving her the literal details. Interpret it. Physician heal thyself. He could do that, perhaps. Decide what it meant even as he began to tell her. Talk himself out of this dumb funk. But what he actually said was, "The second song."

She leaned forward, put her elbows down on the desk, rested her chin on the hammock she made of her palms, and squinted at him. Donny thought she may even have closed her eyes completely.

"The rest of the album, in fact," he said. He felt a need to shore up his case and thought that might do it.

"You don't like it," Eleni said. She spoke quietly.

Did she think he was crazy? Or merely pathetic. He was sinking in her esteem, getting himself crossed off all sorts of lists. The snow outside was gathering on the road now.

He ploughed on. "It's shit."

"So? Big deal."

Donny shrugged. "I don't know. It threw me. It's thrown me. I feel strange."

"Let down," she said.

"I suppose."

Eleni got to her feet. She smoothed the front of her skirt. "I can feel that wine," she said.

Donny held up his glass. Eleni was moving away. She was in the gallery again. Maybe his time was up. She had run out of patience.

He apologized for coming.

She paused; she had been hasty and he could see that she knew it. She told him not to be stupid. "I love seeing you. But this . . . this music thing," she said, "seems very *small*. I know it doesn't feel that way to you, but . . ."

"I know."

He felt about twelve years old. As if he had presented her with a broken toy. Like what had happened was apocalyptic.

He mumbled another apology that she said was unnecessary. She said they could talk about it some more if he liked, but he couldn't do it; the room was too warm for him now. There was, inexplicably, too much of a contrast with the world outside. Strange that he hadn't noticed it before. Eleni took hold of his elbow and smiled, tried unsuccessfully to hold his gaze.

When he pulled open the door to leave, a small silver bell on a brightly colored wool strap tinkled brightly. A woman in a long mink, clutching a gray-eyed poodle in a fitted red jacket, turned sideways to squeeze past him. Eleni would be pleased, he thought. Maybe not about the dog—he assumed that was something she would frown on—but this woman seemed to be in a hurry and she didn't look at him. As he stood in the open doorway, she seemed to focus already on the polar bears. She wanted them; he felt he could discern that with certainty from the movement around him, the expensive scent he lifted from her as she headed in the opposite direction. He had *diagnosed* her intent, he decided. It was as real to him, as clear, as the flu.

* * *

He continued blindly along Queen, but after a block he cut up into Trinity Bellwoods Park and sat in the cold on a stiff and creaking bench. He wasn't alone. Two old men conversed in Portuguese. One of them reached absentmindedly into a plastic bag and cast handfuls of breadcrumbs and rice onto the white path. He looked into the gray sky, watched as from the corners of it, from the furthest points, pigeons collected, swarmed, homed in on him. Soon the path was alive with them. They clambered over each other. Their golden eyes, storm-cloud wings.

Streetcars hauled themselves west. Men in plaid jackets scampered about on scaffolding behind siding that advertised two-story loft spaces. In the dusty doorway of a dilapidated store that seemed to be called Textile Remnants, a woman bulky with layered tweed overcoats arranged a bed of boxes and torn blankets. Hypothermia, Donny thought. Head lice. Schizophrenia. Absentee votes.

He needed to leave. He had arranged a squash game for 6 o'clock because he didn't want to go home to an empty apartment. He knew that if he did, he would stand in the doorway to the kitchen picturing the contents of the refrigerator, taking inventory of the booze, wondering what to drink and eat and in what order. How much was too much? What constituted moderation for today's stressed professional? How much did he weigh? Where the hell was Maria and when would she come home?

The pigeons startled at his rising. The Portuguese men with the bread eyed him suspiciously. It was cold; he had no reason to be here. His was a different language. He passed behind their bench rather than in front so that the birds would settle again. The rice blew about on the ground. But it wasn't rice. He paused. It wasn't bread either. It was some sort of animal fat. And maggots. The grains of rice were actually maggots. And the breeze had died. The creamy mass of them squirmed on the ground.

Donny was on the streetcar heading east. Back toward the towers, the winter noise and end-of-day hubbub. His squash game was in the basement of a hotel. He peered grimly into the failing light. The noise of the carriage, the electric click and spark of it, was comforting somehow. There was the atomic and tinny buzz of a Walkman behind him. The smell of french fries. But then, with a start, he remembered another patient: Adam Govington. Damnit! He had completely forgotten about Adam's appointment.

Adam was going to die. And all of them—Adam, his mother, and his grandparents (the father lived in Denver with an accountant and had nothing to do with them, even now)—were going through the motions. They met to measure the rate of Adam's decline. Donny thought the boy would be lucky to make it to Christmas, and there was nothing he could do about that. He was merely a middleman now. He relayed information from the specialists to the family; he interpreted the graphs, translated the jargon. And he hid the truth from them. The exact thing they came to him for, he denied them. Decided it was better this way—to deliver platitudes, to suggest things were slightly brighter than they really were. Adam could die any day. He was close. It was even possible he didn't show for today's appointment. Or that he wouldn't last long enough to witness the final outcome of the American election, or the arrival of the storm system Donny had heard was gathering over the Rockies. He might miss the removal of the fiberglass moose that had cluttered Toronto's streets and squares for months. Adam Govington now lived at the very edge of the world; he looked over his pale shoulder from the crumbling absolute brink. And Donny should have been there with him this afternoon.

Trouble was—and he panicked at the thought that this might be the real reason he had blown the afternoon off—Adam Govington's mother had recently caught Donny looking at her thigh. His gaze had come to rest on it only in passing. But she had caught him. More than once. Donny had wanted to protest that it wasn't even her thigh, exactly. The short stretch of leg *between* her knee and her thigh proper is what had fascinated him. What was that part of the body called? If anyone knew, he should. She had looked at him icily, evenly, for a moment. But then the moment passed and they were once again discussing her son. She hadn't forgiven him exactly, just decided, Donny thought, that the world could still unfold in a more or less orderly fashion despite his fuck-up, and she should let it go. The doctor to your dying son could be competent and also, at the same time, during the same appointment, a complete and utter asshole. Donny squirmed at the memory.

He collected his athletic gear from the locker at the hotel. It was getting stale; he would have to take it home after the game. Allan was already on the court, playing alone, darting enthusiastically over the hardwood. Donny waited for the ball to get away, to twist madly into a corner and stop, and then he opened the glass door and slipped inside.

Allan was a year younger than Donny and liked to pretend it made a big difference. "It's not just that I work harder than you do to stay in shape," he would say, "I'm also *younger*." He was very tall, very thin, with a thatch of wheatlike hair that he kept short but unkempt. His eyes were green, his skin fair. But today, Donny thought, as Allan served gently into the corner and then loped after the ball, he looked a lot like an underfed wolf forced into a set of tennis whites.

They knew each other from the university. Allan was finishing a PhD in philosophy while Donny completed his residency. They would run into each other at the vending machines, slugging back terrible oily coffee, or hogging window seats at SpaHa, a university hangout. Now Allan ran an organic food shop on Adelaide. It was too far out of the way to make much money. Allan had thought that by setting up next to the fashion district he was guaranteed an image-obsessed clientele, but it hadn't worked out that way. Still, it meant that he and Donny had kept in touch—the odd lunch together, or even a jog up to and around Queen's Park, an occasional squash game and then a pint at the Wheat Sheaf or, if they were feeling more sociable, up two blocks at the Paddock on a Friday afternoon.

Allan leaned against the glass, bent over to catch his breath.

"Working hard?" Donny asked. "How long have you been here?"

"I closed up early."

"Small world." Donny collected the ball, squashed it in his fist. "I did the same thing. I had to get out of there."

"The young soul rebels," laughed Allan. He waved his racket in a way that was an indication for Donny to serve.

They rallied for a while without talking. Donny realized, not for the first time, that much of the pleasure he derived from these games was in seeing Allan struggle. He liked nothing better than to watch Allan tie himself up in a corner, his long limbs betraying him, or smack his racket against the wall in frustration, or come to a skidding halt on the varnished floor as the ball careened past him. He didn't feel guilty about this; he was positive Allan felt the same way about him. Maria had come to watch them once and she was adamant she would never come again.

These gentle opening rallies were also a time when both of them strategized, planned their conversation. What did they want to talk about today; how hard would they push their points?

Donny suggested they get to it. He said he wanted to build up a sweat.

"You seem pent up," Allan said, a little ways in.

Donny was winning. The score was seven to four. He held the ball way out in front of him, delicately, his racket pulled back. He looked over at Allan, whose eyes were fixed on the ball. Tension was evident in his thighs. "Pent up?" Donny said. "*Pent?*"

"It sounds odd when you say it, sure," Allan agreed. "Pent suddenly seems like a made-up word."

Donny served. The ball cleared the service line, but only just, then ricocheted into the corner behind Allan before he could lay his racket on it and died next to the glass. "Eight-four," Donny said, pleased. That was his best serve. If he could repeat it at will, he'd give up medicine.

"So everything's okay?" Allan tossed him the ball and held up a hand. He opened the door to the court and stepped out. He bent over the water fountain, in profile to Donny. The water rose up to meet his mouth in a weak glossy arc. Donny could see the individual bumps of his friend's vertebrae through the thin white cotton of his shirt. When Allan reentered the court his chin was wet and he wiped it with his forearm, which also became wet. Allan pulled up his shirt and wiped his face with it. This was precisely how epidemics were spread.

Donny stabbed at the air with his racket. He felt the blood in him, a rush hour of molecules on the inside track. But then he paused. He thought of his patients. At home around their supper tables, telling their wives and husbands, their children, how their appointment had been cancelled, something about the doctor having an emergency. He thought of Adam Govington. He thought of Maria. Saw her vividly in her orange coveralls, making her way to the top of a slash pile, a drip torch in her right hand like a flaming scalp. Smoke in the air, moose hunters moving through the uncut trees at the horizon. He thought of Al Gore and George W. Bush sitting in their offices. The mass of thoughts in *their* heads. All of them, every one, had more right to be pissed off than he did. And yet he had acted the most dramatically. It was only he who had blown up.

Allan looked at him curiously. "You going to play?"

Donny served. It was a weak effort, the ball sailed on him, struck the wall near the point where it joined the ceiling and rebounded to center court. Allan pounced on the ball, smacked it dramatically at the bottom of the wall. It picked up a wicked spin somewhere in that series of events and bounded in a strange loop past Donny's windmilling arm.

"I'm warming up," Allan said.

Donny took the game comfortably and they began a second. They hadn't spoken again. Actually, Donny supposed that couldn't be true. He vaguely remembered Allan asking if he wanted to go again. And something about grabbing a bite. And Maria, how was she? They had swapped many words apparently, but none of them ran together to form what Donny considered civil conversation. He shouldn't have come, he was still too screwed up. He thought of whiskey and of a newspaper article he had read that said any personality trait you had when you turned thirty you were stuck with for life. If you were a fuck-up at thirty, the reasoning went, then you may as well live with it, or shoot yourself, because the wiring was locked in. The article had annoyed Donny, probably because he was twenty-nine when he read it. He hated it even more now, because he had been unable to shed the memory. The more he tried, the more it cemented itself into the foundation of whatever process it was that allowed him to think. The brain was a mystery to Donny. He vividly remembered dropping a tomato slice into the sand on a trip to the beach with his parents when he was four years old, his father telling him to be a good boy and bury it. He remembered digging the tiny grave. But he couldn't come up with, at this moment, the phone number for his own office.

Allan, though, was saying something.

"Say again," Donny said. "I was miles off."

"Nothing important."

"It's okay. What were you saying?"

"Really," Allan said, "don't worry about it."

Their game was degenerating into a chore. Donny had derailed and needed to get back on track. He was taking out his middle age and his absent wife, and those dumb fuckers south of the border, and Adam Govington, on a pop band. And on a friend. Making them pay the price. After a moment, he told Allan he felt better. He could smell his own sweat, thought he could make out the sharpness of his own anger and frustration.

"But I didn't say anything," Allan said. He sounded a little disappointed. He wanted some credit and couldn't find a way to take any.

They played a few more points. And then Allan said something stupid about Africa, how, if he went there, he would be really big, he could teach them a thing or two about getting goods to market. He combined the comment with a reckless overhead smash that through some complicated geometry sent the egg-sized ball arrowing for Donny's face. He ducked and the ball hit the glass. Allan bent double laughing.

Donny, scowling, collected the ball from the ground and brought back his racket as if to serve before Allan was ready. The man was a gazelle, Donny remembered thinking afterwards, on the way to the hospital, not a wolf at all. The man could move when it really mattered. Because Allan responded to Donny's feint by rushing toward the back of the court, head down. His intention, plainly, was to wheel around, make some miraculous return of Donny's impending and unsportsmanlike serve.

Donny let the racket drop to his side. He moved a step to his right. Not enough to interfere with Allan's progress, but enough to bring him within range. As Allan drew level, Donny spun and pushed hard at his friend, shoved him headfirst into the glass. The noise was unremarkable in these surroundings; players were always colliding with their environment. The injury rate was very high, but rarely was it anything serious. Allan, however, dropped as if he'd been felled by a hunter. A smear of blood on the glass, thickest at the point of impact, diminished as it approached the floor.

Donny gulped. He heard the gulp and he was, he felt, a cartoon of himself. He was two-dimensional, nothing was happening with the weight or import it ought to carry. This, instead of an act of murder, was the Roadrunner, it was Bugs Bunny. For a split second he even saw the animated figure suspended midair, just over the cliff's edge, legs pedalling madly. He shook off the image and tossed away his racket, as if it were a gun. He dropped down next to the body, scraping his knees on the hardwood and depositing a touch of his own blood in that large cell with its begrimed picture window.

Donny had no doubt that Allan was done for. He touched his friend's scalp gingerly, manipulated the loose mess of bone in there, the sharp edges and the soft bottom. Donny pushed. Yep, that was Allan's brain. Resisting the fingertip pressure, but not well. It was an unusual consequence of an impact this moderate, but it happened sometimes. The skull could only take so much. And at only some angles. But hit it wrong and it was vulnerable as fruit. Great plates of bone could come free, float around under the skin. This had happened here. There was no coming back from this. It was simple tectonics; it was how the entire world worked.

He checked for a pulse and found one, but irregular and shallow. It was about what he expected. There was no hurry here. But there was, he knew, protocol. He summoned the appropriate mix of panic and professional expertise, and had the boy at the desk with the towels call an ambulance. He jogged casually back to the court, where one or two onlookers had gathered. And then a couple more, who sat on the bleachers behind them as if this were all part of a game.

He identified himself to the paramedics. They exchanged curt nods. He explained what had happened, more or less, to a policewoman who wrote it all down in a small spiral-bound notebook.

"I have to change," he told her, and pointed to his sweaty and blood-stained clothes. She nodded and Donny escaped to the locker room. He checked his BlackBerry for any messages he might have missed. There was something from Maria: *Donny. Surprise! I'll be home tomorrow. Can't talk about it now. But the weather, you know. Anyway, I'll call you later. Love you.* And another from his office: Adam Govington had taken a turn for the worse, he was at the hospital. Could Donny possibly get in there for a consult?

Well of course he could. He was going that way anyway, wasn't he?

The policewoman offered him a ride.

"It's okay. I rent parking downstairs," he told her. "I'll follow you. If that's okay." He looked at her questioningly. There wasn't anything else going on here, was there?

She said that was fine. But was he okay?

"I'm great," he told her. "I've seen much worse."

"He's your friend, though. And they say it looks bad."

Donny hung his head, as if shamed by her insight. "I'll be okay."

He climbed behind the wheel of his new Xterra. He was still on a honeymoon with this vehicle. It pleased him. Its height above the road, its not-quite-smooth ride and its smart sound system, its awesome roof rack. It made him happy. And as he climbed the ramp and turned on the headlights, filtered carefully onto King, checking the rearview, he realized he would have to be careful. He wanted to whistle a tune, but it would be wrong. It would arouse suspicions, and more than that it just plain worried him. It was inappropriate. Shit happened, he understood that. He hadn't intended to do more than swear at Allan, tell him not to be so fucking racist, so damned superior. But there was little point getting excited about what had happened instead. He gave serious consideration to the notion that he was in shock. And that seemed quite likely. He took his own pulse, measured his breathing, put a hand to his forehead. Yes, he thought, that might be it. He probably shouldn't even be driving.

He saw the ambulance some two blocks ahead. He couldn't catch it. He slipped a CD into the player. Skipped straight to the last track because it was the only one worth listening to. *Grace, she takes the blame*, he heard. *She covers the shame / Removes the stain.*

The real reason for his calm occurred to him as he entered the hospital parking lot. It was about Adam Govington, all of this. With Allan dead, or damn close, Adam would get a reprieve. He was positive. That was the way it worked. It had to. You didn't lose two people in one day. He had offered up Allan to appease the gods. A sacrifice. In return he wanted Adam back. Allan for Adam. It was a fair trade. More than fair. He pulled into a narrow space and found he couldn't open the doors properly on the Xterra. He could have squeezed through the opening, but who was to say his neighbors would be as considerate. He backed out and searched some more. *Because Grace makes beauty / Out of ugly things.*

Donny panicked for a second when he recalled Maria's message. How she was coming home. Which was great. But it wasn't what he wanted. If he got something for Allan's demise he wanted it to be Adam. He loved Maria, though he also wanted to watch that boy's beautiful mother cry with gratitude. Why couldn't he choose?

He found two spots empty beside each other and pulled in. He straddled the line. He turned off the engine and the music and sat quietly with his hands on the wheel. Relax before you go in, he told himself. It's okay. It'll all be fine. The gods know what you want. Those people in there don't, of course, you're not that obvious, you give off only a sense of goodness, a transparent wish that things turn out for the best for everyone. But the gods know. Oh yes, they do.

ABOUT THE CONTRIBUTORS

Jodie Abrams

JANINE ARMIN writes regularly for the *Globe and Mail* and contributes to *Bookforum* and the *Village Voice.*

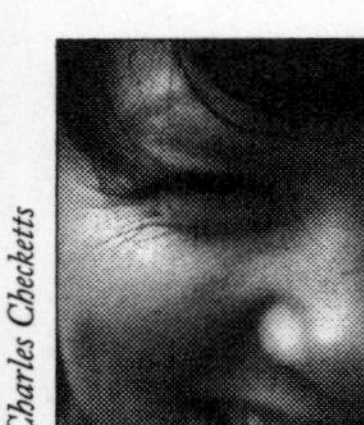
Charles Checketts

HEATHER BIRRELL is the author of *I know you are but what am I?* (2004). Her stories have been short-listed for Canada's Western and National Magazine awards. "BriannaSusannaAlana" won the Writers' Trust of Canada/McClelland & Stewart 2006 Journey Prize. Birrell also works as a high school teacher and creative writing instructor, doing all of this—barely—in Toronto's West End, where she lives with her husband, Charles Checketts.

Danielle Schaub

GAIL BOWEN learned to read from tombstones in Toronto's Prospect Cemetery. Her books include *A Colder Kind of Death*, winner of a Crime Writers of Canada Arthur Ellis Award, *A Killing Spring,* and a series that includes *The Endless Knot*, the eleventh novel of which, *The Brutal Heart*, will be published in 2008.

Anonymous

GEORGE ELLIOTT CLARKE'S first novel is *George & Rue* (2005), an award-winning, critically acclaimed, true-crime story. His second novel, now in progress, is *The Motorcyclist,* a comedy of manners. "Numbskulls" was written in Banff, Alberta; Toronto, Ontario; and St. Petersburg, Russia (May–June, 2007).

Phanindra Deonandan

RAYWAT DEONANDAN is a scientist, author, journalist, and professor. His stories have been published in seven countries and in six languages. He is the author of two critically acclaimed books of fiction, *Divine Elemental* (2003) and *Sweet Like Saltwater* (1999), which won the Guyana Prize for Best First Book. Ever indecisive, he divides his time between Toronto and Ottawa.

Kat Cizek

SEAN DIXON is the author of *The Girls Who Saw Everything* (2007), a novel about the last days of the Lacuna Cabal Montreal Young Women's Book Club. He is also the author of several plays and a YA novel, *The Feathered Cloak* (2007). He lives and plays banjo in Toronto.

Daniel Cianfarra

IBI KASLIK is a novelist and writes for North American magazines and newspapers. Her debut novel, *Skinny* (2006), has been translated into several languages and nominated for the Borders Original Voices Award and the Books in Canada Best First Novel Award. She currently lives in Toronto and her second novel, *The Angel Riots,* is forthcoming in 2008.

Cara Malla

PASHA MALLA'S first book, a collection of stories, will be published by House of Anansi in 2008. He lives in the east end of Toronto, across the street from a prison.

Mary Williamson

NATHANIEL G. MOORE is the author of *Bowlbrawl* and *Let's Pretend We Never Met*. He is the features editor of the *Danforth Review* and a columnist for *Broken Pencil.* He divides his time between Montreal and Toronto.

Ken Mulveney

KIM MORITSUGU was born and raised in Toronto, and has written four novels set in the city: *Looks Perfect* (short-listed for the Toronto Book Award), *Old Flames, The Glenwood Treasure* (short-listed for a Crime Writers of Canada Arthur Ellis Award), and *The Restoration of Emily* (serialized on CBC Radio's *Between the Covers).* She leads walking tours for Heritage Toronto, and teaches creative writing at the Humber School for Writers.

Richard Marks

Christine Murray is a Toronto ex-pat who lives and works in London, England. She writes regularly for a number of Canadian and British publications, and is the editorial director of *Ukula* magazine and reviews editor of the *Architects' Journal*. She is currently working on her first novel, an unlikely love story based in Toronto and London.

Heidi Rittenhouse

Andrew Pyper is the author, most recently, of *The Killing Circle.* His previous three novels are *The Wildfire Season, The Trade Mission,* and *Lost Girls.* He is a winner of a Crime Writers of Canada Arthur Ellis Award, and his novels have been selected as Best Books of the Year by the *Globe and Mail*, the *Evening Standard* (U.K.), and the *New York Times*. He lives on Queen West, around the corner from a sign that reads, *Hobos! Please Don't Poo Here!*

Cylla von Tiedmann

Michael Redhill is the author of five collections of poetry, four plays, and three works of fiction, the latest of which, *Consolation,* was long-listed for the 2007 Man Booker Prize and won the 2007 Toronto Book Award. He divides his time between Canada and France.

Biserka Livaja

Peter Robinson is the author of seventeen Inspector Banks novels, most recently *Friend of the Devil*, two non-series novels, and the short story collection, *Not Safe After Dark.* He has won numerous awards, including an Edgar, a Dagger in the Library, a Swedish Martin Beck Award, a French Grand Prix de Littérature Policière, and five Crime Writers of Canada Arthur Ellis Awards. He recently edited *The Penguin Book of Crime Stories* and he lives in Toronto.

Brian Joseph Davis

Emily Schultz is the author of several books, including the poetry collection *Songs for the Dancing Chicken* and *Joyland: A Novel.* Her new novel, *Heaven Is Small,* is forthcoming from House of Anansi Press. She has lived in Toronto's Parkdale for seven years and is not sure where she will do her laundry once the next condo tower goes up replacing her beloved Super Coin.

Rob Masefield

Nathan Sellyn was born in Toronto. His first story collection, *Indigenous Beasts,* was short-listed for the Commonwealth Writers' Prize and the ReLit Prize, and was the recipient of the Danuta Gleed Award for Canada's Best First Fiction Collection.

Sam Mussells

Mark Sinnett was born in Oxford, England, moved to Canada in 1980, and now lives in Toronto. He is the acclaimed author of a collection of stories, *Bull*, and two books of poetry: *The Landing*, which won the Gerald Lampert Memorial Award, and *Some Late Adventure of the Feelings.* His novel, *The Border Guards,* has been published internationally in several languages.

Jared Mitchell

RM Vaughan is a Toronto-based writer and video artist originally from New Brunswick. He is the author of eight books and a frequent contributor to numerous periodicals. His short videos play in galleries and festivals across Canada and around the world.

Also available from the Akashic Books Noir Series

BROOKLYN NOIR
edited by Tim McLoughlin

350 pages, trade paperback original, $15.95

*WINNER OF SHAMUS AWARD, ANTHONY AWARD, ROBERT L. FISH MEMORIAL AWARD; FINALIST FOR EDGAR AWARD, PUSHCART PRIZE

Brand new stories by: Pete Hamill, Robert Knightly, Arthur Nersesian, Maggie Estep, Nelson George, Sidney Offit, Ken Bruen, and others.

"*Brooklyn Noir* is such a stunningly perfect combination that you can't believe you haven't read an anthology like this before. But trust me—you haven't. Story after story is a revelation, filled with the requisite sense of place, but also the perfect twists that crime stories demand. The writing is flat-out superb, filled with lines that will sing in your head for a long time to come."
—Laura Lippman, winner of the Edgar, Agatha, and Shamus awards

HAVANA NOIR
edited by Achy Obejas

360 pages, trade paperback original, $15.95

Brand new stories by: Leonardo Padura, Pablo Medina, Carolina García-Aguilera, Ena Lucía Portela, Miguel Mejides, Arnaldo Correa, Alex Abella, Moisés Asís, Lea Aschkenas, and others.

"A remarkable collection . . . Throughout these 18 stories, current and former residents of Havana—some well-known, some previously undiscovered—deliver gritty tales of depravation, depravity, heroic perseverance, revolution, and longing in a city mythical and widely misunderstood." —*Miami Herald*

LONDON NOIR
edited by Cathi Unsworth

280 pages, trade paperback original, $14.95

Brand new stories by: Patrick McCabe, Ken Bruen, Barry Adamson, Joolz Denby, Stewart Home, Sylvie Simmons, Desmond Barry, and others.

"While few of the names will be familiar to American readers . . . there are pleasures to be found [in *London Noir*], especially for those into the contemporary London music scene."
—*Publishers Weekly*

LOS ANGELES NOIR
edited by Denise Hamilton

360 pages, trade paperback original, $15.95
***A *Los Angeles Times* Best Seller**

Brand new stories by: Michael Connelly, Janet Fitch, Susan Straight, Héctor Tobar, Patt Morrison, Robert Ferrigno, Neal Pollack, Gary Phillips, Christopher Rice, Naomi Hirahara, Jim Pascoe, and others.

"Akashic is making an argument about the universality of noir; it's sort of flattering, really, and *Los Angeles Noir*, arriving at last, is a kaleidoscopic collection filled with the ethos of noir pioneers Raymond Chandler and James M. Cain."
—*Los Angeles Times Book Review*

NEW ORLEANS NOIR
edited by Julie Smith

298 pages, trade paperback original, $14.95

Brand new stories by: Ace Atkins, Laura Lippman, Patty Friedmann, Barbara Hambly, Tim McLoughlin, Olympia Vernon, Kalamu ya Salaam, Thomas Adcock, Christine Wiltz, Greg Herren, and others.

"The excellent twelfth entry in Akashic's noir series illustrates the diversity of the chosen locale with eighteen previously unpublished short stories from authors both well known and emerging."
—*Publishers Weekly*

DUBLIN NOIR:
THE CELTIC TIGER VS. THE UGLY AMERICAN
edited by Ken Bruen

228 pages, trade paperback original, $14.95

Brand new stories by: Eoin Colfer, Jason Starr, Laura Lippman, Olen Steinhauer, Pat Mullan, Peter Spiegelman, Sarah Weinman, and others.

"Dublin is no longer a small town, but instead a full-fledged city with an intricate history and a life of modernity—the perfect backdrop for the noir genre. The cynicism and despair of classic noir is portrayed within each of these stories. —*MetroLA*

These books are available at local bookstores.
They can also be purchased online through www.akashicbooks.com.
To order by mail send a check or money order to:

AKASHIC BOOKS
PO Box 1456, New York, NY 10009
www.akashicbooks.com, info@akashicbooks.com

(Prices include shipping. Outside the U.S., add $8 to each book ordered.)